How Long the Heart Remembers

HOW LONG
THE HEART
REMEMBERS

a Novel by

Mary H. Hollingsworth

HOUGHTON MIFFLIN
COMPANY
BOSTON
1977

Library of Congress Cataloging in Publication Data
Hollingsworth, Mary H
    How long the heart remembers.

    I. Title.
PZ4.H7412Ho   [PS3558.03498]   813'.5'4   76-43275
ISBN 0-395-25021-8

Printed in the United States of America
v   10   9   8   7   6   5   4   3   2   1

Foreword

MY FATHER was not a successful man as the world knows success, but to his children he was, in a much greater way. Clear and steadfast, his eyes met others' unwaveringly, for he cheated no man; his lips knew only words of truth, for his tongue knew no guile; he lived honorably, for his integrity brought respect from fellowmen; white was white, black was black, for to him there was no borderline of gray; his life proved his faith in God, for all who knew him termed him a good man. What greater riches could a man bequeath his children?

To others he may have seemed an ordinary man, but to me he seemed as powerful as the mightiest Blue Ridge mountain of north Georgia, as solid as the granite near Atlanta, as tall as the tallest yellow pine of south Georgia, as great as the horizon spread over the cotton fields near Fitzgerald, and as sweet as the song of a mockingbird on a fresh spring morning. To others he may have seemed a man not amounting to much, but to me he was a hero.

Therefore

Cano . . . virum . . . profugus fato . . .

My Father
Clemeth Clifton Head

Old age is a time for inward dwelling. As we grow old the present slips away, uncounted; our eyes see only the golden sheen of yesterdays like the moon reflecting the glow of the sun; our ears are tuned to the measured music of bygone years, unheard by those about us. For us there is no future, and all we have left is what our heart remembers.

Contents

PART II   SOUTH GEORGIA

Part I North Georgia

CHAPTER 1

In Dahlonega

ELEVEN-year-old Lillian loved to preach, especially funeral sermons. If she couldn't find any dead birds, biddies or other sundry things fortunate enough to die where we could find them — fortunate because they received a Christian funeral and burial — she let a paper doll die.

On rainy days our favorite play was paper dolls, illustrations of clothes cut from mail-order catalogues. On this rainy afternoon she let one of our newest and prettiest die.

But she didn't get to preach this day; for as she opened the lid of the casket (a kitchen match box), Mama appeared in the doorway and said, "Gloria, you and Lowell go to the courthouse and tell your papa to send me a fire shovel. It's stopped raining now. Lillian, you march yourself into the kitchen and help Jenny peel potatoes for supper. Right now!"

Being the oldest set Jenny apart. She never played with us or joined us in anything. Instead of eating her chocolate teddy bear — Papa brought us each one from work the day before — she saved hers, putting it in a corner of the big clock on the mantle for safekeeping. But while my sisters were in school that morning, I climbed onto a chair, stole the candy and gobbled it before my feet touched the floor again.

Since their return, I had been uneasy, fearing discovery and punishment any minute. I tried to convince myself Jenny should have eaten her candy when we had, but it was no use; so

Mama's interruption was a relief. I was glad to get out of Jenny's vicinity, and more glad to be going to see Papa.

The courthouse was where he worked. The finest and biggest building in Dahlonega, it was built in the middle of the town square. Some said the bricks were hauled all the way from Augusta in oxcarts many, many years ago; others said they were made from the red clay of Lumpkin County — right here; but, wherever the bricks came from, people were mighty proud of their brick courthouse with the big, white columns, and Papa worked there as Clerk of Superior Court.

Until gold was discovered almost a hundred years ago, there was no town, much less a courthouse. There had been nothing but thick woods of hickory, oak, cedar and pine. And Indians. Papa said not to forget them, for they had owned the whole country.

For a long time the Cherokees knew yellow money that white men liked was in their ground, but they kept it secret for fear white men would take the rest of their land. Sure enough, when a white hunter overturned a rock that looked like the yellow of an egg, the secret was discovered and white men came pouring in from all over, squealing like hogs over slop, and boom! There went the woods and Indians. Well, not all the Indians. Cousin Chuck married one.

The miners were a rough bunch of men, and had to have a place to spend their gold; so the town of Auraria was built; but one wasn't enough; so they built Dahlonega, and both were in the Indian territory. They overflowed with people, most of whom weren't good. Barrooms and gambling places thrived and lewd women were like bees around a hive. At night and most of the day decent women stayed off the streets. Some said a murder was committed in Auraria, and the whole mining area soon became notorious for its wickedness.

When Papa talked of the wild days of the gold miners a certain gleam would come into his eyes. He was thinking of his own wild days before he married Mama. That was long after the gold rush, which occurred in his grandfather's time. He would pause in his talk, be silent a moment, then look at me apolo-

[2]

getically and say, "But she was the prettiest thing I ever laid eyes on." Speaking of Mama.

Going down the steep steps from our yard to the street (there was no sidewalk), Glory and I headed toward the courthouse. As we went along we looked in the ditch beside the road; for after a heavy rain, nuggets or particles of gold were often found in ditches and under eaves of buildings, and it had rained a gold-finding rain that day. As a matter of course people looked for it anywhere they walked after a rain.

If we found a small nugget we could buy some candy, maybe even a chocolate teddy bear, and I could put it in the clock so Jenny would never know the difference. I didn't mention my hope to Glory, but before going inside I insisted we look for gold under the courthouse eaves. We couldn't find even a particle, and my heart was heavy. Maybe Papa would give us a penny.

Being timid little girls, we stood in the doorway without speaking. Even if we hadn't been, we would have stood in silence at the scene before us. Papa and his secretary, Miss Gertie Sanders, were standing close together, and Papa had a hand on each of her shoulders, talking.

" — do something. You *must* do something, and that quick. Make Tom marry you. If this gets out — we *can't* let it get out — it might cost me my job."

Miss Sanders was crying. "You have no feeling for me."

Papa almost shouted, "Of course I do! I'm sorry for you, but I have a family to think of. This is election year, and if this gets out — my Lord — can't you see? There'll be a scandal!"

Glory had a quick mind. She said loud and clear, "Mama said for you to send her a fire shovel."

They jumped apart. Papa looked at us wildly, then smiled. "Hello, I didn't hear you come in."

Miss Sanders had hair as red as the flames leaping in our fireplace on winter nights. I stared at it, for I had heard Mama talking to Papa about that red-headed woman. When she saw us she turned to her desk and sat down, wiping her eyes and giving Papa a quick look, which he didn't see.

[3]

As he moved quickly to the fireplace my eyes followed him. Dressed in a suit like the one he wore on Sundays, he looked very important and rich. Since he was Clerk of Superior Court, and working in such a fine place as this, he must be rich. Firelight gleamed on the dark furniture, much finer than we had at home, and on the hearth were a lot of fire shovels. Choosing one, he brought it to Glory. It was brand new.

"Now run along home and tell your mama I'll be home soon."

I watched his hands, which didn't go to his pockets, and, sadly, turned to the door.

The dragged shovel made a lovely sound on the brick pavement and on every picket fence we passed. By the time we handed it to Mama it had lost its brand-new look.

There was no more time for play. Mama's emphatic "Get ready for supper" meant washing our faces and hands. Since we had but one washpan we had to take turns, and of course mine was last.

As Mama bustled about, putting supper on the table, she sang a happy little tune, half under her breath and a little smile played on her lips.

Since it wasn't court week we had no company for supper. When court was in session Mama had to cook for a lot of men who came out of the mountains just to see court. It was the closest thing to a circus they ever got to see, Papa said. The ones who came to our house had no money; the ones who had would go to a grocery, buy cheese, sardines and crackers, and wash them down with corn whiskey brought in a jug from home.

Thus I knew the meaning when Papa sang:

Ha, ha, ha, you and me
Little brown jug
Don't I love thee?

Except for court-week nights, suppertime was a happy time at our house, for Papa told some kind of story that made us laugh or held our rapt attention.

But though it wasn't court week, there was no story that

night. Papa ate his supper in almost complete silence, casting quick looks at Glory and me occasionally.

Mama was silent also, taking her cue from him, and their silence hushed us so we hied ourselves to bed as soon as possible.

In my own narrow bed in Papa and Mama's room I felt relieved. No one had noticed my eating Jenny's candy. Maybe she had forgotten it.

As my parents came into the room I pretended to be asleep, as I did every night; for I was ashamed to let them know I wasn't. They pulled off their clothes before blowing out the light.

Now Mama said, "You didn't laugh or tell one story tonight. Something's wrong."

"There sure is." He drew a long breath. "That secretary of mine has gone and got herself pregnant."

Silence. Then came Mama's voice. "Seems to me it takes two. She couldn't have got herself pregnant." Her voice was sharp and rising.

Papa gave a little laugh. "She goes with Tom Willikin. I told her to get him to marry her."

In an unnatural voice, Mama said, "As I remember, you were once a ladies' man."

He burst out, "My Lord, Bela, do you think I'm guilty?"

Silence. Then she said, "Not really and truly. I don't believe you'd be untrue to me, Caleb. But I'm pregnant, too."

He said, "My Lord!" again.

"Well, as I said, it takes two."

"That'll make us six." I heard him walking up and down. "If I lose the election, what'll we do?"

"The way we've always done — the best we can. What makes you think you might lose?"

He stopped walking. "If it gets out my secretary is pregnant, I'll lose." Now his voice was rising.

"Oh, Caleb, people wouldn't believe you — "

"They'd believe exactly that! Especially that brother of mine. He'd try to make people believe it."

"I know Lish has always been jealous of you, but I don't believe he'd smear his own brother."

"Then you don't know Lish! He's been hating me since I was born. All our lives, whatever he could do to hurt me, he's done."

"You seem friendly enough."

"Civil, that's all. He lives right across the street. I'm the Clerk of Court. I have to be civil to him."

"The thing to do," Mama decided, "is to make that Willikin marry Gertie."

"I told her to see him tonight."

"Well, you won't know anything till morning. Go to bed."

My red eyelids turned dark. Papa had blown out the light, and I could go to sleep. But I could hear them talking low. While the dying fire flickered shadows upon the wall, I went to sleep with Mama's voice, murmuring lovingly to Papa, in my ears.

Papa was right about his brother's hurting him. Tom Willikin didn't marry Miss Sanders right away; somehow, as those things do, the news leaked out. Papa's opponent snatched at it, and, aided by Uncle Lish, he instituted a whispering campaign. Papa was the baby's father.

One morning he came hurrying home and rushed into the kitchen where Mama was preparing dinner. "Bela, the news is out. Hump Jones come to me about it this morning, insisting I fire Miss Sanders right then."

"What has he to do with it?"

"Everything! He's the political boss of this county."

Mama's face turned a little white. "Did you?"

"No, but I'll have to. Bela, I swear to you I'm innocent!"

She came to stand before him. "You don't have to swear anything to me, Caleb. I know you're innocent." In perfect trust she lifted her face to his.

"Oh, Ma!" His arms reached out and gathered her close, and they stood there, crying a little.

Mama pulled away and wiped her nose. "Election is in November. If you could get that Willikin to marry her right away, people might forget by then. It's only February now. November is a long way off."

"I'm going to see him right now. If he don't marry her, I'll have him arrested for bastardy."

When he returned for dinner everything was settled. Mr. Willikin and Miss Sanders would be married that afternoon, and she would no longer be Papa's secretary. Papa wouldn't let her work until she could be replaced, for the simple reason that Hump Jones said no.

Being the political boss of the county, he would do his best to get Papa re-elected, because he not only liked Papa, but also he had married into the Abbott family.

Being in the Abbott family meant quality status; not only that, it meant an almost county-wide kinship; nearly everyone in the county was kin to us, either by blood or marriage; the Abbotts had been in Lumpkin County, Georgia, a very long time.

When the last of the Cherokees' territory was taken from them, the State divided the land into lots, and held a lottery. Each man, widow and orphan was entitled to one chance. My great, great, great grandfather Abbott and his son each held a chance. Some chances were blank, but the two men were among the lucky ones. Both won land and settled down to farm, leaving the chancy gold-digging to others.

Thus the Abbotts came to be among the oldest land-owning families in the county. Quite aside from family, Hump Jones knew Papa was innocent; for if there ever was a man of integrity, Caleb Abbott was that man. However, Hump Jones also knew gossip had ruined the political lives of many good and innocent men.

CHAPTER 2

The Year 1914

THE YEAR proved distressful to us, with only one event to brighten the gloom. The first disaster fell on the first day of March. Papa's mother died.

All winter she had been ailing. In those days no one consulted a doctor unless the ailment was thought to be fatal. If anyone felt bad, the remedy was a purgative; so Grandma kept taking them, but the cure wasn't forthcoming.

Catching her lying down in the middle of a day, Grandpa said, "Mother, you'd best let me call Horace out here or take you to town to see him."

Horace was Grandpa's brother, Dr. Horace Abbott, who lived in Dahlonega, and was practitioner for the whole county.

"Now, Jefferson," Grandma answered, "no man ever saw my nakedness, not even you. I won't begin now."

"But, Anna, a doctor is different. Anyway, one must have seen you while birthing your babies."

"No, they didn't! They felt to do what they had to do, never looking. No man has seen me, and none never will."

Her words alarmed Grandpa even more. The cold bleakness of winter held premonition of death, and his anxiety made him lash out at her. "What in tarnation is the difference between feeling and seeing? I'm going after Horace, right now."

Their love story was almost unique. In town with his father one day, Jefferson spied a pretty girl in a buggy in front of a store. When she saw him staring at her she flashed him the sauciest smile of all her fourteen years. Straightway, he went to the buggy, and though he was only seventeen he said, "I'm going to marry you." Within three weeks they were wed. Now, after fifty-four years together, death was ending their story.

For even from the cursory examination Grandma finally permitted, Dr. Abbott was sure what was wrong: Cancer. "There might be a chance for her if she entered the hospital at Gainesville," he said.

From the maelstrom of weakness and pain Grandma's voice came clear and strong. "I won't go. I've always been a lady, and I'll stay a lady."

Dr. Abbott said, "I assure you, Anna, many ladies go to hospitals to save their lives."

"No lady allows any man to see her nakedness."

Even her family's pleas couldn't change her belief, and she died a lady.

She had been the only one proud of my looks. "Lowell is just like my people," she said, in a tone indicating that the Branes were superior to the Abbotts. But her tone was lost on them. Nobody was as good as the Abbotts.

The Branes lived on a big plantation in Dawson County, were just as rich in worldly goods, and Grandma knew they were better.

Even in this time of great sorrow Uncle Lish had to be contrary. The family was shocked when he disagreed with Papa over the casket they chose. Though the choice wasn't Papa's alone, he made Papa the target of his nastiness. But Papa could be nothing but silent over his mother's body.

Years later he told me he never understood the reason for his brother's hatred. As far back as he could remember, he said, Lish had been hateful to him. He couldn't remember one kind thing his brother had ever done for him. A psychiatrist probably would have discovered sibling jealousy. Then, too, perhaps Papa could have been like the young Biblical Joseph, a little snot — a goody-goody who never did anything wrong — and a favorite of his father.

The bright event occurred well into spring. Late one afternoon Jenny took me across the street to spend the night with a neighbor, who was also my Sunday school teacher. To have to spend the night with her humiliated me, but she made my visit so pleasant I fell asleep without homesickness.

Next morning we found Mama in bed with a baby beside her. Turning back the covers so I could see him, she said, "He's your brother."

Curiously, I gazed on the tiny red face. I didn't know what a brother was, but I soon found out, rather to my dismay.

Everybody in town flocked to see him as if he were the richest gold strike ever made in Lumpkin County. Apparently, my parents thought so: they were always showing him to somebody.

The newborn son wasn't the first. There had been one born before Glory. Having too much blood, he hemorrhaged to death at the age of six weeks. On a snowy November day they buried him amongst the other Abbotts in the Salem Baptist Church cemetery.

My parents named their second son Horace Gregory: Horace, for Dr. Abbott, who delivered him, and Gregory for a famous

Georgia statesman. To Papa's people the second name was alien and it met with their disapproval. Mama said we'd call him Gregory.

He became the center of all attention, except mine. I kept wishing secretly he would go away. My sisters were forever hovering over him; aunts, uncles, cousins, neighbors and friends were constantly coming to see him; and as soon as Papa came home from work he had to hold him. I came to learn that Gregory was part of the family, the same as I was.

Not long after his birth, Mama's parents, my Grandpa and Grandma Walters, came to town to spend the night with us, a very unusual event. They hadn't been among those who flocked to see the newborn son, and it was the first time I remember seeing them; it would be the last for Grandpa, for next morning he left for Milledgeville where he entered the State Hospital to see if his raging headaches could be cured.

He died there June ninth.

The circumstances of his death remain a mystery. All we know is that he lived only three weeks after entering the hospital.

At that time the field of medicine knew little of brain tumor, the probable cause of Grandpa's insufferable headaches. But his case was diagnosed as *dementia paralytica,* and cause of death was so recorded.

Dementia means insanity marked by loss or impairment of memory, will and intellect. Since Grandpa entered the hospital voluntarily, knew where he was going and why, and made the then long train journey alone, he couldn't have been demented. Also, since *paralytica* is merely the Latin name for paralysis, the *paralytica* was as wrong as *dementia,* unless he suffered a stroke in his last weeks of life.

His widow and two daughters made no effort to bring his body home. Though he had been a Southern Missionary Baptist minister, he was buried in the hospital cemetery with only a number marking his grave. He had become something shameful, something to be hidden because he died in an insane asylum.

However, since he died in an asylum, everyone, particularly the Abbotts, assumed he was insane. This was one more club to be held over Mama by Papa's family, who, except for Grandpa Abbott, never forgave her for marrying him or let us children forget it.

On June 28, 1914, an assassination occurred in a city far from the mountains of north Georgia which was to embroil the world in the most costly war in money and lives ever fought to that time: The War for Democracy, the War to End All Wars, World War I.

From his politicking, talking with people all over the county, and from the daily *Atlanta Constitution,* Papa learned the war news and discussed what he learned at home. Though we children didn't understand the full meaning of all he said, we could guess by the tone of his voice and words half said or spelled that what the Germans were doing was even meaner than Uncle Lish's campaign to prevent Papa from winning the election.

Propaganda became horrifying. When the power-mad Kaiser marched his armies across helpless Belgium, stories of the Hun's heinous crimes were rampant.

In Dahlonega hatred grew until anyone with a Teutonic name was in danger of physical harm. An old German couple, residents for more than thirty years, had to abandon their home and flee in the safety of darkness. From mouth to mouth ran the rumor they had been spies. No one seemed to question what spies would be doing in such a remote mountain hamlet.

On everyone's lips was the pitiful song, "Belgium, Brave Belgium, the Smallest of Them All."

We children sang it with relish, but though our hearts were with Belgium, in our play we were the Germans. Marching through the woods, we whacked bushes and weeds to death. Onward and forward we went, Lillian in front. She was the Kaiser.

CHAPTER 3

Lillian and Prestige

W HILE SCHOOL was in session, Saturdays meant a whole day of play for Lillian, Gloria and me. If it was raining we played paper dolls; otherwise, we made a blurred streak going out the back door after we swallowed the last mouthful of breakfast.

Though she was only two years older than Lillian, Jenny didn't play; she helped Mama with the housework, and was as bossy as Mama in keeping the house clean.

Keep it clean they did. It was swept and dusted every day. All the beds had white counterpanes and pillows covered with starched, white slips. The pillows stood against the headboards and over them was placed a ruffled white piece called a bolster, so heavily starched it could stand alone. Nobody dared even to brush against the beds during the day, and at night we went to bed clean as a whistle for fear of soiling counterpane, slips and snowy sheets.

The beds were representatives of our house and lives. Every article had its use and place; if used, it was replaced in its exact spot. There were things we children weren't allowed to touch, such as contents of dresser drawers.

Moreover, Mama cooked three meals a day, breakfast at six-thirty, dinner at twelve, supper at six. No one was late. Monday was wash day; Tuesday, ironing; Wednesday, mending, if there was any, for we took care of our clothes. We had clothes we wore only on Sunday and clothes we wore everyday. We took care of both. Even if the words order and prudence were unknown to us, we knew their connotation.

The mother of four girls (especially Lillian) and a son, Mama needed a helper. Being the oldest, Jenny was that helper, whether voluntarily or by command. Though Santa still left her gifts, we never saw her play. She made my doll a dress, very pretty and quite perfect, but never made one for her own, which remained as Santa left it, unsoiled and beautiful. Already, she was in the alien world of adults, and she never came to know the pleasure we derived from our world of play.

Our house was on the side of a small hill; a wide green lawn separated it from the front street; on the north side grew huge, old oaks that stopped at a grassy pasture; on the south side was a garden space with scattered persimmon trees.

Back of the house, yard, barn, chicken lot and house, and outhouse was a sparse wood ending at the hilltop. To the left was a heavily wooded area; on the right downhill was a picture-book meadow with a shallow brook at the bottom. Across the brook another pastured hill rose steeply and ended at the top — a whole block secured by barbed wire, for ten dollars a month!

We had no lack of playmates and Lillian could climb the big oaks as well as the boys. Often, our play was religious — as well as funerals, there were baptisms. Lillian had to baptize every doll and paper doll we got in Mama's washstand bowl. Once she baptized two chalk dolls Glory and I received at Christmas, and nothing whole was left but their glass eyes and hair.

She was the leader; she invented the games, preached the sermons, climbed trees the highest and started the fights. Wherever action was, she was in front. In Papa's family she was rapidly gaining the reputation that the devil couldn't head her.

Uncle Lish's porch was L-shaped, the short end facing the road and our garden. One afternoon Lillian and Glory and several playmates were climbing the persimmon trees. I could only watch, and watching us all was Aunt Sally, Papa's older sister, from a rocking chair on the short end of the porch.

Aunt Sally was librarian at North Georgia College in Dahlonega; she kept house in an upstairs room of Uncle Lish's house. She was an old maid, as was her younger sister Tish, but both kept hoping, Papa said, to find someone to marry as good as they thought themselves to be.

Now home from work, Aunt Sally sat rocking and watching Lillian climb the tallest tree, which was near the bank dropping most steeply to the road. At the bottom was the barbed wire.

As Lillian climbed high and higher my eyes and feet followed as far as possible under the tree. As she continued climbing the branches began to bend, but still she went up and up. Suddenly, there was a cracking noise; she came tumbling down, knocking me head over heels down the embankment into the barbed wire, which set me screaming.

Shouting, "You've killed that baby!" Aunt Sally came running, untangled me, and took me to the rocking chair, where she rocked and petted me until my tears ceased. All this while Lillian lay unconscious. Unperturbed, Gloria and the others continued climbing.

After many minutes Lillian raised up, shook her head, then stood and looked about her. Seeing her sister and others still climbing, she chose another tree.

Aunt Sally wouldn't let me return to that "wild girl." We sat, rocked and watched them. I envied them not.

After taking a course in library science Aunt Sally gained prestige by becoming the college librarian.

The college was not a small, independent one. The building known as the United States branch mint with the ten adjoining acres was donated for educational purposes by the United States Secretary of the Treasury by the authority of a bill to that effect signed by the President of the United States, Ulysses S. Grant, April 20, 1871.

Seeing a great need for a college in that area, people of Lumpkin County got busy and elected a board of trustees through whose negotiations the college became a branch of the University of Georgia, and gave Dahlonega importance. In 1877 the United States Army inaugurated a military department, and the lively cadets added color and prestige to the town.

No wonder the Abbott family held Aunt Sally in such reverence; she, their kinswoman, was librarian to that majestic college. She herself felt her importance, displayed in the carriage of her person; she held her back as straight, her head as high as any cadet.

She was not the only one in Papa's family to attain prestige. Youngest of the family, Jules married one of the beautiful and wealthy McIntosh girls of south Georgia, thus gaining not only the girl but also a furniture store.

Uncle Lish had married a Texas girl, which gave him prestige; the family admired Aunt Marie because she came from a state bigger than Georgia.

By marrying a poor, landless girl, Papa lost status, but by being elected Clerk of Superior Court, he regained the lost and added greater honor.

This was not lost upon his children, especially Lillian.

Walking in the woods one day, we three spied two big boys trying to dislodge a bird's nest from a tree.

Lillian was furious. She yelled, "You mean boys, git down outta that tree! Don't you dast touch that birdnest! Come down right now or I'll tell my papa on you!"

The boys mocked. "Yi, yi, yi!

Lillian said, "I guess you don't know who my papa is. He's the Clerk of Superior Court, that's who he is. I'll tell him on you and he'll put you in jail!" She grabbed a stick and marched on them, with two little sisters following in fear and trembling.

The words court and jail must have put fear into the boys, for without touching the nest again, they scrambled down, hit the ground in a run and were soon lost to sight.

Self-righteously, Lillian threw down her stick. "I'll teach that poor, white trash not to rob a bird's nest!"

In self-importance we continued our walk, unaware that our days of prestige were numbered.

Spring passed into summer, and on wings of terror death came to hover over our house. Gloria lay sick in our company bedroom on the best bed. We children were not allowed to make any noise or talk above a whisper. We were too fear-ridden to talk normally anyway. What scared us most was that Dr. Abbott practically lived at our house, caring for Glory. From his face whenever he came from the sickroom, we knew he was scared, too; for Gloria had what was the scourge of our mountains — typhoid fever.

It was the sickness that set every mountain family trembling. Whole families would be stricken and at least one would die; sometimes more and, occasionally, the whole family.

Gloria was the special child of our family. In addition to being the prettiest, she was born with a caul over her face — a caul

[15]

endowed one with mystic power. Often Mama would tell visitors with pride, "Gloria was born with a caul," and the people would cast looks of awe at her.

Even without a caul, she would have attracted attention. Her chubbiness, big brown eyes and curly hair made everyone want to cuddle her. Her sweet disposition made her the pet of all who knew her, especially Papa, and I envied her and weighed his attentions to her jealously.

In appearance and disposition, I was her opposite. Though my eyes were brown, they were small, and my darker brown hair was straight. My stuck-out ears added nothing to my angular face. Probably, my physical appearance was a manifestation of an ugly spirit; for I was born howling with rage, and upon the least provocation I still howled.

On the night of the crisis we children were put to bed early, for no noise was to disturb the silent watch in the sickroom. Dr. Abbott sat near the bed, occasionally feeling Glory's feet to see if they were turning cold. Papa and Mama sat on the other side, near the bed, their lips moving in silent prayer. In other rooms women relatives, friends and neighbors tiptoed about, relieving Mama of baby-tending and household duties; for on this night Mama, the mother of the dying child, was the star of the drama.

The night wore on. Three pair of eyes were riveted on Glory's face. Toward dawn her breathing became labored. Dr. Abbott pressed his fingers hard on her wrist, leaning close to her. Her parents clutched each other's hands as they watched.

As light streaked the sky the breathing faltered, and Dr. Abbott seemed to hold his own as he leaned close to the child. She suddenly drew a long breath and as she slowly expelled it, her eyes opened to stare wildly; slowly, they moved around the room and stopped on her parents. Recognition flickered before her eyes closed in natural sleep.

Wearily, Dr. Abbott arose and stretched. "I could stand some good strong coffee," he said and smiled in triumph. His battle with death was won. The fearsome wings no longer hovered.

The next day we children were allowed to stand in the doorway and look at Glory. A frame of bones covered by skin, she was a stranger, staring at us from eyes in cavernous sockets. She looked barely alive.

Before she was well enough to get out of bed, Papa brought four china dolls home. Three had black hair. The blond one he laid on the bed beside Gloria.

She had prestige.

Some weeks later the typhoid vaccine was introduced to our community, which was termed a danger zone. The government had sent the vaccine to immunize the cadets. There wasn't enough for the public, but fortunately for Dahlonega people, there was enough for them. I remember seeing people standing in line far into the night, waiting to be inoculated. We were in that line.

No doubt the vaccine prevented hundreds of typhoid cases, since pasteurized milk, treated water and sewage facilities were far in the future.

CHAPTER 4

Aunt Tish Gains Her Prestige; We Gain the Farm

B ECAUSE OF GLORY'S ILLNESS, summer seemed gone too soon. Our relief and joy over her recovery hadn't ended when October brought school again. When Dr. Abbott said she was well enough to go, we were surprised.

It still seemed summer. The days were warm and sunny. The trees were still green. Flowers still bloomed. But, unnoted by us children, a stirring was in the air.

Election time was fairly upon us, and Papa was out politicking whenever he could spare time from the office. At night his face was gloomy or hopeful. On gloomy nights the household would be quiet, wondering what would become of us. On the hopeful ones our house would again ring with laughter.

The first week of November brought defeat to warm days and to Papa. The whispering campaign proved effective, and we were no longer children of the Clerk of Superior Court.

The day after election Hump Jones came to see Papa. "Now Caleb, don't you fret a bit. I can get you a political job with the State, you being a good Democrat and party man. We ain't going to let your talent go to waste. I'll see you in a few days."

Within a week he was back with a political job for Papa which enabled us to live in the country.

Our living in the country was Grandpa's idea. "With a growing family, you can live better and cheaper on my farm. That new job will let you farm, too."

Uncle Lish had a growing family, but Grandpa made him no such offer. Seeing hope light Papa's face, Grandpa went on, "You'd have to buy a horse, anyway, for that new job. You already got a cow. I'll give you the money to git started."

Papa protested. "What about you? What will you do? That farm and house is your home. Us chillun was born there."

"Tish is raring to move to town. She wants to be somebody, she says, and can't do it in the country. As for the farm, there's enough land for us both. I'll come out by wagon every day and raise my crop. Besides, I can't bear living in the house without Mother."

"Pa, I wish you *could* live with us. We love you."

"I love you and Bela, and the children, too, and wish I could live with you, but I'm stuck with Tish. I'm stuck as long as she ain't married and I don't see no prospects."

Both laughed, then sighed, compassed by the wants and won'ts of life and Aunt Tish.

Pretty in a wan sort of way, Aunt Tish was an artist, painting pictures to hang on walls. Since Grandma's death she was the only one to look after Grandpa, but the country offered no opportunity for her to use her talent commercially, and she was fuming to move to town where she could give oil-painting lessons. As yet, she was the only family member without prestige, and Grandpa felt bound to give her the chance. He figured out a way to do that and continue farming.

Papa's new job began the first of January, so in order to get settled before that we moved to the farm before Christmas.

After supper on the Saturday we moved, we gathered around the fire for a little while before retiring. Suddenly, from outside came a clamorous din made by someone beating on many tin pans. Alarmed, we jumped up.

But Papa laughed. "We're being serenaded by our neighbors. It's their way of welcoming us into the community." He threw open the front door and shouted, "Come on in, folks, and meet the family!"

From out of the darkness people came crowding into our house. At the entrance of a small woman with three boys close beside her, Mama hugged her fiercely. Turning to us children, she said, "This is my sister, your Aunt Lanie."

I, at least, never knew she had a sister, but Aunt Lanie now pushed the three boys forward. "These are your first cousins, Cal, Sid and Midas."

We stared at each other with great curiosity, silent and measuring.

Grandma Walters joined the group. She was taller than either of her daughters, a striking figure of a woman. Her blond curly hair was pulled back loosely into a bun. Her blue eyes pierced through me, and I drew back behind Lillian, then hurriedly sought Papa.

He was saying to Aunt Lanie, "Dob didn't come?"

Her face turned pink. "No, he had to fiddle for a dance."

My eyes caught on a man walking bent like a fishhook; he made no effort to straighten and walk as other people. I tugged at Papa's arm. When he leaned down I whispered, "Why don't he straighten up?"

He whispered, "He has rheumatism. Don't stare at him!"

Forcing my eyes away, I saw Jenny talking and laughing with a slender young man; she was holding her head sidewise, looking up at him from the top of her eyes. That was. odd. I'd never seen her look like that. Her wide gray eyes were sparkling and her cheeks were rosy like a fall apple. Her hair a storm cloud about her shoulders, she was as pretty as Cinderella at the Prince's ball. But she was acting mighty strange.

Papa said she was like a shy, young gazelle; ordinarily, her looks weren't noted, only her brains. Smart in her books, she had her heart set on becoming a schoolteacher, and usually acted like one; but tonight she was smiling without sense and her feet seemed to be dancing, though she was supposed to be standing still. Not liking what I saw, I sought Lillian. She could explain.

She was pretty, too, with her honey-colored hair and light brown eyes, but her looks also went unnoticed. No one in Papa's family held much hope for her; she had no mind for books nor did she bear the least resemblance to a shy, young gazelle. Lillian was a filly, galloping over green fields, her mane flying in the wind; untouched by whip and unbroken by bit, she reveled in freedom and sun.

What was the essence of Lillian? Can one bottle the sunshine of a cloudless June day? Can one take the songs of every bird and make one lifelong song? Can one name the reasons for children's happy laughter? Can one take all the colors and fragrances of every flower and make them everlasting? Even her name held summer sunshine.

Lillian.

Gloria and I loved her. She could preach sermons, invent games, climb the tallest trees, outrun, outfight any boy her age; she wasn't afraid of the Devil, and led us in paths of joy. She was Lillian, unmatched and incomparable.

I found her still standing with Glory and our cousins, but her interest had flown. Her eyes were fastened on a tall, dark young man. She, too, seemed a stranger. Dismay seized me, and I hastily sought the person on whom I could depend not to change — Papa.

He was talking to a small man with gold teeth and a tall woman with a very dark complexion. Mama came to them, and he said, "Ma, this is our Cousin Chuck and his wife Raven."

Cousin Raven! The family always carefully explained she was a full-blooded Cherokee Indian. The only difference I saw between her and white women was that her skin was darker.

Someone hollered out, "Sam Grindle, how 'bout a song?"

The bent-over man turned in the direction of the voice. "Ah, who wants to hear me sing?"

A chorus responded, "We do!"

Pulling a small metal object from his pocket, which I later learned was a jew's-harp, he clenched it between his teeth, and began to play by flicking a piece of it with a finger. Removing the object, he sang:

> When I am gone to yonder shore
> No more to wander here alone,
> I'll be with Jesus around the throne
> When I am gone, when I am gone.

It seemed he had already gone and was an angel, for his voice sounded like one. Sadness overwhelmed me, and my eyes sought Lillian. She had made her way to the side of the tall, dark young man, her eyes still on his face.

When Sam ended his song Papa asked if everyone would like to sing. When all answered *yes* he brought out our hymn books, and the evening was filled with hymn singing.

My sadness increased, however, because Lillian was sharing the same book with the dark young man, and her eyes stayed on him more than on the book.

After the people left we girls went to the back porch to urinate. Lillian asked Jenny, "Did you notice Erastus Redder?"

"No, which one was he?"

"The man I was singing with."

Jenny replied, "No, I didn't. I was singing with Dave Colley. He's coming to see me."

Dumfounded, Lillian asked, "You mean he's going to be your beau? You mean you're going to start *courting?*"

"I told him I'd ask Papa. And I am."

In wonder Lillian repeated, "You're going to start courting."

"If Papa will let me. Oh, Lillian, wasn't he pretty?"

Abruptly, Lillian said, "I never noticed. Gee, I wish Erastus had asked to come see me."

Shocked, Jenny said, "But Lillian, you're not even twelve."

"I don't care! I don't care how old I am or ain't. I love Erastus Redder."

I loved Erastus Redder too.

Glory said, "You'd better not let Papa or Mama hear you say that, Miss Lillian, or I know which end of you would be redder."

"It surely would," agreed Jenny. "You're not old enough to start courting. You have to be at least fourteen."

Lillian tossed her head. "I'm going to start courting when I'm twelve. In April I'm going to court Erastus!"

"You can't do the courting. *He* has to, and he'd never look at a twelve-year-old girl, I'm sure."

Lillian said, "I'll make him look at me. See if I don't!"

Jenny admonished, "You'd best behave yourself and be a lady."

Glory said, "I'll tell Papa on you if you don't."

Sidling close to Lillian, I took hold of her hand to let her know I was on her side.

CHAPTER 5

Catamounts and a Horseless Carriage

THE NEXT morning Papa woke us by standing in the doorway singing:

> Oh, peas in the pot,
> Hoecake's a bakin'
> Go down to the barn
> And wake up Jacob!
> Go down to the barn
> And wake up Jacob!

After breakfast Lillian, Gloria and I explored our domain.

From the road running by the front (and leading to town), our house was almost hidden by a grove of oaks when they were in leaf; the white house itself was surrounded by a large sandy yard, and faced north; from our front porch we could see towering peaks of the Blue Ridge Mountains.

Near the steps of the back porch, which ran the length of three rooms, was the housed well. Many country people still used water from springs, but the more enlightened had roofed, housed wells covered with lids. Water was drawn by means of a windlass, rope and pulley. I soon learned to stand out of the way of the flying windlass when the bucket zinged to the bottom.

Lifting the lid, Lillian said, "If you look into a strange well and make a wish, it'll come true if you don't tell what you wished." She silently made a wish, then helped Glory and me to look while we wished. I don't know what Glory wished (perhaps that Lillian would be a lady), but I could guess what Lillian's was; so I too wished Erastus would start courting her.

From the backyard a path sloped to a level tract, ending near the road leading to town. On this stood the stables, barn lot, and big barn, with its shelter under which were kept the wagon, cider press, plows, harness and Papa's twists of homemade tobacco.

Returning to the backyard, we inspected the log corn cribs and smokehouse and found a path to the apple orchard. The trees were easily climbed, offering no challenge; soon tiring of so easy a diversion, Lillian headed for the split-rail fence separating the orchard from a thin wood, which soon ended in a wide meadow. At the end ran a brook, and beyond it a little way stood a thick dark wood, which didn't look inviting; so we followed the brook downward to a thicket of willows embracing it, and found a pool several yards wide and about four feet deep. Immediately, Lillian named it our washing hole.

Stripping off all her clothes except her drawers, she said, "I'm going in washing," and was soon thrashing about in the icy water. Glory and I followed her at once.

Since all the washing we ever did was in washpans and washtubs, being able to wash in plenty of water was wonderful, though our teeth began chattering instantly.

Our marvelous time lasted only a few minutes. Papa's voice was very loud. "What do you girls think you're doing?"

Lillian said, "We're washing."

His face was white. "Ain't you got no better sense than go in washing in winter? No, you ain't! You'll git pneumonia, sure. Come out of that water, right now! I've hunted high and low for you — scared to death. Thought you was lost."

While we dressed he continued to berate us. "You needn't think just because you're in the country you can become as wild as rabbits. Hurry up! Dinner's ready. We got to eat and go to Sunday school."

Lillian exclaimed, "Sunday school! In the evening?"

"Country churches have their Sunday school in the evening 'stead of morning 'cept preaching days. Preaching's just once a month. That day both's held mornings." Pointing to the thick, dark wood, he asked, "You see them woods at the edge of this pasture?"

We looked and nodded.

"Don't ever go into them woods. Back over there" — he pointed — "there's caves in the side of the mountain where wildcats and catamounts stay, and they roam all over them woods," pointing again to the dense wood. "Wildcats and catamounts will kill you in a minute."

Glory's big eyes became bigger. "What's them?"

"Wildcats look like house cats, only they're big as a big dog; catamounts are yellow and big as a calf. You wouldn't have a chance against one. They pounce on you 'fore you know it. You ought not to come even this close to them woods yonder — no telling when one might come out and kill you."

Dividing her hair in a straight line from front to back, Lillian wore it in two big braids, one on each side of her head. Habitually, she tossed them much as a horse tosses its mane. Now she tossed. "I ain't skeered of any old wildcat or catamount." She gazed into the forbidden wood daringly.

Giving her a long look, Papa said, "You ain't scared of the Devil! I'm not just trying to scare you. I don't want my chillun to be cowards, but I don't want 'em to be fools, either. Lillian, you may not be scared of 'em, but I mean you'd better mind me and never go into them woods. Do you understand me?"

She nodded, but there was a gleam in her eyes Glory and I understood only too well. But we would never go into the woods no matter what Lillian said. So we thought.

After dinner Papa hitched our horse, Nell, to the wagon; it was a cheaper make than Grandpa's because it had no wagon seat; so he put two kitchen chairs in front for him and Mama and spread an old quilt in the back for us girls. Mama would hold Gregory.

Since the sun was shining brightly, Jenny took her parasol. Young ladies couldn't be the least browned by the sun. Lillian decided she was as much a young lady as Jenny; so she took her parasol too. Glory and I didn't own one. Jenny shared hers with Glory and Lillian shared with me.

Though the church was only three miles away, going by wagon made it seem ten. Deeply rutted by winter rain and ice, the road was filled with holes hub deep. The ride was so bumpy Jenny and Lillian had difficulty holding on to their parasols.

Suddenly, we heard a loud, strange noise. Coming toward us was something that was likely to split our eardrums and make our eyes pop and necks crane like a giraffe reaching for leaves of a high tree.

"A automobile!" shouted Papa, pulling Nell to a stop as far as he could on the side of the road. Jumping from the wagon, he ran to hold Nell's bridle; for her ears were flicked forward.

"Don't worry, Papa!" Lillian shouted. "I'll skeer it with my parasol!" She began waving it threateningly at the oncoming car.

Thinking two would be more effective, Jenny waved hers too. But the automobile was soon passing. Nell whinnied and trembled. Papa tried to reassure her and look too, for we all gaped to see a buggy running along the road without a horse.

Shaking his fist at the disappearing car, Papa shouted, "Scare a body to death, will you? You infernal, ungodly automobile!" Climbing into the wagon, he said, "I ain't got no use for them things. They're against nature. Now you take things contrary to nature and they're bound to be against God."

The small, white frame church was set on a cleared, level

place at the foot of a low hill. Concord Church was so new it didn't as yet have a graveyard. When we arrived numerous wagons, buggies and oxcarts were in the churchyard.

Before entering the church, Papa said, "Women and children on the left, men on the right." So we children followed Mama to a bench on the left while Papa seated himelf with men on the right.

The church had no organ, and who had ever heard of a piano? Sam Grindle, the song leader, used a tuning fork to set the pitch. Matching his voice to it, he began singing:

> There's a beautiful home beyond the dark river,
> There's a mansion by faith I can see;
> And the Savior is there His faithful to welcome.
> There's a beautiful home for me.
>
> Home . . . on the banks of the river,
> Home . . . where the ransomed ones gather,
> Home . . . with the angels forever,
> On the beautiful banks of the river.

Sam didn't have a home, we later learned; he lived with his brother Banty and his family right up the road from us. No woman would marry him bent double as he was; so he loved to sing about home.

Since he was the children's Sunday school teacher, I learned he liked to talk about home, too. Every Sunday he would tell us how beautiful the heavenly home was and how we should all live good lives so we could go there when we died.

All children were good in those days. They knew better than not to be. Being good meant sitting still and silent, creating no behavior problem. Though churches hadn't dreamed of nurseries, children's noise never disturbed services, for children were taught they were to be seen and not heard.

After Sunday school, children hovered about their mothers, who swapped the latest news and recipes. Mama was the only woman wearing a ready-made dress and hat; the others wore dresses of calico, cambric or gingham, and tatting or crocheted lace-trimmed bonnets. Bright red flannel was the most popular for the little girls' dresses, but Mama eyed red flannel with disapproval and none of us ever wore it.

Since the serenaders were among those present, we weren't total strangers. Many others were relatives we had never seen, and we soon became acquainted with them. But Aunt Lanie, her boys and Grandma weren't present. Later, Mama explained Uncle Dob did fiddling for dances and desultory gold-mining for money and didn't make enough to buy his family Sunday clothes. Though Aunt Lanie ran a grist mill, she made only enough flour and meal for bread. And since Grandpa's death, Grandma lived with them.

The men also gathered in the churchyard to talk, and Papa had to tell of seeing the horseless buggy.

Tater Collins, whose land adjoined Grandpa's, said, "One of them things will never take the place of a good horse."

Jettie Gridley, who wasn't quite right in the head, spoke. "A horse ain't near as good as a team of oxen. You can't beat them. You can plow with a horse, though, but you can't plow with one of them horseless buggies."

An old, white-haired man with a flowing white beard spoke. "They call 'em automobilly wagons. Nobody'll catch me in one."

Joe Toose said, "I wonder who it wuz. I never knowed anybody in these parts rich enough to own one. 'Tain't likely somebody would come all the way from Gainesville in one."

Papa said, "They're rightly called automobiles. I've seen one before. The Shores in Dahlonega have one, but the one we saw wann't it."

Remembering Papa had just moved from town where he was Clerk of Superior Court, the men fell silent while Papa began steering the talk to his new job — as cattle inspector and dipper.

"I hear tell spotted fever is rampaging agin in the upper part of the county. The government says it's caused by ticks biting cows." Seeing their interest, he continued. "Ticks can be kept off cows if they're dipped in disinfectant twice a year. They say spotted fever kills more people than typhoid."

Joe Toose said, "My Polly had it once. Nearly died."

The old, white-haired man said, "I buried my first wife and two children from it."

"If people would just dip their cows, it'd cut out all this spotted fever," Papa said.

"How would you go about dipping a cow?" Banty Grindle asked.

"Why, the government's got a vat and pens set up near Cavender Creek, close to town. Dipping's free. All you do is drive your cow there, she's dipped and penned till she dries and you drive her home."

"Does it hurt her milk?" Joe asked.

"Not atall. Not in taste or production."

Since all present were experienced with Rocky Mountain Spotted Fever, they wanted their cows dipped. Thus Papa's new job was begun.

CHAPTER 6

Dipping Cow Problems and Town Education

As we were driving from the churchyard Papa pointed to the top of the hill on which set the one-room, one-teacher school that he didn't want us to attend.

"That's Dewey School. Your great-uncle, W. K. P. Abbott, donated the land to build it on, and named it for Admiral Dewey who won the Spanish War," he told us children. "Your great-uncle is brother of your grandpa, and he's called Red Polk by the family. Another Polk Abbott was brother to your great-grandpa, and he was called Black Polk. They believed in handing down family names in them days," taking a dig at Mama for not naming Gregory two family names.

She wouldn't let it pass. "What did you want me to name him, White Polk?"

Papa laughed weakly.

"Why did they call 'em Red Polk and Black Polk?" asked Glory.

"'Cause of the color of their hair. Now, you see them tubes at the top of them ladders — across the road from the school-house?"

We nodded. Two large water tanks were at the top of very high frames, all made of wood. From the tanks ran pipes to a wooden trough about a foot wide and two feet deep, which ran along the side of the road, and on around the mountain to a gold mine, Papa explained, to wash dirt from the gold.

"Why don't you mine gold, Caleb?" Mama asked.

"I'm a farmer," and he looked at her in surprise.

"Seems to me more profit would be in digging gold than in digging grass. It would be easier mining gold," she said.

"My pa is a farmer," he said.

"And his pa was a gold miner," she reminded him.

In 1852 Great-grandpa Abbott sailed around the Horn to California, nearly died of starvation aboard ship, but reached the coast before the crew had to eat each other. After two years of mining, he returned home with enough gold to launch his many sons as doctors, merchants and farmers in addition to building himself such a substantial home it is lived in today, still beautiful and sound.

All this was Lumpkin County history, also the gold of the county. And, Mama, weary of not having gold while the dirt under her feet contained so much, continued. "Why, there's enough gold left right here in Lumpkin County — "

But Papa wouldn't let her finish. "Every man has a right to his own calling." They looked at each other.

Glory asked, "Will we ever have to go to Dewey School?"

Papa replied, "I hope not. I hope you chillun finish town school and go on to the college."

That was the beginning of what we later termed "Caleb's pipe dreams," for even then doubt was in his mind whether he could find the hundreds of dollars needed to educate his children.

But he tried to make his dreams come true. Before moving to the farm, he had rented a furnished room in Hall Villa, a big apartment and rooming house, for Jenny, Lillian and Glory. During the week they would live there in order to attend town school.

The room contained a double bed for Jenny and Lillian, a cot for Glory, a dresser, a table to eat and study on, and four chairs, but no cookstove. Cooking would have to be done over the fire in the fireplace which had pothooks.

Doubtfully, Papa eyed it. "Reckon you can cook on it?" he asked Jenny.

"I think so."

"Jenny, you'll soon be fourteen, a grown girl. You'll have to do the cooking and looking after Lillian and Glory — make them study and behave. Reckon you — "

"I reckon." But she looked nervous.

Turning to the other two, he said, "You'll have to mind Jenny, help her with the housework, behave yourselves and study hard."

Seeing the look on Lillian's face, he hastily assured her, "It'll only be till school is out, then you can come home. Besides, I'll come after you on Fridays after school, and you can stay home till Monday mornings; so you won't stay but four days and nights by yourselves. If I take you outta school now, you won't make your grade, 'cause there ain't no school in the country till July."

As far as Lillian was concerned he could take her out, but she knew she had to do what Papa said. Anyway, she told me later, living like that might hold a lot of fun.

Turning to me, he said, "Lowell, stop staring at that light!"

Hanging from the ceiling by a thick wire was the prettiest light I ever saw. Whereas the light in a kerosene lamp came from a wick, this light came from four tiny wires inside a glass globe not half as big as a kerosene one, and the light was almost as bright as the sun. I couldn't keep my eyes off it.

Papa said, "That's a 'lectric light. Ain't you never seen one before?"

I shook my head.

"Well, stop staring at it, I told you! It'll put your eyes out."

*

So it was that from Monday mornings until Friday afternoons, the three girls were away from home. At first, the house was lonely. Mama was always busy about the house. Papa was away seeing that cows were dipped. Gregory was too young to know anything about paper dolls and funerals. I had to amuse myself.

I came to like playing alone; for I could let my dolls and paper dolls do as I commanded and not as Lillian and Glory said.

Nevertheless, on Friday afternoon, from the time Papa left for town until the wagon came rolling back down the road, I couldn't stay away from the window facing the road.

When Lillian entered the door the house would come to life with laughter, shouts and running feet, not to mention slamming doors.

I followed her around like a puppy, not wanting her out of my sight. As soon as I could get her and Mama together long enough, I'd say, "I'm gonna sleep with Lillian tonight," which meant Gloria would have to sleep with Jenny. This was no fun since Jenny would go to sleep immediately.

Sleeping with Lilliam meant much whispering, pinching, slapping, tickling and giggling in the dark; best of all, she would tell stories, some she read or heard and others of her own imagination; so Gloria and I vied for the privilege of sleeping with her.

For a while the first one who said it during the day would be the one; it got so both would say it the moment our eyes opened to a new day. Finally, weary of it, Mama said, "Both can sleep with her every night," thus making two little girls happy.

This rule held until Gregory became old enough to demand his turn, then came others to demand theirs; so Mama was forced to make each take turns again. For many years we kept strict account of whose turn it was.

Had Lillian been a different person she could have ruled us as a tyrant. But she wouldn't have been Lillian; none of us, she least of all, was aware that she did rule us, but with love.

For a few years Glory and I enjoyed being the only eligibles. In order that each be close to her, she slept in the middle. On the first night she had to make a rule.

"Move over. I ain't got room enough to cuss a cat. I can't even turn over." She began pushing us toward the bed's edge, then stopped, and said, "I know. Let's all lie the same way, and when I say 'spoon' or one of you say it, all turn the same way. That way we'll have more room."

We might as well have been Siamese triplets.

Before long Jenny brought Papa bad tidings of Lillian. "She won't study. When I ask if she has her lessons, she always says yes, but I never see her study. What's worse, there's an old Holy Roller woman living down the hall, who talks about Jesus all the time. Lillian practically lives with her after school until bedtime, and nearly all Lillian talks about is Jesus, too."

Thoughtfully, Papa said, "Well, I can't take her out of school now. I'll see what I can do with her."

He found us playing paper dolls in the back room. Opening the door, he gaped at the stovewood, which he had to cut, arranged on the floor in three houses. This took a lot of stovewood.

"Christamighty! What is all this? So-o, this is why the wood box stays empty!"

"Oh, Papa!" we laughed.

Sitting on the floor with us, he let his eyes travel slowly over our play paraphernalia. He saw with his eyes, but his mind couldn't grasp the meaning of the world so familiar and dear to us. He was a Gulliver caught in the land of Lilliputians.

He shook his head, trying to fathom this world and the one of the Holy Roller. Abandoning the effort as useless, he plunged into the world of Lillian. "Lillian, what's this woman's name who lives down the hall from you in town?"

"Valentine Bounds, and Papa, you ought to hear her pray."

"Have you heard her?"

"Sure, I hear her every night when we're in town. We pray together and Jesus comes and stands in the room with us."

"Now, Lillian!"

"But we feel Him, Papa!"

He was silent a long moment. "Instead of going to her apartment so much, hadn't you ought to be studying?"

[32]

"We git my lessons first. Don't take but a few minutes, then we pray and git up her Sunday sermon."

"Her sermon?"

"Why, yes. Mrs. Bounds preaches every Sunday at a church."

"M-m-m. Ain't you in her way when she's gitting her sermon?"

"No, I help her."

"Listen, Lillian, you mustn't go to her apartment every night. She'll git tired of you. Once a week is quite enough, and I'd rather you not go at all."

"But who'll help her git up her sermons?"

"She can git them herself."

"But, Papa, who'll help me git up my lessons?"

"Can't Jenny?"

"No, she's too busy gitting up her own. She sits up to way in the night studying. Some nights she don't even take her clothes off — just falls across the bed, shoes, corset and all on."

"*Corset?*"

"*You* said she was a grown girl now, and all grown girls wear corsets, she says. In the mornings I have to lace her up, and she says the corset pinches awful."

"How do you know she goes to bed with all her clothes on?"

"We can't sleep good 'cause we can't blow out that 'lectric light, and I wake up and see her sound asleep with all her clothes on."

"You gooses! Don't you know you don't blow out a 'lectric light? There's a little knob at the top of the globe you turn and the light will go out. When you want it back on you turn that knob agin. You tell Jenny, be sure and tell her, *I* said she don't have to wear a corset."

"I told her Mrs. Bounds don't wear one, and she's grown, but Jenny said Mrs. Bounds ain't a proper person."

"Jenny must be a proper person, I suppose. Lillian, you stay away from Mrs. Bounds!"

"I can't, Papa! Mrs. Bounds says Jesus won't talk to her unless I'm there, and she can't git her sermons unless Jesus talks to her; so I have to be there. Besides, I'm going to be a preacher just like her when I git grown."

[33]

For a long moment Papa looked at his second daughter. He had to get her away from that Mrs. Bounds. Yet he just couldn't take her out of school now. Getting an education was the most important thing in life. It meant a better job, a better life — why, it taught a person how to use the brains God had given him. Only a few more weeks, then he could bring her home. But Lillian, a preacher!

He rose and left the room, and we resumed playing. It was as though he had never interrupted.

He sought Mama in the kitchen and told her all Lillian said, ending, "I tell you, Bela, I can't bring her home till school is out. That Mrs. Bounds must be crazy."

"Why," Mama said, "my daddy would turn over in his grave if he knowed a grandchild of his was associating with a Holy Roller."

"That's who she's taking it from!"

"What?"

"Preaching, that's what. She wants to be a preacher and she inherited it from your pa!"

Mama sniffed. "There's worse things than being a Baptist preacher. I could name a few."

"Now, Ma, I didn't say — "

"If Lillian wants to be a preacher, she can be one!"

Without another word, Papa picked up his hat and headed for the barn. As the door closed he heard Mama's last words:

"I dast say a woman can preach as well as a man any old day!"

After he took the girls to school Monday he arranged for them to stay with his uncle and aunt, Dr. and Mrs. Horace Abbott, until school was out. They had a big house and only two children, who were about the ages of Gregory and me. Needless to say, both loved Lillian immediately. Since he had to move their belongings from Hall Villa and notify the girls, it was later than usual when he returned, but he came with a satisfied mind. No longer would Lillian have access to Mrs. Bounds.

Entering into her new environment with her usual whole-heartedness, Lillian soon forgot Mrs. Bounds. And, as usual, she let her heart rule her head. Before school was out she became entangled in a situation which ended town schooling for her and Gloria.

Much to the annoyance of our aunt and her cook, a next-door neighbor was letting her chickens run loose. Not only would they come into Aunt Deena's yard, but also they would come inside the house and fly onto the dining table. Because there were no screens in those days, open doors offered easy access for chickens, flies, etc.

Constantly having to shoo the chickens out, both Aunt Deena and the cook voiced their strong disapproval, which Lillian overheard. Her loyalty demanded action.

Finding a hen on the table one day, Lillian caught it and without hesitation, took it to the backyard, wrung off its head, then threw it into the yard of the neighbor, who brought it to Aunt Deena. "This is my hen and you killed it!"

"No, I didn't, but I'll be responsible for it."

"I'll sue you!"

"Go right ahead, but I'll sue you for letting your chickens be a common nuisance."

Though no lawsuits issued, bad feelings resulted, but Aunt Deena wasn't bothered by the chickens again.

Knowing Lillian had killed the hen and thinking it marvelous, our great-aunt told Papa, but his reaction was far different from his aunt's. He decided country school might not be such an inferior education after all, so when town school ended in April Lillian and Gloria came home for good.

Since Jenny would now be a "sub-freshman" in North Georgia College, she went to live with Grandpa, Aunt Tish and Aunt Sally during school terms. When Grandpa moved to town Aunt Sally moved back home with her father. All concerned were determined that nothing would defeat Jenny's ambition to become a schoolteacher.

In his new job Papa had to go to remote mountain cabins to induce owners to have their cows dipped. Since town families owned cows, they had to be induced too. Uncle Lish lived in town. And owned a cow.

Not wishing to make his authority too obvious, Papa didn't

bother the town people for a while. There was enough in the country to keep him occupied for some time, and occupied he was, many days until long past dark. The job was proving to be a big one, and he was given a helper.

Papa carried his usual conscientiousness into his new work, and discovered being a government man was not eating pie.

After some dipped cows died, no doubt from pneumonia, but many people believed from disinfectant, some, including Uncle Lish, let it be known that they wouldn't allow their cows to be dipped, and any government man coming onto their premises would be shot.

Papa was a peaceable man, and a little gun-shy. He said he never knew an Abbott who wasn't. "None of 'em has ever been in jail, but none has ever been a sheriff, either," he said with a little laugh. But he was no coward. He was a family man.

"Born in ignorance, bred in ignorance, they'll die in ignorance" was his summary of the situation, and he turned in his resignation the last of March, but not before he dipped Uncle Lish's cow.

Fairly well educated, Papa had taught school before his marriage, and wasn't as ignorant as some natives. Fairly well educated too, Uncle Lish couldn't use ignorance as an excuse. The enmity he felt toward Papa wouldn't allow him to submit to orders from his younger brother, but Papa had the backing of the law.

When forced to submit Uncle Lish ceased speaking to him, and ordered his family to act accordingly. In the following fall they moved to Texas, and for over twenty years the silence between the two families lay unbroken.

CHAPTER 7

Lillian and Diggers of Grass

With no other source of income, Papa became a digger of grass in earnest; at least, he became the sower and plower, we girls became the diggers.

By the time Lillian and Glory came home in April, the seeds he had planted were two to four inches high and growing, but not as fast as the grass amongst them.

Unable to plow and hoe too, Papa introduced the art of hoeing to three reluctant students. He was no stranger to farm life, as he had been born and raised in the house where we now lived; and his instructions were lucid and ample enough for us to construe their meaning: get the grass out of the cotton, corn, etc.

After buying each a hoe, he took us to his cotton field for our first lesson in chopping cotton. "Chop out all the cotton except two stalks to a hill, and leave about a foot and a half space between each hill." He showed us by example while we watched in silence. He made cotton, grass and dirt skid through the air, but his accomplishment didn't impress us.

Taking our hoes, at Papa's insistence, we began chopping a row each. For a round or two Papa went with us to see how well we could do. Then, trusting his cotton crop to our inexperienced and unwilling hands, he departed to plow corn.

In the very early morning our shadows stretched long before us, drops of jeweled dew lay heavy on tender leaves and the cooing of mourning doves echoed the sadness in our hearts. Imprisoned within walls of limited space, we were bound by alien and unwonted fetters that chafed and restrained spirit and body; they transferred energy into narrow channels of uncharted courses; they fashioned our wills to warp and woof of sun, grass and dirt, and embroiled us in the struggle of reality.

Reality embodied rows and rows of cotton to be chopped, and

after a dozen or so rounds our struggle was wavering. The sun beamed high in the sky, bringing sweat to forehead and lips; the new exertion started fatigue growing in unused muscles. Blisters formed on our hands from the friction of hard hoe handle against flesh, and feet grew more reluctant to go forward.

Looking up from our rows, Glory and I saw Lillian standing still, hoe handle under her chin and her gaze directed to the distant rail fence separating field and wood. When she saw us looking at her, she said, "I saw Roger climbing over that rail fence. Before I left the house I told him he couldn't go nowhere today. I'm gonna whip him good when I git home." Roger was one of her many "sons" and her favorite, despite her threat and ferocious look toward the wood.

"How come you made him stay home?" Glory asked.

"Yesterday I hung my best mattress out the window to sun, and for pure meanness he climbed on the housetop and poured a bucket of syrup all over it. He ruined my best mattress!"

Glory and I broke into laughter, but she turned an outraged look upon us. "I told him to stay in his room all day for that mean trick. I'll wear him out when I git home. See if I don't!"

Her look and words couldn't erase the ludicrous picture, and she joined our laughter. Soon we were sitting in the middle of the field in an uncontrollable fit of mirth while grass and cotton continued to grow unmolested.

When our laughter subsided Lillian got up, brushed the dirt from her dress and said, "I'm thirsty. Let's hurry and finish our rows and go to the house for some water."

Quickly, we finished, threw down our hoes and went. On the way Lillian broke a switch from a black gum bush, and proceeded to beat bushes (stand-ins for Roger) all the way.

Mama saw us at the well. "What're you doing back so early?"

"We got thirsty," Lillian said.

"Dinner'll soon be ready. No need to go back until after dinner."

At the thought, we became sorrowful. We looked longingly toward the thin woods in which we played; hearing noisy blue jays in nearby trees, we thought of other birds: "Phoebe! Phoebe!" "Chick-a-dee! Chick-a-dee!" calling from the deep wood; we could close our eyes and see the dappled shade of new leaves. Our hearts constricted at the thought of waiting hoes. The afternoon sun would be much hotter.

When Papa arrived for dinner, he asked, "Did you finish?"

Lillian's mouth opened, her mind knowing how little we had done; she shook her head, unable to say words. Then she held out her blistered hands.

Papa said, "Oh, phaw! Put a little turpentine on 'em, and they'll soon go away." He seemed heartless. And relentless.

Needing a better excuse, she said, "We got thirsty."

Papa said, "You ought to've finished that cotton. I wanted you to hoe corn this evening."

Lillian's mouth opened wider. We were entangled for fair. Stretching before us were endless days of hoeing.

Papa continued, "When you go back after dinner, take some jars of water and set 'em in the shade to keep cool. But finish that cotton before you come home."

All three of us swallowed sudden big lumps in our throats.

In the late afternoon Erastus Redder came down the road on a big, white horse, but he never slowed the horse from its gallop or glanced sidways to notice a twelve-year-old girl who stood still to watch him as long as he was in sight.

After that day Lillian always liked to work in fields near the road, for Erastus often passed on his galloping white horse, which never paused in its gallop; nor did the rider ever turn his head to glance at Lillian, gazing after him with her heart in her eyes.

In odd moments she began singing the lonesome song:

> I have loved you, yes, dearly loved you
> More than all this world can know;
> But you slighted me for another,
> And I say forever go.
>
> At night while you lay asleeping,
> Taking in your sweet repose,
> I'm a poor girl, broken-hearted,
> Listening to the wind that blows.

*

[39]

Shivers would run over me at her singing, and I hated Erastus for not loving her; for her song sounded as mournful as winter wind moaning through tall pines.

Papa was no slave driver; we didn't spend all our time digging; sometimes we were free to lose ourselves in our make-believe world.

Lillian's imagination had grown. We no longer played funerals. She was now a full-fledged preacher, preaching sermons from a rock pulpit in our play church. Her sermons always had the same result: weeping by the three of us.

Planks across rocks were the benches. Though Glory and I, sometimes Gregory, were the only living congregation, the benches were filled with sticks, substitutes for people.

We were different people, too. Lillian was Mrs. White and had a house full of children, though no mention was ever made of her husband. Of her children Glory and I knew three sons, Alfarette, Arbuckle and Roger. They were ever giving their mother trouble by climbing on tops of houses, cribs, barns, etc., from which they inevitably fell.

Gloria was Mrs. Green; she also had a house full of children, though their escapades remained unknown since we were too busy listening to those of Lillian's children.

Being too young to choose, I was given the ugliest name, Mrs. Brown, but I was too grateful to be Mrs. Anybody to protest. I too had a house full of children, identical to Lillian's.

Each built a playhouse near our "church" in the cool, thin wood adjoining the meadow; thrushes, phoebes, peewees, chickadees and other birds poured forth their songs to our welcoming ears; sunlight sifting through the trees made intricate shade patterns on the ground, and we could lift our eyes and see the sunbathed meadow dotted with daisies and Queen Anne's lace.

Once a week Lillian held church services. When Gregory was present we had difficulty making him sit still; he would never join our weeping, but would gaze at us with wonder in his big, gray eyes. To our household he had become the object of adoration, a very fit object, too, having grown into a rosy-cheeked boy with golden ringlets and merry laugh.

Since he was the only male child and still the baby, Mama wasn't eager to trust him to our care. Her distrust wasn't altogether unsound; for one morning we slipped him away. The air was chilly, and we put his red winter cap on him.

The meadow and brook were so enticing that morning that we abandoned our old playhouses. Lillian said, "Glory, Greg will be my little boy. Lowell can be your little girl. I'll build my playhouse across the branch, and you build yours on this one. Then we can cross the branch to see each other."

Finding an uprooted sapling, Lillian laid it across the brook at the narrowest place, which was also the deepest. Carefully, she carried Greg across, and soon two playhouses were ready for visiting.

Lillian decided to visit us first. With Greg straddling her hips she started across the slender footlog. When she reached the middle, the sapling gave way; she and Greg tumbled into the water and, for an instant, were unseen.

When Greg's red cap rose to the surface and went floating downstream, Glory and I began screaming, but the water churned and Lillian emerged grasping Gregory. She pulled him to the bank on our side.

Wiping water from his face, he gleefully shrieked, "I been babsized! I been babsized!"

That was the only baptism of Lillian's which was unintentional. That, too, was the end of our sneaking Gregory out to play. Realizing that he and Lillian might have drowned, we quickly went home. Lillian and Greg stayed in the smokehouse while Glory and I smuggled them dry clothes. For the rest of the day we stayed in the yard, sobered by what might have been.

Spying a gourd vine near the washpot, Lillian said, "Vina Washpot lives near us and comes to play all the time. See, she's right beside you, Glory!"

Glory looked. No one was there. I could see no one either.

Prickles were at the nape of my neck. But Lillian's eyes focused just beyond Glory.

"I can see her plain as day. Her hair is black and curly, her eyes are big and green, and she has freckles on her face. She's always laughing at something. She's mean, too. Just yesterday she filled the sugar holder full of salt, and nearly died laughing when her Papa tasted the salt in his coffee. She stuck a pin through the cushion of her Mama's rocker, and laughed and laughed when her Mama sat down on it, and jumped two feet in the air."

By then Glory and I were enthralled with Vina Washpot, even if we couldn't see her, and accepted her presence as natural. Living through Lillian, she was our constant playmate; like a shadow she followed us wherever we went, and her escapades often enlivened a dull day of digging.

Our cow was dry. We bought buttermilk for supper from Tater Collins and family, who lived about a mile away through some woods and across a creek. Going for the milk, of course, fell to us girls, but we didn't mind. Walking through the woods in late afternoon was a pleasure, but crossing the creek was quite another matter.

Crossing was by means of a footlog, the flat side of a split log. By long use it dipped close to the water in the middle where the water was deepest. Since there were no handrails, crossing was perilous at any time, but crossing while the creek was swollen by rain and running swiftly took courage indeed.

We had to do this one day when the rushing, angry water lapped the log. I backed away. "I ain't crossing."

For once Glory was my staunch supporter. "I ain't either."

Lillian said, "You won't have any milk for supper."

"We don't care."

"If we don't git that milk, we won't have *any* supper."

We considered empty stomachs, looked at the footlog, and decided on empty stomachs.

But Lillian did not. She broke a short stick from a black-gum bush for each of us and stuck them in our mouths. "Here, chew on this real hard as you cross, and you won't be skeered. Now, follow me!"

Without hesitation, with milk bucket in hand, she crossed; following her, chewing as fast as jaws allowed, Glory and I crossed. Sure enough, no thought of fear entered our minds. Getting across crowded out all else.

CHAPTER 8

Indian Graves, the Chestatee and Thunderstorms

THROUGH LILLIAN'S IMAGINATION and curiosity a new road was always beckoning us. What she couldn't think of, Mama said, was frost-bit.

One road, though, lay unexplored so far by us girls because we hadn't noticed it. A little way beyond our house, it branched to the left and was hardly more than a trail. Bordered by dense, dark woods, it ran past the Johnson house on the bank of the Chestatee River to dip through a shallow ford and climb to the Colley house, perched high on a hill facing the river.

One night at supper Papa said, "In the woods on the river road are three Indian graves. Cherokees. They used to own all this land around here. When any died the others just piled a heap of rocks on 'em. Well, these graves near the road are rock piles nearly as high as this house. If you go stand close to 'em, and say, 'Little Indian, little Indian, what are you doing there?' they'll answer nothing, nothing at all."

To think of dead people talking made the hair on our scalps rise. We had never heard of dead people talking. But then, Indians could do anything. We could hardly wait until next day to hear them.

Papa told us how to find the road — just beyond our peanut patch — and said the graves were to the right a piece down and near the road. But the graves were far enough in the wood for the big, thick trees to provide a gloomy and fearsome place.

Lillian, Glory and I tiptoed close to the big piles of rock.

Lillian whispered, "Little Indian, little Indian, what are you doing there?"

We stood shivering and listening.

Silence.

Glory said, "Lillian, maybe you didn't say it loud enough."

So Lillian said louder, "Little Indian, little Indian, what are you doing there?"

Again a long silence. Something must be wrong.

Shaking with fear by then, we clutched each other, but Lillian was determined to hear the dead Indians talk. She said, "Let's all shout it together. They might be hard of hearing. One, two — "

So we shouted, "Little Indian, little Indian, what are you doing there?"

And listened. And waited.

And waited.

We tried repeating the question one by one, shouting it one by one; whispering it one by one; in quavering normal voices one by one; and all these in unison.

But the little Indians answered nothing, nothing at all.

When crops were laid by at the end of June, Dewey School opened for the first session, and would remain open until harvest. Though their school had ended only in April, Lillian and Gloria had to go. Papa wanted his children to obtain a good education, and every little bit counted.

Children then had to buy their own books and supplies; also, since Jenny was going to summer school, he had to pay tuition; so he stood in need of cash. He persuaded Uncle Dob to accompany him and they secured a job high in the mountains at a sawmill. The distance being too great to commute, they batched in a cabin during the week.

While Papa was away we children discovered Mama's terror of thunderstorms, which came with furious ferocity and brought mighty wind, hail, thunder and vicious lightning. In town we had a storm cellar, and Papa. That summer we had neither.

Whenever Mama saw boiling dark clouds tinged with pink over the mountains, she closed windows and doors and took us into the parlor, which had no chimney.

When wind began tossing trees into twisting paroxysms, thunder became a continuous rumble and lightning mean, yellow streaks, she would fall to her knees and begin fervent praying. "Oh Lord, save us from this storm! Have mercy, oh Lord, and save us — " And on and on, over and over, she made her plea known to the Lord. When it seemed destruction was upon us, she burst into horrible weeping.

Of course we children would, too. All but Lillian. In vain she would try to interest us in games we normally loved, such as "Wire Briar, Limber Lock," "Slap Hands," or "What'cha Got There?" But we were deaf and blind to everything but Mama's terror.

Even if Mama had not had cause to dread storms (she had experienced a cyclone when she was fourteen), her fear wasn't without reason. Wind rocked the house and often toppled huge oaks; lightning scooted across the floor in blue balls or lit the room with blue streaks; hail as large as bird's eggs beat the house and castigated the earth; and thunder shook the house and made the earth tremble.

It was indeed a time for trembling. If Lillian did, we never knew. When it seemed the earth would be destroyed, she brought out black-gum toothbrushes, stuck one in each of our mouths and told us to chew hard. Then she would sing:

> Be not dismayed, whate'er betide,
> God will take care of you;
> Beneath his wings of love abide,
> God will take care of you.
>
> God will take care of you,
> Thro' ev'ry day, o'er all the way;
> He will take care of you,
> God will take care of you.

*

Her confident voice would soothe us, Mama's weeping would subside, and the storm itself would end. As soon as Mama said it was safe to open doors, we would hasten to the front porch to eat the accumulated hail.

After one of the most violent storms anyone ever remembered, Papa and Uncle Dob came home to stay. They couldn't risk leaving their families alone at the mercy of such weather, they said.

It was just as well, for it was almost harvest, school was out and Jenny came home for two weeks before entering college.

CHAPTER 9

The Young Lady, Grandma Walters and the Mad Dog

J ENNY'S COMING HOME meant she wouldn't stay in town during the week and would help with the harvest for two weeks. Since she was now a young lady, she could have no ray of sun darken her milky skin, so she covered every inch with old clothes and a wide-brimmed hat.

Though proud to know Jenny was a young lady, I didn't want Lillian to be one. Her skin was honey-colored with freckles scattered over her nose. I didn't want her wrapped up like Jenny while in the fields or hurt by pinching corsets.

One day I asked Jenny, "Does it hurt to be a young lady?"

And she told me, "Yes, in some ways, like pinching corsets. But then, you have to pay a price for everything. At first, I didn't want to be grown-up, but now I do, so I have to pay for it by wearing corsets and tight shoes. You see, there are good things in being grown-up — like courting." She blushed.

She had been courting since we moved to the farm. All through spring, on Sunday afternoons Dave Colley called on her. They walked out to the orchard. The apple trees held up their sweetness to a cloudless sky, and she leaned on the June apple tree while they talked there.

My envying eyes watched them. When I got to be a young lady, I was going to look just like Jenny in a white dimity dress with a pink ribbon sash, and have a big pink bow in my hair, which would be flowing like a dark cloud over my shoulders. I would be courted by a sweetheart just like Dave, a tall, slender young man with black hair and sad brown eyes, sort of like the eyes of our dog, Nig.

Just as Dave had to Jenny, my sweetheart would propose to me while showers of apple blossom petals blew around us. Only I wouldn't tell him I was going to be a schoolteacher and couldn't marry him. Papa and Mama were married, and I wanted to be married, too, though Jenny seemed not to want to be; for she didn't intend to marry Shad, either.

When Dave stopped courting Jenny, Shad Grindle began. He too came on Sunday afternoons. They didn't walk to the orchard, but sat on the front porch facing the Blue Ridge Mountains. Shad didn't mind Jenny being a schoolteacher; he was one already, so they had much to talk about.

Their courting was slow. All through summer and harvest an aura of romance swirled around Jenny like invisible mist; even her outlandish garb worn in the fields didn't vanquish it. We three eyed her with a little awe; but to our surprise, she did as much field work as we.

All four did more in less time because Jenny was there to prevent our watching every bird flying over and listening to the latest escapade of Vina Washpot. Nor did we pause to watch Erastus Redder galloping by on his white horse.

While we were picking peas one day, she said, "I want to tell you all a secret, but you must promise not to tell Mama."

Though not knowing what a secret was, I promised with the other two. Coming close, Jenny said in a low voice, as if we were surrounded by people instead of pea vines, "When spring comes we're going to have another brother or sister. Mama's going to have another baby."

"Another one?" Lillian asked, not altogether pleased.

Jenny nodded. They looked at each other.

"I hope it'll be a brother," Glory said. "We have enough sisters, *I* think."

Saying nothing, I wondered how Jenny knew when Mama didn't. It must be a surprise for her. I knew about surprises. Sometimes when I would be doing something very quietly so Mama wouldn't hear, she would suddenly appear in the doorway.

"Surprised you, didn't I? Now march yourself into the dining room, where I can keep an eye on you."

Surprises made me feel bad, so I wouldn't tell her, even when we were alone in the dining room, where we stayed most in winter. It had our very long dining table, a lot of chairs, a fireplace and the back door, which opened onto the back porch. A window faced the barn, which was down a little slope.

The fireplace was the focal point. To the right was the door to the kitchen, which had only casement windows. In it were the cookstove, some shelves, a kitchen safe where dishes were kept, a lot of nails on which hung cooking utensils, and a wash bench on which were set a water bucket, washpan and a cake of lye soap, which Mama had made.

In our bedroom were two double beds for us four girls. Between the beds was the passageway from the dining room to our parents' room. Our dresses were hung on nails around the walls. We had never heard of a clothes closet, and I doubt if any house in the area had one. Nor any coat hangers.

Not long after Jenny returned to school, Grandma Walters came to live with us. She slept in Jenny's bed, which meant Jenny, when she was home, would sleep with Grandma; so Glory and I would have to sleep with Lillian, our one consolation.

Since Grandpa's death, Grandma had tried living alone, but couldn't make a living, so she moved in with Uncle Dob and Aunt Lanie; then, unable to endure Uncle Dob's drinking, she moved in with us. The only things she had to move were her clothes.

"I could never 'bide whiskey," she said.

Her parents were Scotch-Irish, and Grandma's speech held

the brogue; she also talked at a fast clip, and both made her talk seem comical to us children.

Her Scottish blood showed, too, in her frugality. She was more saving than we. When she wanted to make a fire in the cookstove, instead of striking a match to the kindling, she would get a shovelful of coals from the fireplace, put them in the stove, lay kindling on top and blow the embers into flame. Most of the time this took some doing. She would blow, blow and blow. "Good for the lungs, saves matches, too," she told us.

Once when she stooped to get the coals she raised her head too quickly and whacked it sharply on the fireboard.

"LordGodAlmighty! I wish thar wanna fireboard in Lumpkin County!"

We three girls laughed, not because she bumped her head, but because of her speech. Mama though we were laughing at the former, and at the first opportunity she told us, "Don't you young'uns ever laugh at my mama agin. She's had a hard life, and I don't aim for a passel of young'uns making it harder."

Then she told her mother's story:

Before the Civil War Grandma's parents owned a big plantation and a lot of slaves. When the war began Grandma was fourteen. Her two older brothers and her pa had to go fight, leaving Grandma, an eight-year-old brother, and her mother, whose hands were crippled by rheumatism.

Every slave left and Grandma had to do everything in field and house. She didn't know how to do anything, but she learned by doing. She plowed, planted, and reaped; she cut down trees and split wood; she learned to cook, weave cloth and sew.

For over three years the menfolks were gone. They were too far off for furloughs, and if it was their time of trial and tribulation, it was also that of the homefolk.

Coffee couldn't be had, so Grandma parched corn or made tea from sassafras bark. Salt couldn't be found, so Grandma dug up the dirt on which salt from curing meat had dripped, boiled and strained the water and used it. Syrup was used for sweetening. They had no shoes, so she made them out of quilts.

Soon after the men came back, her family lost the plantation because they couldn't pay the taxes, and they had to start renting. All worked harder than any slave ever had. "You young'uns don't know what hard work is. Just look at Ma's calloused, sprattled hands!

"Then she married Pa who didn't have nothing. In them days nobody had nothing. But Pa never did git nothing, so Ma had to help make a living right on. While she's living with us her life is going to be as easy as we can make it. I won't have her laughed at and aggravated by you young'uns. Remember that!"

We remembered, though it was hard on certain occasions. Like the time our dog Fetch snatched the chicken head, which was Grandma's favorite piece.

Papa killed chickens by chopping their heads off. Grandma wrung their necks, threw the heads and bodies down to bleed. This time Fetch watched from under the house. As soon as the head hit the ground she streaked out, snatched it, ran for a crib, crawled under and dined in safety.

Grandma burst into the house at a run, vowing, "I'm ganna kill that dog! See if I danna. She got my chicken head, and I'm ganna kill 'er! Shure as I live I'll kill 'er! Won't nobody know what wenna with 'er, but I'm ganna kill that dog!"

She had no use for dogs, and we had two, Nig and Fetch. Nig had belonged to Papa's mother and was left when Grandpa moved to town. Fetch was our own, much loved even by Mama. Grandma made no move to make friends with them.

Nor did she with us children. She seemed simply to ignore us, centering most of her attention on Mama. They did many chores together and seemed to have a lot of fun, laughing and talking.

But while Mama was sewing, Grandma was out in the woods gathering wood to be used under the washpot. Since we three girls were usually in the fields, we paid no heed to where she was stashing the wood. In our goings and comings we often saw her moving toward the pasture gate with her arms loaded.

Then one day, free from field work, we went down to the cow shelter where we had labored so long and hard to make a real playhouse, and stood gazing in utter dismay. Our beautiful white rock miniature fireplace had been toppled by an armload of washwood, our pretty oak sapling beds made by Lillian were smashed and washwood was piled all over our lovely playhouse.

Crying and working, we threw out every stick and soon had the playhouse clean again, but we couldn't rebuild the fireplace or mend the beds.

Lillian vowed, "I'll never forgive her for that! Never, **NEVER**, *never!*" Gloria and I also made the vow.

From that day Grandma was considered our enemy. But, remembering what Mama said, we said no word to anyone but each other. Being such a stranger to us, Grandma also said not a word but put all the wood back under the shelter and piled more on, and we hated her fervently and completely.

One afternoon Papa took Lillian and Glory to help gather corn; Mama went to see her sister Lanie, and left Greg and me with Grandma, who went to look for more washwood; she left Greg and me playing in the white sand of the backyard; for the weather was warm and sunny.

Sometime later I noticed a strange dog coming into the yard, an unusual happening; I also noticed how big and mean he looked, which sent a shiver of fear through me.

My fear was well founded; the dog made straight for Nig lying nearby and jumped on him, snarling and growling. Always a coward, Fetch tucked her tail between her legs and crawled under a crib.

Taking Greg by the hand, I led him to a safe distance, I thought, and stood watching, my heart in my mouth; for it was plain Nig was no match for the big dog. Somehow he broke away and fled to the barn. But the big dog didn't follow. Saliva dribbled from its mouth, its eyes were red and mean. I took Greg's hand again and was backing away when, to my horror, the dog advanced on us.

Though scream after scream tore out of my throat, I couldn't get my legs to move, and we stood facing a horrible death. Then there was Grandma, rushing between us and the dog.

In a voice I knew to obey, she said, "Mad dog! Git Gregory on the back porch and stay there!"

Her voice activated my legs, and I pulled Greg onto the porch, and turned to see Grandma meet the dog head-on. With one hand she caught hold of the dog's upper jaw, with the other she

[51]

got hold of its tongue and began pulling. In the struggle she got the dog's head between her legs and, with superhuman effort, held it; with both hands she pulled the tongue until it ripped from the mouth; flinging it down, she caught the dog's upper and lower jaws, prying them apart until the bones snapped, and the lower jaw hung useless. All the while the dog was wrestling her all over the yard, but when she heard the bones snap, she let go and came running onto the porch steps, half falling, half sitting.

The dog also began running but in an odd manner, not toward anything in particular; the running became a stagger, then the dog fell to the ground, jerking and writhing in the blood pouring from it.

I looked at Grandma. She had slid half down the steps, and was panting as if she had run long and fast; sweat was streaming from her face. She made no effort to wipe it away; she just sat, sweating and panting, her hands all bloody, and slick from slobber.

Crying quietly, I crouched near her. Her eyes focused on me, though filled with horror still, and she said between gasps, "Now you — know — why — I ain't got — no — use — for dogs. Always — going mad — biting — killing."

Deep shudders began to shake her, and she stopped talking. Abruptly, she began crying and tears mingled with the sweat running down her face. Gregory and I joined her terrible weeping. After a little while, it spent itself.

She began to speak haltingly. "Saw a baby boy die — 'bout size — Gregory — had fits — like mad dog — horrible death — horrible way — to die. I hate — dogs — can't bide 'em." She nodded toward the now still dog. "Mad. Woulda got you — and Gregory. Thank GodAlmighty — I heard — you scream. Come running. Danna breathe a word to your ma — oughtn't to know — Gregory — too little — tell. Danna say a word to 'er!"

I nodded, still looking at her, and in looking I could understand something of the way she was. Most of her life had been spent in the pristine struggle of survival. Was it any wonder she couldn't see the little ways of children and could only see things like safety, food, shelter and provision for the morrow?

I wanted to cower at her feet and kiss them, to throw my arms around her neck and hold her tight. I could not. She had never touched me, and now I couldn't bring myself to touch her.

She never laid a hand upon any of us children in anger or loving-kindness, but now I knew she would fight to save our lives, counting her own as nothing. Fascinated, I couldn't tear my eyes away from the woman who sat shuddering, sweating, bloodied and slobbered. She was my grandma, and I was glad she was. So glad that little prickles shuttled up and down my spine and came out of my mouth and heart in sudden laughter.

She scolded. "Hush that laughing. T'ain't nothing funny!"

"Oh, Grandma! I'm so glad you're my grandma!"

Like the sun breaking through dark clouds, she smiled at me, then got up slowly and stiffly, climbed onto the porch to the wash shelf. Over and over, she washed her trembling hands, emptying one pan of soapy water, filling it again and again, washing and washing until I thought she would wash away her hands. Finally satisfied, she went into the house to change her clothes.

When she came out, she said, "Let's go to the barn and wait for your papa."

We didn't have long to wait because Papa was about to go get Mama. Grandma did a lot of talking in her clippity way, and Papa's face grew white and the eyes of my sisters grew big as they listened.

At the end Papa looked at Grandma with tears in his eyes. "I don't know how to thank you, Sarah."

Tears were in Grandma's eyes, too. "No need. I'm glad I was there, Caleb."

"You've got to have a doctor examine you. We'll go after Bela, then go on to town to see Dr. Abbott." Turning to Lillian, he asked, "Reckon you can look after the little 'uns while we go?"

Her answer was hearty. "Yes, sir. I sure can."

Before they left Papa buried the dog and its tongue, then spread clean sand over its blood. He wanted to make sure Mama wouldn't find out until much later, and we all agreed not to breathe a word to her for a long time.

Papa told Mama her mother had to go to the doctor because

something was wrong with her stomach. They found Dr. Abbott at home, and Papa managed to get his uncle alone and tell him the story, and why they had to keep it from Mama. After the doctor examined Grandma and found no broken skin, he declared it a miracle. No broken skin meant she would be all right. Next morning Papa put Nig in a big box at the barn and told Mama he was sick. As days passed it was evident he was. Every day we took him food and water, and the day came when he couldn't eat; then came the mad fits which we watched with tear-filled eyes. One day he died. Papa buried him in a grave-yard all his own and marked his grave with white rocks. Lillian didn't hold a Christian funeral. We were too busy crying, including Papa.

Never again did we girls mention hating Grandma, though she continued piling washwood in our real playhouse. We abandoned it and returned to our playhouses in the thin wood.

CHAPTER 10

Winter and Christmas

HARVEST TIME meant more than gathering in from the fields, which Papa, Grandpa and we girls did. It was a preparation for winter.

Though Mama and Grandma had canned corn and tomatoes during the summer season, now they made crocks of kraut and hominy, and dried green beans, pumpkins, apples and anything else they could find.

When harvest of fields was garnered, Papa and Grandpa went into the deep wood to cut oak and hickory. Since they never ventured there without their guns, they often brought squirrels home for supper, our first taste of wild meat.

Grandpa took his wood home, and we children stacked ours on the back porch until it could hold no more, then we stacked rows in the yard until we had enough to last till spring.

Our world was soon imprisoned by winter and our way of life

changed. There was no field work or play in the thin wood, for snow lay deep on the ground. We three had no yearning for the outdoors, for we could hardly endure any time away from the fire.

Grandma's coming ended Papa's tale-telling at supper but, afterward, he would take Gregory and me on his lap while Lillian and Gloria sat near, and tell us stories. His knowledge of children's stories seemed endless; through him we learned the magic of fairies and elves; and, more important, we learned of the people from whom we were descended.

However, not all evenings were spent thus. On some, we popped corn over the fire, then Grandma and Mama would make popcorn balls by rolling the popcorn in molasses. Or Mama would boil a pot of chestnuts over the fire or both women made candy from molasses, and sometimes we got out the hymn books and sang.

Days drew close to Christmas and we girls began thinking of Santa Claus, inspired by Papa's singing:

> Up on the housetop reindeer pause
> Out jumps good old Santa Claus
> Down through the chimney with lots of toys
> All for good little girls and boys.

We couldn't have been better.

Christmas Eve morning Papa woke everybody shouting, "Christmas Eve gift! Christmas Eve gift, everybody!"

Since he said it first we were supposed to give him a gift, but we didn't because we didn't know the meaning of the word. He didn't know that, and all day he teased us by asking, "Where's my gift?"

Though he knew very little enjoyment himself, he tried to share what little he knew with us. On this Christmas Eve he was trying to bring us the shining magic of Christmas.

Coming in with an armload of wood, stamping snow off his shoes, he'd say, "I thought I heard sleighbells around the rooftop while I was gitting that wood. You young'uns had better start listening."

Throughout the day, he'd say, "You young'uns better be gitting ready for Santa Claus. I'm sure he's on his way." He went about singing:

> I think I hear the sleighbells ringing,
> The merry, merry sleighbells jingling,
> The bells of Santa Claus!
> The bells of Santa Claus!
>
> Then crack, crack, crack the whip!
> Old Santa makes them swiftly fly!
> Crack, crack, crack the whip!
> Old Santa makes them fly!

So we listened for Santa's sleighbells, but could hear only the cold wind sweeping around the house, though that didn't lessen our anticipation. Lillian made certain the dining room chimney was cleared of excessive soot; we hunted a pair of stockings without holes, pinned them together with safety pins, ready for hanging on the back of a chair at bedtime.

Then Papa told us, "After supper, we're going to church for the Christmas tree program," and the afternoon stretched endlessly.

After an eon of time supper was over and we were on our way. Wrapped in coats, caps and quilts, we children hovered together in the back of the wagon while in front Papa and Mama rode in two kitchen chairs, with Jenny and Grandma in others behind them.

Since Nell had to pick her way over the snowy road, our pace was slow, but we finally arrived and entered the church to the singing of "Joy to the World."

Rounded and tall, the tree stood proudly with lighted candles on its green branches and strings of popcorn wound in tantalizing loops from limb to limb. Underneath were small paper sacks on which all the children's eyes were glued.

After Preacher Crickett offered a prayer, we sang, "Hark, the Herald Angels Sing." Then came the sonorous voice of the preacher reading the old but ever new Christmas story. After another Christmas song, he gave the benediction, then asked the men to come and give out the sacks.

Every eye watched as a sack was placed into the eager hands of every man, woman and child. The minute the sack exchanged hands the owner opened it, pulled forth the contents and began eating.

My heart pounded until I too was handed a sack. In it were an orange, an apple, some bunched raisins, a stick of peppermint and one of lemon candy, some Brazil nuts and English walnuts. Reverently, I lifted my orange from from the sack and put it to my mouth for an immediate bite, but my eyes chanced on Lillian.

Holding her orange carefully, she was turning it around and around under her nose, taking deep smells. Lowering her face, she touched the orange lovingly with her lips, took another big smell, and returned the fruit tenderly to the sack; she withdrew the peppermint which she began eating.

Though my stomach clamored for the fruit, I did exactly as my sister did. It would taste better eaten when she ate hers. But my stomach rebelled at such treachery, and I appeased it with the peppermint.

Though it was past our bedtime, we girls lay awake in the darkness, listening for Santa's sleigh. At every pop and creak the house made, we were sure Santa's sleigh had settled on our housetop, but, not hearing any noise in the dining room where our stockings were hung, we choked back disappointment, and strained our ears again.

"Santa Claus has been here," Papa said from our doorway.

Opening our eyes to darkness, we saw Papa's silhouette in the light from the dining room. Throwing aside the covers, we rushed into the room where Papa had a roaring fire. Not waiting to see our joy or disappointment, he returned to bed.

On each of the chairs where our stockings were sat a doll. Mine was dressed in blue-checked gingham dress with matching bonnet, but it wasn't pretty because it had a cloth head and painted-on face. Gloria's was exactly like mine, but dressed in pink. Picking hers up, she took a quick look and put it down again. There was a small box for each of us also. Opening them, we found a tea set consisting of a teapot, two cups, two saucers and two plates. She stared at hers, then replaced the lid. Then we looked at Lillian.

She was holding a doll larger than ours, and its head was not of cloth. We saw it had painted blue eyes and blond curly hair, and the face was familiar.

Lillian was staring at the doll in dismay. When she looked at us the truth was plain in her eyes. "She's just like Grandma." At our dismal nods, she looked at the doll and said decisively, "Her name is Minerva."

Gloria and I glanced at our dolls with their cloth faces. We had no name for them.

"What else did you git?" Gloria asked.

Lillian picked up a woven straw thing with a handkerchief inside. "A handkerchief holder."

We had a third gift: a picture to hang on the wall. Lillian's was the prettiest, depicting a blooming apple tree by the rail fence of a meadow; Glory's was a mother holding an infant with a white filmy thing over her head; mine was a fat, little girl in her gown coming downstairs. The pictures were peculiar gifts. Years later I realized the walls of our house were bare of pictures of any kind.

Jenny didn't get up to see what Santa left her, so we looked at her chair. It held a picture of a young girl and man at a garden gate with lots of different colored flowers around; a handkerchief holder with one inside like Lillian's; and two silk hair ribbons, one pink and one blue. She had no doll.

Being the baby, Gregory hadn't got up, either. His chair held the most wondrous things of all: a monkey on a string, a red ball and a little red wagon.

Lillian said, "I wish I was a boy! I'd rather have what Greg got than what I did."

"Me, too," Glory and I echoed.

Our attention turned to our stockings. In one we found two apples, some Brazil nuts and bunched raisins (there were no seedless ones then); in the other, we found an orange, some

English walnuts, two sticks of peppermint and two sticks of lemon candy. Eating one each of the candy and the raisins on the spot, we saved the rest for days to come.

Many days passed before we ate our oranges. We kept toting them around, smelling them and anticipating the eating until at last we could no longer resist the pleasure of tasting.

Several days after Christmas, Glory and I were playing alone for once. She said, "I know how much our dolls cost."

I looked at her.

"Nineteen cents. I looked them up in Sears, Roebuck catalogue. I know how much Miss Lillian's cost, too. Twenty-nine cents."

Her information was lost on me. I missed the connection of Sears, Roebuck and Santa Claus.

CHAPTER 11

Aunt Sally Marries; Jode's Offer

LATE IN JANUARY Papa returned from town with exciting news. Aunt Sally was married.

"Christamighty, Bela, you ought to see him — dried-up persimmon. But *she* thinks she's found someone as good as her at last. I don't care how many farms he owns, I don't see how he can do her any good, him so much littler than she is — umph — umph," noticing us children with our big ears stuck out. "Anyway," he added hastily, "we're to go to Tish's for a big supper tomorrow night, 'cause they're leaving for south Georgia — where he lives — the day after." He looked at Grandma doubtfully. No mention of her had been made in the invitation. The Abbotts didn't socialize with Mama's people.

Grandma read his look and sniffed in disdain. "You needn't worry 'bout me, Caleb. I wanna go if I was invited. I'm just as good as they are, if they don't but know it, and it might be I'm just a little grain better. I'll just fix a bite o' supper here for me and Mr. Couch."

"Who?" Papa asked in unison with Mama.

"Mr. Thomas Couch, that's who. He's been wanting to court me, so I may as well let him."

Papa said, "Mrs. Walters, that man has already buried two wives. You don't want to be the third, do you?"

She sniggered in scorn. "Who said aught 'bout marrying? All I said was I'm going to let him do a little courting. I wouldn't marry a man the sun ever shone on. That I wouldn't!"

Papa laughed. "Well, all I have to say is rats like cheese as good as mice!"

Quickly, Grandma's eyes lowered to her lap, and her face turned pink. "LordGodAlmighty, Caleb, I'm shamed o' you!"

We went to Aunt Tish's for supper and Grandma prepared supper for her beau, Mr. Couch.

Sure enough, Uncle Willy just about came up to Aunt Sally's shoulders, but his blue eyes from behind thick-lensed glasses were steadfast, and he gave a nice, pleasant impression. He owned three big farms and a big house full of fine furniture.

All he did was ride around on a horse overseeing his tenants. Upon a horse he must seem bigger than he was. Two years past he buried his first wife. They had several children, so Aunt Sally had not only got a husband but also a family. One thing was certain — he was a sure enough gentleman, Aunt Sally said, thinking mostly of all he owned.

He wasn't the only man we met at the supper. To our surprise, Aunt Tish had a beau there. His name was Jode and he was kin to the Shores, the richest family in town. "He comes from a FINE family," Aunt Tish made a point of telling Mama. "He's a railroad man. Up here visiting kinfolks a few days." Kinfolks weren't all he was visiting.

Not at all short like Uncle Willy, Jode towered over every man present, even Papa. When my eyes got up to his face I liked his eyes. They were as blue as the October sky.

I heard Grandpa tell Papa in private, "I'm mighty afraid Tish has her hooks in him."

"Well, Pa, any old time you want to come back home, come on. You know we'd love to have you. You know that, don't you?"

"I know that, Caleb, and I'd love to the best in the world, but seems you have enough."

Papa laughed. "I don't think I'll have Mrs. Walters long. She's started courting. Thomas Couch."

Surprised, Grandpa said, "Why, he's a fine man. He's had bad luck with wives. Owns a big farm. People say he has money." He looked at Papa squarely. "Mrs. Walters is a fine woman — smart — downright good-looking. Had things been different I'd have courted her myself."

It was Papa's turn to be surprised. "Why, Pa!"

Both men were silent a moment, thinking had things been different — then Papa said, realizing his father was unhappy in town, "Pa, why don't you come on back home? We love you!"

Grandpa said, "We'll see about it later on. Sally's leaving and if Tish marries too, I'll need somewhere to go. I'd rather live with you, Caleb, than any of the children."

Papa laid a hand on his father's shoulder. "Thanks, Pa. Just remember the farm is yours. You know they say there's no place like home. You come on back any time you're ready."

Grandpa's sweet face lit up with a smile. With his long brown beard he looked like the picture of Jesus in our Bible, I thought.

He said, "We'll see, Caleb, we'll see."

It seemed Jode and Papa had known each other before. Papa asked him, "What are you doing up here so far from a railroad?"

"I'll tell you, Caleb. You know Josh Hammock down at Gainesville?"

"Yeah, I know, the mule, horse and cow trader."

"Well, my run ends at Gainesville now, and I get a few days off between runs now and then. I got to talking to old Josh, and he thinks we can make a lot of money selling hogs."

"How's that?"

"He wants me to go up into the mountains and buy a lot of them old hogs running loose up there."

"You mean them long-nosed briar-rooters?"

"Yeah. Said we could buy 'em for a dollar or two a head, drive 'em to Gainesville, fatten 'em up and sell 'em for five or more dollars a head — said we could make a thousand dollars outta the deal."

"M-m-m. Jode, you'd better watch Josh Hammock — he's a blue-nosed mule skinner from way back. He's put over some mighty shady deals. Know'd him from my court days."

Jode looked wise. "You don't have to worry 'bout me atall. I've done some skinning myself. He can't skin me no more'n I can him. He told me to git 'em and he'd feed 'em. But I'll keep my eyes peeled."

"You'd better. Josh is out for the easy dollar."

Jode thought a minute, then asked, "Say, you wouldn't want to go with me to git them hogs, would you? I'd pay you a dollar a day. I need help."

Papa considered. He had a family, and it'd be a rough trip. Besides, them mountaineers could be right ornery. "I don't know. I got a family, Jode."

"It won't take a week and I'll pay you fifteen cash dollars as soon as we git the hogs to Gainesville."

Fifteen dollars would buy a lot of things (that was in 1915). He could use the money, with Mama pregnant and Jenny in town school. "Let me see what Bela says."

Mama acquiesced. Fifteen dollars was a lot of money. She told Papa, "I'll be all right. Ma's there."

Early the next morning Jode and Papa set out on horseback for the mountains to round up the hogs.

CHAPTER 12

Grandma Courts; Sam Grindle Dies; Skinned; a New Brother

WHILE HE WAS GONE two things happened. On Sunday afternoon Mr. Couch came rolling up in his topped buggy to court

Grandma. The other surprised everybody. Sam Grindle suddenly died.

Since there was no fireplace in the real parlor, the courting was done by the fire in our parents' bedroom while Mama and we children stayed in the dining room. It was a little odd to know our own grandma was courting, and we couldn't decide whether we approved. Whether we did or didn't, the first Sunday was only the beginning.

Sam died the following Tuesday. Since he had been bent double for over twenty years, his death posed a problem as to how he could be laid straight in a coffin. No coffin could fit him since his body was like the upper part of an S. Then someone thought of buckling him down in a regular one; so six men used all their strength to hold him straight while others did the buckling, and Sam lay straight for the first time in more than twenty years.

Since he had lived with his brother and family only a short distance from us, Grandma decided it was her bounden duty to attend the wake. Mama couldn't, being rather obviously with child, and children had no business there, so Grandma lit the lantern after supper and went.

To think of Sam dead made us children sad. His fine voice would be missed in Concord Church, for everybody liked to hear him sing. We recalled how lonely his song sounded the night of our serenade.

Lillian gathered Glory, Greg and me in the cold back bedroom, and preached a funeral sermon for him, and all of us cried to think he'd never sing on earth again, but we cheered up to think of him singing around the great, white throne of God.

At bedtime Mama locked all the doors; the house was a little fearsome with both Papa and Grandma gone, and we were a little uneasy about going to sleep.

Far into the night we were brought awake by a pounding on the front door and Grandma calling, "Bely, Bely, let me in! Let me in, Bely! Quick!"

Scrambling out of bed, we all went to the door. In her excitement Mama fumbled with the lock before she got the door open; all the while Grandma kept pounding and hollering.

Mama got the door open and there stood Grandma, her blond hair tumbling about her shoulders, her eyes wild with fright. She rushed inside, slammed the door and turned the key, all the while exclaiming, "LordGodAlmighty! LordGodAlmighty! I never seen nothing like it in my whole life! LordGodAlmighty!"

"Ma, Ma, what in the world?" Mama asked

Grandma went to Mama's room where coals still glowed in the fireplace, threw on more wood and stirred up the fire. She was without her coat, and was shivering.

Curious, we stared at her white face while she stirred the fire.

Her tongue went at its usual fast clip:

"Lost all my hairpins running down that road. Dinna wait to light my lantern. We was all settin' thar, pretty as you please, paying our respects to the dead, talking how good he was. Then we looked up, and thar he was, settin' up in his coffin! Every head o' hair rose clean up! Mighta been then I lost my hairpins. I tell ye, Bely, I never seen nothing like it, never!" She paused as a shudder shook her.

Wonderment was in Mama's face. "You mean to tell me that Sam Grindle come back to life?"

"Don't know where he did nor dinna. Never waited to find out. Nobody did. Never saw such scrambling. Wanna a chair left upright! I tell ye, Bely, it was enough to make anybody run. There he was, laid out pretty as anybody, then all of a sudden't, thar he was, settin' up in his coffin!"

By this time our mouths were wide open.

"I swan!" Mama said. "Reckon Sam did come back to life?"

We couldn't find out that night; for a hundred wild horses couldn't drag Gradma back to the Grindle house. Still wondering if Sam had returned to life, we all went to bed.

The next day we learned he hadn't. The buckles had broken.

Papa was gone little more than a week. One afternoon he came riding in with fifteen cash dollars jingling in his pockets, but he was not spending a dime before he consulted Mama.

Gathered around the fire after supper, we heard about the trip. "We went up to Neel's Gap, then cut across and went up Cooper Creek."

"Did you see any wildcats and catamounts?" Lillian asked.

"No, but we heard plenty screaming at night. We saw bears and lots of deer. Mighty rough country up in there, but purty — mighty purty. But rough. And lonesome."

"Where'd you sleep at night?" Mama asked.

"With the mountaineers. Once't they found out we was buying hogs, they were powerful friendly. Didn't have to use our camping stuff atall.

"When I first saw them hogs, I couldn't believe what I was seeing. Their snouts, I know, was a foot long and I could count every rib they had. At the first cabin we stopped at, Jode bought over fifty, a dollar a head. We started back, buying as we went. We done all right with bedding them down at night till we got to old Ebe Shalter's house. Ebe, you know, always come to town court week with a jug. Well, that night he got out a jug. Him and Jode — "

He looked Mama squarely in the eyes because she was looking at him oddly — "I did not! You ought to know me better than that!"

"I never said a word!"

"No, but your eyes did!"

"What happened?" Glory asked.

"During the night, somehow them old ridge-runners got outta their pen. It took us two days to round 'em up. Hadn't been for that, we'd been home long before now."

"What did Josh Hammock say about them hogs?"

"By the time we got 'em to Gainesville, Jode was sick of 'em — said he never wanted to look at another hog as long as he lived — so he sold 'em outright to Josh at three dollars a head."

"How many was they?" Mama asked, her eyes turning shrewd.

"A hundred fifty-three."

Mama was silent a minute, then said, "That made Jode make a profit of two hundred and ninety-one dollars." Very quietly.

"Yeah. Josh shore got skinned that time," Papa said.

With meaning emphasis Mama said, "Josh won't the only one."

"Now, Ma, I agreed to go for fifteen dollars."

[65]

Mama nodded. "Ignoramus!"

Grinning sheepishly, he replied, "Yeah, guess I was."

No more mention was made of the hogs, for he had made fifteen cash dollars, which was better than no money at all.

Since Papa killed so many squirrels and rabbits, Grandma had plenty of brains to eat, enough to content anyone, but I guess it took more than brains to content her, for Mr. Couch continued to court her on Sunday afternoons.

We three decided we didn't approve of Grandma courting; so we would stand as near as possible to the closed door of the courting room and sing:

> While the rich man sleeps on his velvet couch,
> Dreaming of his silver and gold,
> The orphan lay on a bed of snow,
> Murmuring, "So cold, so cold."

Singing the word *couch* louder and more emphatically than any other, we hoped it would stop him from courting Grandma. But it didn't. As far as we could tell, they didn't even hear us no matter how loud and often we sang.

That spring we three girls helped Papa do the planting. He made the rows by plow while Lillian followed, dropping seed so many inches apart; Glory and I followed her to cover the seed just so deep with our hoes. It was painstaking work and tiresome. Nights of heavy sleep seemed only begun when Papa would rouse us. Time to get into the fields and plant, plant, plant.

One May night Mama told us girls we could sleep in the parlor bed. This was kept ready for company; we weren't allowed to touch it, much less sleep in it. We never thought to ask why we could sleep there; we just washed extra clean and hurried to bed before Mama changed her mind.

The next morning we found that Dr. Abbott had been to our house in the night and left a big, fat baby boy. Our new brother had a pug nose and big blue eyes. Grandma said he looked like her pa; Papa said he looked like his Uncle Grover; but Mama said he looked like himself and his name was Justin, and she said it firmly. When she saw how amazed Papa was at the strange name, she let him add the middle name of his brother, Jules, *Francis*.

As weeks passed Justin became a happy, gurgling baby and held our adoration. "He's better than the gold in the ground," Lillian would say, bouncing him high on the bed when Mama was at a safe distance. That wasn't often, for hoeing season was upon us. The seeds we carefully planted miraculously sprouted and were now several inches high. We three again became diggers of grass.

Jenny was still in school. At the end of this term she would stand her state teacher's examination; if she passed, which we did not doubt, she would be a schoolteacher in the fall, the goal for which she had strived for so long. We didn't complain at the loss of what help she could have given. It was easier to let her become a teacher than to get her into the fields anyhow, Papa said.

Justin and grass weren't the only things growing. Mr. Couch was wanting to marry Grandma. A man as old as he couldn't have wanted anything else, Papa said. His last wife had been dead over two years and he needed someone to look after him.

But Grandma was in no hurry to marry; she seemed happy with her chores at our house. Her best was rocking Justin. In the afternoons she would sit on the front porch and rock him back and forth on her knees.

CHAPTER 13

Education and Miss Keene;
Protracted Meeting

THE LAST WEEK of June Papa said, "When school starts next month, I may as well start Lowell in the primer."

When he returned from town Saturday he brought me a slate

with pencil and sponge and a primer reader. I too was going to be educated.

Miss Keene, the teacher, rang the bell. On that first morning we entered school carefree and anticipating, but it was the last day that we did.

She said, "You will remain standing until I assign you a seat. The boys will be seated on the right, the girls on the left."

Something in her voice made us halt in our tracks.

Lillian mumbled, "The sheep on the right, the goats on the left."

Miss Keene rapped sharply with her pointer. "There will be no speaking aloud. Anyone speaking aloud three times without permission will be soundly whipped," and she pointed to a bunch of switches near her desk.

Smiles were wiped from faces and eagerness died, and we soon hated the teacher whose black eyes pierced through us and sent a chill of fear down our spines.

The bunch of switches was replaced often. Every day she whipped some boys, and sometimes girls. Other students had to witness the horrifying spectacle of Miss Keene's white arm going up and down, up and down, cutting the air with a terrible swishing as she brought the switch down on a victim's back.

Strangely enough, Lillian, Glory and I escaped her vicious lash. We did so by being quieter than mice; however, every time we endured the painful sight Lillian's eyes held a look of righteous anger.

On a Monday morning in August Miss Keene said, "Protracted meeting began yesterday at Concord. We'll attend morning services. We'll march down and take the back seats on the left, which are reserved for us. School rules will apply, so any misbehavior will be punished."

There would be no misbehavior. Not only were we aware of her switches but also we were well experienced in church attendance. Moreover, we knew protracted meeting was where one got saved from sin. Being saved was the most vital requisite of life after the age of accountability -- twelve years old; so protracted meeting was not to be held lightly.

As we entered the church the choir was standing and my surprised eyes found my mother there. For the first time I became aware of her appearance. Her white straw hat offset her black hair and the wide brim framed her oval face. Her white blouse with rows of lace insertions and edges, and white batiste skirt enhanced the effect and she seemed a heavenly being. Almost blind with pride, I stumbled to my seat and became aware of the singing:

> O they tell me of a home far beyond the skies,
> O they tell me of a home far away;
> O they tell me of a home where no stormclouds rise,
> O they tell me of an unclouded day.

After the song, Deacon Grizzle was asked to pray. Being filled with the Spirit, he often shouted aloud before rising from his knees. His fervency was well known, used and anticipated in church meetings. The longer he prayed the more his ardor increased, with frequent "Amens" from preachers and "Amen" members.

Among the congregation there was a stir like a freshening breeze. The Spirit was being felt. God was coming down from His great, white throne and filling the little country church with His power. Women began shouting "Glory! Glory!" and "Hallelujah! Glory to God!"

At last the prayer ended and Benny Wimpy, song leader since Sam's death, put the tuning fork between his lips, gave it several twangs, took it from his mouth and began singing: "Are You Washed in the Blood of the Lamb?"

Fervently, the congregation joined in.

When the song ended, Rev. Ridley, the visiting preacher, went to the pulpit, opened the big Bible to a certain passage, adjusted his eyeglasses and took a good look at the congregation.

He was an old man. The top of his bald head seemed a crown for the fringe of white hair encircling it. Though a little man, his vibrant spirit made him seem larger. As he stood now gazing out over the congregation, he drew all eyes, and people grew silent under his searching gaze.

"A while ago," he began, "we sang of a heavenly home. Everybody here wants to go there when they die. If you didn't, you wouldn't be here. Some are prepared to go. You've been saved from your sins. But some of you have not been. You're sinners, but you want to be saved, and don't know how. I'll tell you. You git born of the Spirit and washed in the blood of Jesus Christ. You do this by praying until you know you're born agin! You can't go to heaven unless you are born agin. You can't be sinners and go to heaven.

"Jesus prepared heaven for the born agin. He also prepared a place called hell for sinners. Hell is a lake of hellfire and brimstone. I'm gonna read you a story telling of God raining hellfire and brimstone on some sinners," and he read the story of Sodom and Gomorrah (Gen. 18: 20-32; Gen. 19: 12-25).

When he ceased reading he stood looking over his eyeglasses until we wondered if he would ever speak again. Suddenly, he gave the Bible a sharp *whack!* Everyone gave a little jump and sat straighter.

"According to this Bible, sinners will be destroyed. They ain't a person in this church today that don't believe the Bible. SINNERS" — his voice began to rise — "do you want to spend eternity in a lake burning with hellfire and brimstone?" he screeched. "No, you don't. Then git saved from your sins!" His voice descended to normal.

"I don't know what yore sins are — could be anything you're doing that ain't right. It stands between you and God. Just like in the days of Abraham, the cry of wickedness goes up to the Lord. He knows what you're doing. If you don't repent and turn from yore wicked ways, the Lord will destroy you like he did them wicked people of Sodom and Gomorrah. He rained hellfire and brimstone" — his voice rose in crescendo, his white hair trembled and his eyeglasses slipped to the end of his nose — "on them wicked cities!" He paused, then his deep bass rolled forth, "YES, HELLFIRE AND BRIMSTONE." Again he stood looking out over his glasses at the people, his words reverberating in the silence.

"Now, sinners!" he suddenly screeched, "do you want to be burned by the hottest fire God ever invented? Do you want to be cast into the lake of hellfire and brimstone where the worm dieth not, where there'll be gnashing of teeth, and eternal darkness, where you'll be tormented forever?"

His voice returned to normal. "Or do you want to live in a city of gold, where a river of pure crystal water flows from the throne of God, and there by the crystal river grows the tree of life? How would you like to sit down by that river under the shade of that tree? How'd you like to walk on streets of gold? We all know what gold looks like. This county is full of it. Just think what a city built of gold would look like!

"Jesus is there. That's the best thing about heaven. Think how it'll be to look on the face of Jesus, the Son of God! They say His eyes are filled with mercy. SINNERS! Will He look on you with mercy?

"The Bible says He will judge people on Judgment Day. It says He is a righteous judge, meting out justice with undisputed wisdom. He is the One Who will say, 'Depart from me, I know ye not.' Will He know you? Righteous people will be sent to enjoy life with Him in the city of gold, but the wicked will be cast into the lake of *hellfire* and *brimstone,*" and his voice rose to its highest screech, where it hung quavering until vocal chords, protesting the burden, choked off sound; whereupon, Preacher Ridley flung out his hand to the people, pointing accusing fingers. Then, gathering the force of his whole body into his voice box, his deep bass thundered, "YES, HELLFIRE AND BRIMSTONE!"

If the Spirit hadn't struck sinners with fear and trembling, Rev. Ridley's voice had. When the call went forth for sinners to come to the mourners' bench while Christians sang the invitation hymn, sinners poured down the aisle to kneel at the bench.

The song was hardly finished when from somewhere in the church a woman began to sing:

> On Jordan's stormy banks I stand,
> And cast a wistful eye
> To Canaan's fair and happy land,
> Where my possessions lie.

*

[71]

Everybody joined in

> I am bound for the promised land,
> I am bound for the promised land;
> Oh, who will come and go with me?
> I am bound for the promised land.

There arose a joyous ecstasy of laughter. Without looking I knew the laughter was coming from Cousin Totie. Every meeting day she got happy with the Spirit, and her happiness always overflowed into that ecstatic laughter. Never rising from her seat, she would sit, holding one hand high, and laugh and laugh until the Spirit subsided.

Not so with Aunt Jencie Grindle. Up and down the aisle she'd go, shouting and clapping her hands at every step. "Git ready, chillun, we're gwine to Glory!"

Other shouters, men and women, joined Aunt Jencie. Since I saw and heard shouting every preaching day, it wasn't new, but in a protracted meeting more people shouted. My eyes wandered from one to the other, but they had a hard time keeping up.

As sinners knelt at the mourners' bench, Christians came to kneel beside them; when all those wanting to be saved were praying, the shouters also came to pray with them. Voices of sinners and Christians arose, beseeching Jesus to have mercy and save sinful souls. It was indeed electrifying to hear a sinner scream, "God, have mercy on me!"

From time to time sinners rose, shouting that they were saved, and their joyous praises would be joined by others, while cries for mercy continued.

If a sinner couldn't "pray through," he or she was urged to go home and continue praying until the conversion experience came. This had to be physical and spiritual. The sinner had to know without a doubt he had been born into the kingdom of God. To do this a sinner prayed until the burden of sin vanished, whereupon he was filled with a great surge of joy and a new outlook on life. Earthy values would change to spiritual.

Night services were attended with parents. Mothers took

quilts for pallets on which to place sleeping babies and young children. At the feet of us three girls Mama spread a quilt for our two brothers. She had to sing in the choir and Grandma sat with other old ladies while Papa took his place with other men in the "Amen" corner.

One of the mourners who couldn't pray through the first night was Leila Colley, Dave's sister. She was told to continue to pray at home.

These hours of soul's travail were known as "seeking the Lord." Since Leila was absent from both school and morning service the following day, we assumed she was having a difficult time finding Him. But when we arrived for the night service we saw her with her family near the front.

Before preaching a testimony meeting was held so people could tell what the Lord had done for them. Leila was the first to rise. Her face was radiant. "Last night," she said, "I was lost, but tonight I'm found! Jesus washed my sins away! Last night I went to the mourners' bench, but couldn't pray through. I prayed all night and all day. Tonight I was in my room upstairs when I heard Mama calling me; so holding the lamp, I was going downstairs when Jesus spoke to me; He said, 'My child, thy sins are forgiven!'" She began weeping from joy. Through her tears, she continued. "Such light shone about me! That old kerosene lamp was as bright as the sun! The whole house was filled with light!" So full of feeling she could speak no more, she sat down.

A quavering old voice rose in the stillness:

> Amazing Grace! how sweet the sound,
> That saved a wretch like me!
> I once was lost, but now am found,
> Was blind, but now I see.

Others joined in and soon the whole congregation. There were numerous "Amens!" Men and women began shouting. So many people were going up and down the aisle shouting I couldn't keep count.

Preachers Ridley and Crickett were shouting, too. People began shaking hands with each other in pure pleasure of

Christian fellowship, going all over the church to everyone they knew.

I saw my father and mother meet each other, falling into each other's arms, and they stood shouting together. Then Grandma Walters joined them, throwing her arms around both, and they shouted together.

By that time Lillian, Glory and I were crying and would have joined them, but we had to take care of our brothers.

Some time passed before the church quieted. Then from his seat at the back a well-known figure arose. He was Tig Beckly, the drunkard. In a trembling voice he said, "Folks, I'm a lost man. I've been trying to pray, but my heart's a stone. The Spirit has left me. The Lord says, 'My spirit will not always strive with man,' and He's gone and left me to my bottle. I'm going to hell. 'Tain't no use praying for me. I'm a lost man!" Shaking, he sank to his seat and covered his face with his hands.

Instead of his prepared sermon, Rev. Ridley preached on the text Tig quoted, and the invitation hymn, "Where Shall You Be When the Last Trumpet Sounds?" was added incentive for sinners to go to the mourners' bench.

The Spirit was not only felt in church but throughout the whole community. And there was no doubt the Spirit of the Lord was in our house.

It was evident in Papa's saying a longer grace than his customary, "Lord, give us thankful hearts for these blessings," Glory and I cheerfully washing dishes, Mama and Grandma singing hymns as they went about their chores.

So no one noticed how quiet Lillian had been lately. Though she was thirteen, a year over the accountability, we never considered her a sinner; for wasn't she always preaching sermons to us children?

It was getting dusky dark that Friday before the Sunday closing of protracted meeting. Mama was cooking supper; Papa was at the barn, feeding Nell, Lily and her calf; Grandma was there, too, milking Lily. Glory and I were in the dining room, peeling potatoes and caring for the boys playing on the floor.

Suddenly, Lillian came into the room singing:

*

Down at the cross where my Savior died,
Down where for cleansing from sin I cried,
There to my heart was the blood applied;
Glory to His name.

Glory to His Name . . . Glory to His Name . . .
There to my heart was the blood applied;
Glory to His name.

I am so wondrously saved from sin —

She broke into shouts of joy, practically dancing around the room, laughing and shouting.

Coming to the doorway from the kitchen, Mama, amazed, said, "Why, Lillian!"

But Lillian danced out the door, heading down the path to the barn, shouting and singing, "Glory to His Name! I am so wondrously saved from sin! Glory to His Name!"

Coming up the path with a filled milk bucket, Grandma saw her and set the bucket down. Looking through the window, I saw them running toward each other. Grandma opened wide her arms and Lillian went into them, throwing her arms around Grandma's neck. Then *she* began shouting. There they were, hugging each other, talking and shouting. They would walk a little way, then stop to shout and talk some more. Then both began singing "Glory to His Name!" to the top of their voices, and thus they came to the house. Mama had also been watching through the window, and turned to meet them on the back porch. Such shouting I had never heard nor have I since.

Papa's coming from the barn rescued the milk, saved supper from burning and brought us back to normal, though he too was happy Lillian was saved. In fact, he seemed more happy over her being saved than he had over Jenny's salvation while we lived in town. He seemed to think Lillian needed saving more than Jenny.

At that night's service she testified to her conversion, then thoroughly enjoyed herself participating in the shouting and praying for sinners while Glory and I tended our brothers.

In the Sunday morning service the doors of the church were

opened so that recent converts could become members. The candidates had to tell their conversion experience, and the officials judged whether they had had a truly saving one.

Becoming a church member was an honor and a grave responsibility, not to be taken lightly, so children under twelve were not accepted. This we had been taught from our earliest years, and it was the reason neither Glory nor I had gone to the mourners' bench. We weren't sinners yet.

But Lillian was thirteen, her experience was adjudged a true one, and she would be baptized along with accepted others in the pond formed by Cane Creek Falls that afternoon at three o'clock.

But the protracted meeting had no effect on improving Miss Keene. She continued the whippings until the term closed. We saw no more of her and heard a year later she died of typhoid, but former pupils were certain she died of pure meanness.

CHAPTER 14

The Foreshadow of Things to Come

THE FOLLOWING Sunday morning Grandpa, Aunt Tish and Jenny came driving up in Grandpa's buggy.

Hardly waiting to take off her hat, Jenny said, "I'm a school-teacher! I passed the teacher's examination, and was assigned a school in Wilcox County. I'm leaving in two weeks."

Papa's hands trembled in his lap. Looking at her, he said, "Wilcox, eh? That's in south Georgia. Will you be close to Sally?"

Sensing disapproval, she said, "Yes, it's in south Georgia, but not close enough to stay with Aunt Sally. My school is over twenty miles from her house, and I have to board in my school district." Seeing the look on his face, she exclaimed, "But, oh, Papa! I'll be making money! Real money! Think of that!"

The eagerness of the bird about to try its wings caught at

Papa's heart. He smiled. "Oh, pshaw! I guess you'll be all right. I was just thinking it might not be so long before you git married and make me a grandpa, and you *know* I'm too young for that!"

Her face turning scarlet, she laughed and turned to Mama, who was wiping her eyes furtively with the corner of her apron. "Aunt Tish said she'd help me make enough clothes, if you could get the cloth. I'll need many nice ones, being a teacher."

Aunt Tish said, "I thought I could help her make hers as I make mine. I'm going away, too."

Papa jumped to his feet, overturning his chair. "Where do you think *you're* going?"

"I'm going to Atlanta to take a art course. I got a right to my chance in life, ain't I?"

Sparks flew between brother and sister. Papa stuck his hands in his pockets. "What about Pa?"

I was glad Grandpa was out looking over his crop.

Tish answered. "He's going to live with Sally."

Amazed, Papa asked, "You mean he's leaving north Georgia?"

"Why, yes, Sally and Willy are coming after him in their new Ford, and Jenny's going back with them."

Taking his hands from his pockets, Papa slammed one fist into the other. "I'll be damned if he is! I'll just be damned if he is!" Almost beside himself, he glared at his sister. "When did you Miss High and Mighties decide all this? WHO give you the authority to order Pa to do this and that? WHO do you think you ARE?"

With Papa looming over her Aunt Tish looked very small.

He went on, "Pa ain't going nowhere. If you want to go off, Pa can come live in his own house. God knows we want him bad enough. We *love* him!"

At the insinuation, Tish winced, but lifted her head to ask triumphantly, "Where would he sleep?"

An unwilling and ignored witness, Grandma Walters now spoke. "He can have my bed. I'm going to be married next Sunday and won't be needing it anymore."

Everyone turned to where she was sitting in a corner.

Mama said, "Why, Ma!"

Papa said, "Mrs. Walters, you don't need to marry anybody. There's room here for us all. Why, you and Pa might just git up a case and git married later on. Never can tell!" He smiled at her.

Aunt Tish's mouth went into a grim, straight line. Things weren't turning out as pat as she had thought. The very idea of her pa marrying that trashy Bela's mother brought a quick decision. "I can put off going to Atlanta, I reckon. I ain't in no hurry."

Grandma spoke to Papa. "Caleb, I know I don't *have* to marry Mr. Couch, but I want to!" Her face turned pink, and she lowered her eyes as she added, "You was right about them rats."

For a long moment he looked at her, then laughed, firmly convinced she spoke true. She joined his laughter while Mama looked from one to the other in bewilderment.

"What has rats to do with marrying?" she asked.

"Everything, Bely, everything!" her mother told her.

Turning back to his sister, Papa asked, "What does Pa say to all this — you and your big plans?"

"Well, I ain't told him exactly," she admitted.

"Just been sorta nagging?"

"I been talking about it. Sally said that country down there was fine farmland. People making money hand over fist. I thought Pa might be more satisfied down there, away from this rocky land."

"You hadn't give a hoot about his tending this rocky land in all your life! There's more important things in life than making money. You want him to leave the country he was born in, eh? His pa and ma was born here, and their pa and ma, and *their* pa and ma. His wife, our mother, is buried in Salem Church cemetery with them all. That means nothing to you!

"This is his land, his home! You didn't think about that. You didn't think 'cause you didn't care!" He picked up his hat. "I'm going to find Pa. You passel of women git in the kitchen and cook some dinner!" As he went out the door he muttered something about "infernal women, always fignigling and fignagling."

Both Mama and Grandma were silently appalled at Aunt Tish's scheme. Jenny was too enthralled with her own future to be much concerned, but the rest of us children couldn't think of life without Grandpa. Since our moving to his farm, he had become an integral part of our family circle. We didn't want him to go way down to south Georgia. It was all Aunt Tish's fault, always wanting to be something she wasn't. As we looked at her our eyes became hostile.

Mama and Grandma were tripping over each other in words, talking about the wedding. When Jenny broke in with questions about enough cloth for her clothes, Mama assured her absent-mindedly the cloth would be bought next day. Her doubt banished, she joined the talk.

Turning to Lillian, I saw she was girding herself for battle with Aunt Tish, and a shiver of premonition ran through me. I didn't like the atmosphere. It was too cloudy and torn. When I saw Lillian following our aunt to the well, I went to look for Papa. Something was wrong with our world, and I wanted him to make it right again.

I didn't have far to look. He and Grandpa were at the barn, currying their horses. As I came up Grandpa smiled and said, "Hey, darling!" Papa didn't say anything, just looked at me hard. Sidling past him, I sat down on an empty cider keg.

"Well, Pa, what do you think of my plan to plant more cotton next year? Don't you think we could git more money for it than apples and cabbage?"

Grandpa replied, "No, this ain't cotton country. Raisin' cotton is for big farmers. We ain't. We're family farmers, and make enough. Let well enough alone." Then pushing back his hat, he looked at Papa. "What's ailing you? You been beating around the bush ever since you come down here. Now, out with it!"

Papa stopped currying and faced his father. "It's Tish."

Grandpa grinned. "She's bent and determined to go to Atlanta."

"Pa, why don't you come and live with us? Mrs. Walters is gitting married next Sunday. We got plenty of room, and we all want you. Why don't you git your duds and move in? Let Tish go to grass!"

Grandpa's eyes twinkled. "I will when it's time. Tish ain't going nowhere yet. She ain't got the money."

[79]

His own twinkling, Papa said, "More ways than one to skin a cat, eh? Listen, Pa, this is your house and this is your land. All you have to do is come back."

"I know that, Caleb."

Turning their attention to currying, they finished and let the horses out into the barn lot. Their eager talk in planning next year's crops held no foreboding of the future. Neither was aware of how deep and wide would be the fignigling and fignagling of women.

When we returned to the house the passel of women were putting dinner on the table, the clouds had scattered and the pieces were together again. I noticed Grandma and Aunt Tish talking together. She could now afford to be civil to Grandma, who would soon be out of her brother's house and would be the wife of a man nobody dared call trash.

At the table my eyes were compelled to return again and again to Aunt Tish. Despite the anger she had incited that morning, she talked as if no words had passed between her and Papa. In fact, she was rather gay, laughing easily, and even teasing Grandma about her forthcoming marriage. But I didn't like the look on her face when she thought no one was watching her. She looked just like our cat after eating a mouse, and her eyes kept going from Grandpa to Papa, and in them was a slyness that made me uneasy.

After they returned to town, I felt better, and soon Lillian, Gloria and I went to play. As soon as we were alone, though, Lillian said, "That Miss Tish. She thinks she's the boss of everybody. I let her know a thing or two about us."

"You didn't *fight* her!" I said, shivering at the thought.

Glory, who had been a witness, said, "She let her know she couldn't up and send Grandpa down to south Georgia away from us."

Blazing with her triumph over an adult, Lillian boasted, "I told her this was our home the same as it was Grandpa's, and she might as well try gittin' us to go to that old south Georgia as to try to git Grandpa to go."

We laughed and laughed at the brightness of the remark Lillian made to hateful old Aunt Tish.

CHAPTER 15

"They Ain't a Rock Big enough to Stump Your Little Toe on"

GRANDMA and Mr. Couch were married in our parlor. Since it was the first wedding we children had seen, we sat silent and wide-eyed throughout the ceremony.

Though she carried no flowers, Grandma made a lovely bride in her white waist and skirt trimmed with lace. It was the first good look we had at Mr. Couch, and we were pleased to see the same sweetness of expression as our Grandpa Abbott's.

Satisfied that Mr. Couch would make a good Grandpa, we were sorry we had sung *velvet couch* so loud behind the courting door, and as they drove away in his topped buggy, which showed he had money, we felt forlorn.

Who would get up washwood now? Who would rock Justin while Mama did her work? We brightened. Maybe we could take turns and get out of field work. Since we had to be at Aunt Tish's for supper and had to hurry, we couldn't know the answers then.

When we arrived, we saw Uncle Willy's new Ford, black and shiny, in front of the house. Aunt Tish wasn't just bragging when she said Uncle Willy had a lot of money.

In the backyard Grandpa and our new uncle were cutting stovewood. Papa stayed to help, but we went into the house.

Both aunts were busy cooking. And talking. When we entered, the talking ended abruptly, leaving a peculiar silence, broken by Aunt Sally's welcome. Though she now had money, she was as friendly as ever.

At supper, when everyone had been helped to all the good rations, Aunt Sally said, "Pa, you and Caleb ought to see that farmland in south Georgia — you wouldn't believe your eyes. They get a bale of cotton to the acre, and the corn grows twice as high as it does here. I never saw such rich land! Don't have to buy much fertilizer atall!"

With a twinkle in his eyes, Grandpa said, "We don't buy any here. Just clean out the stables at planting time."

"Pa!" Aunt Tish remonstrated, disgusted that he would mention such a thing at the supper table.

Uncle Willy put in, "Can't be beat for farming, that land can't. People gitting rich hand over fist raising cotton."

"The big farmers," corrected Grandpa. "Me and Caleb are little farmers — family farmers. Don't need much cotton here. No market."

Looking through his thick-lensed glasses, Uncle Willy said, "Down there little farmers are truck farmers. Raise vegetables. Sell 'em fast as they come in. Some have two crops a year. Raise peanuts, watermelons, strawberries, sweet potatoes — anything. Good market."

"The climate's good, that's why," Aunt Sally said. "We don't have ice and snow. No big freezes, just a little frost. A neighbor raises strawberries, and makes a fortune every year, and not much work, either. I'm thinking of starting a dairy. Big cow country. And they raise hogs in droves."

Grandpa was now listening with interest. His life had been filled with years of hard labor in hilly and rocky fields with little financial return, and he was getting old; this new land of Sally's sounded like easy money with easy effort.

She added, "'Nother good thing about it is there's no hills or rocks. The land's as flat as my ironing board."

"No rocks?" Lillian asked, unbelieving.

"They ain't a rock big enough to stump your little toe on."

But we children liked rocks. In my mind flashed the pasture on Grandpa's farm. I could see the big, outcropping gray rocks, some almost as big as a house, lichen covered and filled with nooks and crannies we spent hours exploring, and the beautiful milk-white, smaller ones scattered everywhere. We wouldn't like a land with no rocks.

Papa now spoke. "You all can have that flat land. I'll keep the hills. We may not grow as tall a corn as you, but we sure do make it. We made so much this year we ain't going to have room to put it."

"We'll have a log-rolling, Caleb, and build a new crib. May as well have it while Sally and Willy are here," Grandpa said.

Aunt Tish said, "Pa, them things are going outta style."

He gave her a hard look. "Not when I need a new crib."

Papa looked at Mama. At her nod, he asked, "How about Tuesday? That'll give us time to git word to everybody."

Aunt Sally said, "Fine. I want to see everybody before going back."

CHAPTER 16

The Logrolling and Lillian

On TUESDAY the sun was barely a rim over the horizon when wagons and buggies filled with relatives from near and far, friends and neighbors began rolling into our yard.

Men went to the deep wood with their axes and women went about cooking the big dinner. Children were set to fetch wood and water until men began snaking in logs, then older boys were set to skinning off the bark.

When food was being dished up, Mama blew on the conch shell to summon the men, who came hurrying into the yard. Washing-up supplies had been placed on the battling bench, and I went there to find Papa.

When I saw Uncle Willy talking to Grandpa, I listened.

Uncle Willy was saying, "You got a pretty stand of timber."

Grandpa looked sly. "Oh, that ain't all the timber I got."

"Ever think of selling any?"

"Don't want to. Don't want to cut down my trees."

Staring in disbelief, Uncle Willy said, "Huh. You got thousands of dollars just standing there."

"Let 'em stand. I don't need thousands of dollars."

"Well, no, but woods oughtta be thinned now and then. Been

thinning mine, but our longleaf pines are bigger and higher than yours. I wish you'd come down and see my country."

"Tish and Sally want me to move down there, lock, stock and barrel. But I'm too old to go to a strange land."

"Why, you're not old! And where I live ain't a strange land — it's still Georgia. I wish you would just move in with us. You can have your own room and all the land you want to tend. You could make right much money raising strawberries — easy work. Just plant 'em and let 'em grow."

Again Grandpa was interested, but he said, "I don't know. This is where I was born — know everybody, everybody knows me."

"You could come back on visits."

"Yes, I could do that." They turned to wash up.

I hoped Grandpa wouldn't go. We'd never get to see him again. Troubled, I returned to the house.

People hadn't finished eating when Lillian whispered to me, "We gotta sneak off or we'll be washing dishes till the sun goes down. Meet me in the oak grove."

There I found Lillian, Gloria, and several boys, all cousins.

Lillian said, "Tell you what we're gonna do. We're going up to them wildcat and catamount dens on the side of that mountain. We'll kill one. Won't they all be surprised when we come draggin' a dead catamount back to the house?"

In his slow way, Jim said, "So will I. What're we gonna kill it with?"

Lillian said, "Why, rocks, of course. All of us will throw rocks into the dens until one's dead. Maybe we'll kill two. Papa said them dens was just full of wildcats and catamounts."

Unbelieving, the boys hooted their derision, but they were weary of skinning logs and wanted out as badly as we girls wanted out of washing dishes. Moreover, they didn't believe Lillian was that brave.

However, through the dark, green wood west of our house, much like the children following the Pied Piper, we followed Lillian. No sun penetrated the denseness, and fallen leaves from time immemorial made a soft carpet.

Abruptly, we came out into sunlight, facing the rocky foot of a mountain which rose before us. Through the rocks ran a narrow path which Lillian followed, walking with sure feet.

Glory nudged my elbow and whispered, "She musta been here before. She knows exactly where them dens are." I nodded.

Lillian said, "Better be gittin' yourselves some rocks. We're almost there." Pointing to three caves in the piles of rocks, she came to a sudden halt.

"What we'll do," she said, "is divide into three groups, one for each den. Cal, you be head of one; Jim, you be head of one, and I'll be head of the other. When I count three, start throwing!"

Standing in front of a den, we made ready.

Lillian counted, "One, two, THREE!"

A barrage of rocks sailed through the air, and hit all around the dens, but none fell inside. No movement or noise issued from either den.

"They ain't no wildcats nor catamounts in them caves," Jim said.

"They are, too! Papa said so! If you don't believe him, I dast you go into one and see!" Lillian said hotly.

"I don't believe him, but I ain't fool enough to go inside one to find out. Let's go home. We ain't got no business here."

Glory declared, "We'll git a whipping for coming over here. Papa told us not to come into these woods. He said them wildcats and catamounts roam all over them."

Her face brightening, Lillian said, "That's how come we never heard 'em, too! They're all out roaming."

Instantly, we looked behind us, all around us and at each other. I reached out to grab Jim, the tallest, but he moved and began walking back toward the house, not exactly running but at a very fast pace. We also moved at a very fast pace.

Back at the house we found people going home and a new corn crib, its raw logs gleaming. The dishes were washed, too.

After the day's people, the house was strangely silent, so we found ourselves in the backyard. Breaking our listlessness, a whinnying and mooing came from the barn lot. Nell and Lily were demanding attention.

"Nell needs taking out for a run, but I have to cut stovewood," Papa worried.

Lillian said, "I'll take her!"

"I have to milk and you have to tend to Justin," Mama said.

There, we had the answer as to whom she would entrust Justin.

Eagerly, Lillian said, "I'll take him! I can hold him with one arm and guide Nell with the other." Seeing doubt gathering, she hurried on. "You know how gentle Nell is! I've had the other young'uns ride with me, and never hurt a one!"

That was true. Each of us had ridden with Lillian. That none had ever got hurt was no credit to her. Barebacked, she would get one of us behind her; once out of housesight, she would prod the horse into a gallop; her braids loosening in the wind, her hair streaming out behind her like a flag, we would go galloping, galloping all over the farm; and the one behind her would hang onto her waist for dear life. It was better to leave the baby in my care than to have him go horseback riding with Lillian.

But Mama yielded to her pleading and off they went on Nell, Lillian holding Justin in front of her — which was a mercy; however, having been confined all day, the horse walked eagerly with her ears cocked forward. Uneasily, I watched them jounce away.

The sun dipped to the treetops. Mama was warming supper. Papa was sitting on the back steps showing us how far he could spit. Mama came onto the porch. "Seems to me Lillian's been gone long enough to be back."

Papa said, "They'll be back before long." Nevertheless, he walked across the yard in the direction they had gone, and stood listening. Then, after returning to the steps, he walked back. It would soon be dusk, the time wildcats and catamounts began their nightly prowl, and it was commonly known that both had jumped from trees onto the backs of horses. He'd better start looking.

Again, he listened. This time he heard a faint call for help. Following the sound, he began running, with me right behind him. I knew she'd hurt that baby.

In no time he outdistanced me, but I followed his crashing through the woods. As we ran Lillian's cries became stronger, and the direction they were guiding us was toward the dens we

[86]

had rocked that afternoon. As we came nearer, however, her cries came from the west of them, and the terrain became alien.

Abruptly, I came out of the woods and almost ran into Papa, who was calling, "Lillian, Lillian, where are you?"

"Over here, in the water. Nell's on top of me!"

"My God!" Papa groaned. "Where's Justin?"

"On the bank. Hurry, git Nell off my leg!"

He waded hurriedly into the water, hollering, "I'm coming. Is Justin all right?" But he had the answer as Justin bellowed a cry.

Not knowing how deep the water was, I stood trembling on the bank. I could see Nell in the water and it seemed Lillian was under her. On the opposite bank sat Justin, bellowing in anger and fear.

"Whoa, there, Nell," Papa said gently. A moment later he said, "Giddup, now. Come on, git up! You ain't dead!" There was a thrashing of water, then Nell rose to her feet. "Whoa, Nell, whoa there! Lillian, can you stand up?"

She tried, but sank back to sit in the water. "It's my leg."

Papa said, "Ugh! Let me take Justin to Lowell. You be still till I git back." He brought me Justin, then brought Nell and handed me the reins. There I was, juggling Justin and the reins while Papa brought Lillian in his arms and sat her down to examine her leg.

The bone was intact. "Thank God, you're all right. And the horse."

He got her on Nell, got me on, then handed me Justin, who had quieted. We started home in silence.

After a way, Papa said, "What I want to know, Lillian, is what in tarnation was you doing way over here?"

"Just ridin'."

Papa grunted. "Just ridin'!" he snorted in derision. "I know exactly what you was doing. You was making Nell jump that creek. Now wann't you? And she couldn't."

Lillian said, "She can, too! She's jumped it plenty times!"

There was an ominous silence. Then, wearily, Papa said, "I just don't know. I just don't *know*."

"Don't know what?" she asked.

"What's going to become of you!"

While we struggled through the wood Lillian was silent. I heard her breathing deeply. Her leg must be hurting; a quick pain shot through me; my arm tightened around her waist. Her head was bent, her body straining against something. I realized she was crying.

As we came into our yard she lifted her head and flung back her hair. "It won't all my fault!" she cried out passionately. "Nell was frisky and wanted to run, and the wind felt so good coming against my face that we was at them dens 'fore I knowed it!" She stopped to draw a long, quivering breath, then blurted, "I did so want to see a wildcat and catamount!" She broke into body-racking sobs as Papa helped her from Nell, and I heard him gasp in astonishment.

CHAPTER 17

Lillian's World; Jenny's World

WITH HARVEST upon us we had no time for play, much less chasing wildcats. We helped Grandpa gather his and he helped us; so from sunup to sundown we were all busy — we with our field work and Mama with kraut and hominy-making and storing vegetables.

One afternoon Lillian and I were gathering tomatoes; the autumn sun made them hot, but that never hindered Lillian's voracious appetite. Taking a bite from one, she chewed slowly, thoughtfully, letting the juice run down her chin and drip onto her dress. Her light brown eyes held my dark brown ones.

"No, Lowell, I won't ever go to them dens no more. And if Papa *would* let me ride Nell agin, I wouldn't make her jump. The Lord saved my life that night. He told me so."

Though the sun was hot and bright, a shiver went through me. I could feel my scalp prickle, not wholly from her words. There was a knowing in her eyes I didn't know, and I was held motionless.

She went on. "He told me I hadn't been taking proper care of my body. He said He give us our bodies as houses for our souls, and we'd better be careful with 'em."

Her eyes left mine at last, lifting to the sky. Gulping down the last of the tomato, she said loudly, "I've been a disobedient child, Jesus. Forgive me!"

So intently did she look and listen that I, too, lifted my eyes to the sky, but could see naught but big, fat white clouds like blobs of white butter. My eyes returning to her, I saw her lost in rapt attention and her head nodded in understanding. Her eyes, wide with wonder, found mine again.

Though little shivers were running wildly through me, I was earthy enough to accuse her. "You did *not* see Jesus!"

Giving me a sweet smile, she said gently, "Yes, I did. He had on a long white robe whiter than any milk, and his hair hung about his shoulders. His eyes, oh, his eyes! They're full of love! And his smile, how sweet! How sweet it is! See that white cloud over there?"

Against the horizon was a pile of white clouds illuminated to a gloried shine by sun rays. She was pointing to them. "Look close and you might see Him. Look quick! He's fading away!"

I gazed until my eyes hurt, but I couldn't see Him.

She said, "I promised Him I'd be a better child, and I will!" She yanked up a tomato vine, and the force set her down hard. Surprised, she sat silent, breathing deeply. Then tossing her braids, she laughed. "That was swift and just punishment. I lost my temper. He always punishes us for what we do wrong. Never forgit it. What we sow we shall surely reap!"

Going to the onion row, she pulled up one, wiped the dirt on her dresstail, skinned it with her fingers and took a big bite. Pulling a hunk of corn bread from her pocket, she crammed a piece quickly into her mouth, but that didn't prevent water in her eyes from spilling over and trickling slowly down her tomato-stained face.

In south Georgia Jenny's school began in September and lasted eight full months with only short holidays for Thanksgiving, Christmas and Easter. We marveled that people there deemed going to school more important than gathering harvest.

In her letters she told us she liked teaching, but the people ate such nasty things as possums, goats, terrapins and sausage stuffed in hog guts. Of course they washed them first, but her stomach refused such nauseous food. The only vegetable they had was something called collards, a cross between cabbage and turnip greens, and field peas; she often went to bed hungry because both were infested with worms.

Dismayed, we made sure Grandpa knew what people ate down there, but he wasn't dismayed at all. "What they need to learn is some good north Georgia farming; they must be plain ignorant to raise just two vegetables, then let worms eat them," he said. "Sounds like they's a snake in Sally's Garden of Eden." He laughed at his own joke.

Ah, there was, there was, but it had naught to do with vegetables, and the snake wasn't in the garden but in the family.

CHAPTER 18

The Deceiver; a Forced Decision

Now that harvest was over Grandpa and Papa began cutting winter wood. One Saturday at dinner Grandpa said, "Caleb, I'm thinking about spending the winter with Sally and Willy. I'd sorta like to see that land of their'n."

Papa dropped his fork. His eyes flew to his father. When he retrieved the fork, his hand was trembling. "If you go," he told his father, "you won't come back."

Grandpa flared. "What in tarnation makes you say that? I'll be back in time for spring plowing."

Papa looked at his plate. When he looked at his father again, his eyes were glistening with tears.

Grandpa didn't notice. Continuing to eat, he said between bites, "You can git Fergus Anders to help finish hauling your wood. I got enough for Tish — she'll be gone most of the winter anyhow."

"Where she going?" Mama asked.

"Atlanta, to take that course she's been fuming about. She ain't gitting no younger, so I thought I'd — " he broke off and looked at Papa and saw his distress.

Papa asked, "Pa, what made you change your mind about going to south Georgia? I thought you said — "

"Jules is bringing his family up next week in his new Buick. I rode in Willy's Ford. I'd sorta like to see how a Buick rides." He looked sheepish. "Besides, I wanna see what their wonderful country looks like. They'll stay a few days and I'll go back with 'em."

My parents looked pleased. It was very seldom Jules and his wife came up to visit. I couldn't remember them.

Papa was worried. "If Tish is leaving to take that course, why don't you move your things on out here before you go, and live with us when you git back?"

"Tish is keeping the house in town. She won't be gone but six weeks."

Papa swallowed. "Well then, how come you want to stay the whole winter down there?"

Grandpa put down his fork, pushed back his plate and looked at his son. "Caleb, Jules has been down there long enough to marry and have two young'uns, and I ain't never been to see them. Sally's down there, too, now. I want to go see 'em. They ain't nothing to do up here in winter noway. What you so all fired up about?"

"I don't know," Papa said slowly, thinking. "I feel uneasy somehow, you going way down there. No, it's more'n that." He looked at his father. "I don't know what it is makes me so uneasy. But I am."

"Oh, shucks! I'm a grown man, Caleb. I can look out for myself."

But he didn't know that the easiest person to deceive was himself and that his own children were his best helpers.

Papa answered, "I know that, but all's not right someway."

Grandpa laughed. "I know what's the matter. You ain't been far from me since you was born. You hate for me to git outta your sight.

Papa replied gravely, "I hope that's what it is."

Uncle Jules looked like Papa, only fatter, shorter and younger, and he laughed more. Life had treated him kindly. To judge by his new Buick touring car, it still was.

Mama and Aunt Adah had much to talk about — mostly their husbands. From their talk one would think they had caught the most valuable men in the State of Georgia.

But Papa and Uncle Jules weren't enjoying themselves. Down at the barn, Papa was currying Nell while his brother watched.

Papa said, "We shore made a good corn crop this year, had to build a new crib. Had a logrolling and got it done in a day."

"So Sally was telling me. Shucks, you people up here are way behind the times. Logrollings went out with the last century. Another thing. So you raised enough corn to fill three cribs. How much money are they worth? A hundred dollars? That ain't much. All year you work for a wagonload of cabbage and apples. What are they worth, fifty bucks? Why, Caleb, you don't know what good crops are! Down my way, farmers getting rich, hand over fist, raising cotton, a bale to the acre, a hundred bucks a bale!"

"Don't reckon I'll ever be rich," Papa said.

"Trouble is, Caleb, you don't wanna be. You never tried to be, either. No ambition."

"I wanted to be a lawyer," Papa said, straightening up.

"Oh, that. You never had the money."

"I'd had enough if Pa hadn't sold that cordwood."

Uncle Jules knew the story; we knew it; for, once in a while, Papa let escape the one regret of his life, though most of the time he held it a fast prisoner.

Grandpa told the young Caleb he could have all the cordwood he could cut during summers for college tuition. All one summer Papa labored in the deep wood for college tuition. Then an emergency arose for which Grandpa had to have money. He had no recourse but to sell Papa's wood. That ended Papa's wood cutting.

Though he borrowed money for the first semester, he had to drop out in the second; then, intending to re-enter the following autumn, he taught school for tuition. During that time he met Mama, and the nearest he ever came to being a lawyer was the two terms he served as Clerk of Superior Court.

Now Uncle Jules clapped Papa on the shoulder. "Be practical, man! It's too late to think of college for yourself. But you got chillun you can send. Listen," he said, his face as solemn as if at a funeral, "you'll never make enough money up here to send them. In south Georgia farmers are making thousands of dollars a year off cotton. Why don't you move down there where you can make some money? You could make enough to send every one of your young'uns to college. Give them the chance you didn't have. Why don't you move?"

"I don't have land down there, and no money to move on."

"Aw, I'll fix that. I'll find you a place to move, if you'll come."

"I dunno, Jules. Pa said he'd be back next year in time for spring plowing."

Grinning slyly, Uncle Jules said firmly, "No, he won't."

Puzzled, Papa looked at him.

"That's all fixed. Sally and Willy are going to keep him."

Papa exploded. "*Keep* him! He ain't *that* old yet! Why, he ain't but sixty-eight! If he lives with anybody, he'll live with us, right here in his own house on his own land!"

"Caleb, when a man gits as old as Pa, all he needs to do is putter around. Pa's worked hard all his life, and he needs to ease up. Willy's going to let him tend as much land as he wants — raise strawberries or truck-farm. Whatever he wants. That land down there is rich, and it'll grow crops such as you've never seen. Down there, Pa won't have a life-and-death struggle in plowing rocky hills. His life will be easier. Would you have him up here, scratching around these rocks till he dies?"

Papa's shoulders slumped, and he said thoughtfully, "What does Pa say to all your big plans?"

"He's going, ain't he?"

[93]

"For this winter, he said."

"Oh, he'll stay, once he sees that land and country. No snow nor ice. No rocks nor mountains. He'll stay," Uncle Jules said confidently.

Papa swallowed a big lump in his throat. "The farm — who'll look after it if I move?"

"Oh, he'll sell it!" Uncle Jules said airily.

Papa couldn't believe that. Looking his brother in the eyes, he said, "I can't believe Pa would sell the land his Pa bought for him. I can't believe it!"

Uncle Jules said, "I didn't want to say this, Caleb, but you sorta force me to. He'd sell it if it wann't for you. He knows if he sold it you wouldn't have no place to go."

Papa's face turned white, as if Jules had stuck a hunting knife clean through him. He tried to cry out his pain but couldn't.

Jules didn't notice. He went on. "I come up here to see if I could get some sense into you. You been thinking what you want to do, not what's best for your wife and chillun. For God's sakes, get them out of this bone-pore country that's as good as dead and into one that's rich and living!"

Papa found breath to mumble, "We're doing fine here."

"Fine!" Jules mocked. "Bet you ain't got ten dollars in your pocket! And look at the clothes of Bela and your chillun! They ain't had decent dresses since you moved out here." His voice became solicitous. "Caleb, I want you to have a better life than you all are having. Don't you want to better yourself?"

His brother's words showed Papa how wide the gulf between them, and stirred anger to lash out at him. "I want to stay on the land bought by our grandfather. I want it to stay in the family, to be handed down from generation to generation. We was born and raised in that house. I want my children raised there, on the land of my father, in the house of my father. Don't that mean nothing to you?"

Jules laid a hand on Papa's shoulder. "You're just plain sentimental, Caleb, and just plain foolish. I want to give my wife and chillun a better chance in life, give them things to make life

[94]

easier than my mother and her chillun had. Pa. Well, he sees things my way. You ain't thinking what's best for your family. You ain't thinking what's best for Pa. The rest of us want to make his life easier in his old age."

Papa said stubbornly, "His pa bought this farm for him outta the gold he dug in California. I don't see how he could want to sell it."

"He'll sell, all right. Just you move and see! Another thing. Pa knows he's gitting old, and most of his chillun have left here. When Tish marries, you'll be the only one here."

"Are Tish and Jode gitting married?"

"Didn't you know? They're gitting married next summer. They're gonna buy some land from Willy and build a house down there."

"Why, *why* do you all want to live down there?"

"It's a land flowing with milk and honey."

He didn't mention gnats, mosquitoes and sandspurs.

Papa shook his head. "I don't believe it, and I don't care what the rest do. I want to stay here."

"Caleb, Caleb, ain't you ever gonna do nothing?" It was Jules's turn to be hopeless.

Papa did a strange thing then. Turning to Nell, he pulled her head down and rested his face against it. His arms reached up and around the horse's neck. The horse nuzzled him, and man and horse stood loving each other.

When Papa faced his brother, he said, "You be looking for a farm for me. I might move to that Garden of Eden of yours."

"You'll git rich raisin' cotton, Caleb! See if you don't!"

Papa wasn't wanting to be rich, he was wanting to talk with his Pa one more time. He told Jules, "Soon as I make up my mind, I'll let you know."

That afternoon Uncle Jules and his family returned to Aunt Tish's. The last words he said to Papa were "I'll git you that farm, Caleb, in time for spring plowing."

Papa grunted, "I ain't decided yet."

All during supper Papa was quiet, not talking much and not

laughing at all, which was unlike Papa. He acted as if he faced Judgment Day at sunup.

When Grandpa arrived next morning we were surprised.

"I was coming into town to see you this evening. Didn't think you'd be back out here 'fore you left," Papa told him.

"We don't leave till Saturday," Grandpa said, surprised too.

"I thought you'd be busy gitting your stuff together."

"I got that up yesterday. What's eating you? I come out here to help you today, now that Jules is out from under your feet. Anything you want me to do?"

"Yes, there is. I want you to go git all your stuff, and move out here with us. Forgit about going to Sally's."

Fire kindled in Grandpa's eyes. "Now that'd be a tomfool thing to do after I promised Jules I'd go back with him. I told you, Caleb, I'll be back in the spring."

Papa could hear his brother saying, "He won't be back." Now he said, "You might not want to come back after seeing their Garden of Eden. Fact is, Jules and Sally don't think you will."

"Oh, pshaw! Their thinking don't mean much. Their talk makes the land sound good, though, and I might like it. The way they picture it, all a farmer has to do down there is plant the seed. Jules musta sold you on it. He said you was going to move down there, too. That's why I come to see you today. They ain't no use of me coming back if you ain't here."

"I'll be here if you don't want to sell the farm. Do you, Pa?"

"I don't know. I'm gitting old. And tired. The money would be enough to last me for the rest of my life."

Papa swallowed. "But, Pa, your pa bought this land for you. Don't you want to keep it?"

Grandpa said, "Pa give each of his young'uns money to get a start in life. I bought land with mine. A time comes in every life to make a choice. I'm facing it. So are you. I can keep this farm, stay on here with you, but would it be the best thing for us? We'd have no more than we got now. That ain't much. You got a houseful of chillun, and more than apt, more to come. Can you raise them on a wagonload of apples and cabbage a year?"

Papa's heart was sinking fast. "I sent Jenny to town school so she could be a teacher."

"You done a good job with Jenny. But you got others to school. In south Georgia you might make enough money to make teachers out of all your girls, and doctors out of your boys."

One thing was sure and clear. His pa had been considering selling the farm. Or else he'd been talked to, hard and and fast, for his words were almost exactly the ones Jules spoke yesterday.

Papa swallowed hard to keep from crying. He couldn't say, after his father's words, "Pa, I don't want to move to that strange land. Let me stay in the house where I was born. Let me plow the land I plowed when a boy. Don't make me move!" No, he couldn't say, "Give me the farm your pa give you."

Grandpa seemed to know Papa's thoughts. "I can't give you this farm, Caleb. I have other children. If I don't sell it now, at my death it will be sold and the money divided amongst you. If I sell it now, I'll have enough money to keep me for the rest of my life; the rest will be divided amongst you when I die."

"How much would you sell it for?"

"At least fifteen thousand. With all the timber, land and a good house it's worth that."

Papa had less than a hundred dollars cash. It was his pa's farm. He would have to get his own. He had forty acres in the woods. No house, no money to build one, and it would take years to clear for crops. Now he said, "I hate to see this farm get out of the family."

His father said, "There's a time to hold on to old things, and a time to let 'em go."

Papa said, "Then you've just about made up your mind to sell."

"Not yet. I want to see that land down there first."

"That leaves me straddling a fence. Do I wait here till you decide or go ahead and let Jules find me a farm?"

"Caleb, you're going to have to make that decision."

Even while Papa considered debating it, he knew what he had to do. He had to move to south Georgia.

CHAPTER 19

Grandpa's Decision

We didn't go see Grandpa, Uncle Jules and his family off.
Papa said we'd probably see them again soon enough. He also
said there was no use in hauling any more wood, for we might
not be there to use it. With his words all the sorrows in the world
came to live in his face.

Grandpa had been in south Georgia hardly a month when he
wrote to say he liked it there and would stay. Willy would let
him tend all the land he wanted, but he aimed not to tend much;
he was going to take life easy. "The land is flat with no rocks,
and farmers use what they call 'guano' for fertilizer. The
climate is so mild you need no coat, only a sweater. It's my
honest opinion you'd like it down here. Plowing is easier, and I
think you could make a better living."

Soon after Christmas Uncle Jules wrote he had found a farm,
and for us to come as soon as possible since spring plowing
began earlier there. We were to come to Ralston, where he lived,
and he would help us get settled because the farm was only
twenty miles away.

Papa sold his forty acres to move on; we stacked the good,
solid furniture in the smokehouse, left the stored harvest, and
out of all the food Mama prepared for winter, she took a flour
sack of dried apples. We stuffed our personal possessions in tow
sacks and bundles.

This took time. As we gathered around the fire after supper,
Papa tried to answer our questions.

"Where is south Georgia?" Glory asked.

"A long way from here," Papa said in his teaching voice.
"We're in north Georgia, and Georgia is the biggest state east of
the Mississippi River."

"Never mind the Mississippi," Mama said, her light brown
eyes glistening with hope. "Maybe Jenny can live with us again."

Papa said, "No, she's in Wilcox County, fifty miles above where we'll be living in Coffee."

Mama sighed and depression settled upon us.

Seeing our gloomy faces, Papa said, "We'll have to take a long train ride to git there."

Mention of a ride lifted the gloom.

"What," demanded Lillian, "is a train?"

From Jenny's letters we knew about south Georgia, but we didn't know about trains.

Papa's forehead wrinkled as he tried to picture a train. "A train is a engine pulling lots of cars on iron tracks." His fingers explored his smooth black hair.

Mama said, "I don't see why they have a engine to pull cars. I thought cars went by theirselves."

Having once ridden on a train from Gainesville to Atlanta and back, Papa now displayed his superior knowledge. "Not them kind of cars. You're thinking of automobiles. Train cars are different. They're long and black with a lot of sofas."

Thirty-five miles south, Gainesville was the nearest place to catch a train. Usual transportation between there and Dahlonega was the mail-hack, something between a buggy and a wagon.

Mama said, "The mail-hack won't hold us all."

"I got Rover Shore to take us in his automobile. There we catch a train to Atlanta, and here I want everyone of you chillun to stay close to your ma and me. In Atlanta we have to wait two hours before our train to Ralston comes. In them big city terminals are white slavers — they could be some in Gainesville. They kidnap chillun and make white slaves outta them, girls especially."

His dove-gray eyes became stern as they lit on each of us, beginning with Justin, the baby on Mama's lap; Gregory, three years old and still wearing aprons; Glory, his eyes lingering; his eyes passed me quickly; then on to Lillian, frowningly. "None of you git outta our sight. Don't forget that."

A chill ran down our spines and we could feel prickles in our scalps. Our ignorant eyes grew large as we considered the prospect of being kidnaped; not that we knew what kidnaping was, but, because of Papa's solemnness, we knew it was something terrible; so we promised to stay close to our parents. That is, Lillian, Glory and I did. The discussion seemed lost on Gregory and Justin.

But his tight lips broke into a smile, his face lit with hope and he said, "In south Georgia, we'll git rich raising cotton!"

We all broke into laughter as we said one to another, "We'll git rich raising cotton!"

Snow was on the ground and spitting lazily into the cold air the morning we left Dahlonega. We had spent the night with Aunt Tish in town. In the early morning two Fords stopped in front of the house to carry us to Gainesville. Our parents and the boys got in one and we girls were told to get into the other. The drivers piled sacks and bundles at our feet.

The side curtains of the Ford, put up to keep out as much cold as possible, prevented our seeing out except through the windshield and the not too clear isinglass of the rear window. Awed and a little scared, we three never uttered a word all the way to Gainesville.

CHAPTER 20

The Train

BOTH FORDS pulled up to the terminal at the same time. Papa herded us inside a room with a lot of benches like a church. Grouped together, we stood until Papa and the drivers brought in our sacks and bundles; not that we worried about them, but we just didn't know to sit. Finding us a bench, Papa told us to sit down while he got the tickets. "Don't forgit what I said about them white slavers," he ended.

Even to them we wouldn't have been tempting. Not Mama with a baby on her lap and another clinging to her skirts, flanked by three growing girls in long, shapeless garments.

Subdued by the strangeness, we sat silent and close to Mama, who now opened the box of biscuits and sausage Aunt Tish had prepared for us, for it was past noon.

Suddenly, a deafening noise split the air and our ears. BANK, BANK, BANK, bank, bank, bank! It was louder than thunder. Smoke as black as cyclone clouds swirled at furious pace past the big windows while the racket kept on and on, BANK, BANK, BANK!

Loud as it was it didn't shut out the screams coming from Glory's and my wide-open mouths; for at the first *bank* we jumped to our feet and clutched each other in terror.

"Judgment day has come!" Glory shrieked.

"Judgment day! Judgment day!" I echoed.

Papa came running. Grabbing his coattails, we both screamed; "Judgment day! Judgment day!"

Sitting down, he pulled us close, whispering fiercely, "No, it ain't! A train engine's making that noise! Hush! Stop that hollering!" He petted and soothed us into quietness, then looked at us with sad eyes. "I hadn't realized you all was so all-fired ignorant. Guess it's time I was gitting you outta them mountains."

Mama handed him a biscuit and he began eating.

With a toss of her braids Lillian said, "I knowed that was a train all the time."

Though she hadn't acted as scared as Glory and I had, we didn't believe her. Papa said she wasn't afraid of the devil, but that didn't make her know more than we.

A loud voice hollered, "At-lanta! ATLANTA! All aboard for Atlanta!"

Gathering sacks and bundles, we hurried outside and were nudged along by Papa toward a long, black house with a lot of windows. It was hooked onto a big black thing that was puffing and blowing as if it had been running very fast. Papa didn't give us time to stand and gaze, but we did get a glance. That was enough. The thing made me think of hell. Black smoke poured from the chimney and white from the sides. Something was burning in it for sure.

A kind man helped us up the high steps and through a narrow door. We were in a long room and between two long rows of sofas. Finding two facing each other, Papa settled us, then returned to the terminal for the rest of our sacks.

My eyes watched him go out the door, then began roving. That was the prettiest place I had ever seen; the walls were so shiny I could almost see myself; the sofas were not only soft but were also red like roses; on the floor between them was a red rug; next to a window, I noted the curtains were red, too.

I saw Papa coming, his arms laden with sacks. He hadn't reached the steps when the train began moving. We were leaving him! I wanted to tell Mama, but no sound would come from my mouth. Nursing Justin, she didn't see my beseeching eyes. Rising to go to her, I saw Papa running. In another minute he stood beside us, breathless and laughing.

"I almost got left! Had to jump for it!" he said, sitting beside Mama.

My weak knees gave way, I plunked back on the seat, tears flowing.

Reaching over, his strong arms lifted me onto his lap. "What! Crying! Don't you know we're on a train?"

Blinking away my tears, I was going to tell him the reason, but when our eyes met there was no need. He knew. I soon noticed with disapproval that other passengers were continually passing up and down the aisle. Why couldn't they stay in their seats and be quiet?

"Oh," Papa explained, "they have to go for a drink of water or to the toilet."

When Mama had to take us, we found out about this. Soon we children were going to the toilet to push down the handle to see the water run. Nor did we get over the wonder of the water fountain. There was no need for a dipper. All you had to do was hold down a button thing for water to rise high enough for you to lean over and drink. I guessed it was the ever-flowing fountain we sang about in church.

Lillian was now by the window with Gregory on her lap. Facing Mama, Papa sat next to Lillian; Glory was beside Mama with Justin stretched between them. Next to Papa, I was on the aisle side.

Between trips to the toilet and water fountain, I looked at people. My gaze fastened on the woman across the aisle. Where her nose should have been were two big holes.

Papa saw. "Stop gaping at that woman!"

"But Papa, how does she keep the rain out?"

Glancing at the woman, he said, "She's got on a bonnet."

Occasionally, a big, black man with flashing white teeth passed through. He wore a red cap, and always seemed in a hurry.

Having been a teacher, Papa still loved to teach, and when chance allowed, he not only taught us children but also other people things he knew and others didn't. Now he taught us about trains.

I started him by saying, "I wish we had a house like this."

"This ain't no house," he said, "but a train car. The pale man is the conductor, and the Negro man, the porter." He paused, and I watched his Adam's apple go up and down. More was coming. "This car is hooked on to a lot of others, some in front, some behind, and all are hooked on to the engine — the big, black thing you saw with smoke coming out. In the engine are the engineer and the fireman. The engineer guides the train — keeps it on the track — and the fireman keeps the fire going. The fire is what makes the engine have the strength to pull the cars. The engine and the cars are called a train."

"How does fire make strength?" I wanted to know.

He said slowly, "I don't know everything, and that is one I don't."

I returned my gaze to the woman without a nose.

Though Gainesville was only about fifty miles from Atlanta, it was well after dark when we reached there, for the train stopped every few miles, either to let somebody off or take somebody on or both. In between stops the train moved slowly, though we seemed to be flying. But the train finally approached the big city, and the conductor came, hollering, "Atlanta! ATLANTA! All out for Atlanta!"

Gathering us together, Papa whispered fiercely, "Stay close to us. Remember what I said about the white slavers!"

[103]

As we left the train to climb the high steps leading to the waiting room, all of us, except Mama, who was carrying Justin, were loaded with sacks and bundles.

The waiting room was huge. Herding us like a flock of sheep, Papa counted heads, fearing we would become lost in space. Besides, the huge columns supporting the ceiling caused confusion in direction, and almost immediately we saw conspicuously displayed on them big white placards reading:

BEWARE OF WHITE SLAVERY

Lillian read the words aloud; though we didn't know the meaning, the fact that they were there made our skins prickle. Hardly daring to move, we sat close to our parents.

But Gregory couldn't read nor did he know the meaning of printed words. A little later Papa discovered him missing. His face turned white. "Stay right here," he cautioned. "I'll find him." But he feared Gregory would never be found. The white slavers had him.

I couldn't bear Papa out of my sight again, so I held on to his hand as he strode around the vast waiting room, looking for a three-year-old boy with golden curly hair and merry laugh.

There was a fruit stand on the farther side from where we were sitting, and there it was that we caught sight of Greg's golden curls. Being at no loss for words, he was regaling the stand-keeper with family history while munching an apple. In his other hand was a banana. I looked at the fruit enviously.

Gathering Greg in his arms, Papa glared at the man. "Trying to kidnap him, eh?"

The man smiled. "Oh, no, sir! I was trying to git him to tell me his name. I knowed he was lost."

"If you knowed he was lost, why didn't you bring him back to us instead of tempting him with your old fruit?" Papa gave my hand a tug and we walked away, leaving the man open-mouthed and scratching his head.

We finished eating the sausage and biscuits, then busied ourselves getting water and going to the toilet. It didn't seem long until our train arrived; we settled down on this for the night, for it would be sometime next day before we arrived at Ralston.

[104]

But I couldn't sleep very well. The train people didn't blow out the lights; the conductor was always coming through hollering "Tickets"; another man would come through hollering, "Sandwiches, peanuts and candy"; people kept getting on or off. Just as I would drop into sleep, one or the other woke me.

When at last no men came through hollering and the train quit stopping to let people off or on, I became aware of the whistle's mournful and lonely cry. It made me think of times flowing fast as the moving train into the past, to be no more.

From the known we were hurtling through darkness into the unknown, and I wished we were rushing back to Grandpa's farm, back to the red, red hills where trailing arbutus blossomed in early spring, chestnuts ripened in the fall and snow lay deep in winter.

I wanted to go back to times that the crying whistle was telling me even now were ended. Turning my face to the soft sofa, I cried with the whistle, lonely in the night for all the things my heart remembered that would never be again.

Part II   South Georgia

CHAPTER 21

A New Home, a New Status

THE TRAIN was the world. Time became the mournful crying of the whistle; the man hollering, "Sandwiches, peanuts and candy!"; the staccato singing of the conductor, "Tickets! Tick-ETS! Tickets!"; the swaying car carrying people this way and that as they went up and down the aisle; the shiny walls reflecting faces; the soft feel of the sofas; the cold water forever spurting up to thirsty mouths; the foul odor of train smoke; and under and over all was the clickety-click of the wheels running over rails.

So we were unprepared when the world came to an abrupt

halt, the conductor suddenly appearing, hollering, "Ralston, Ralston, next stop!"

Papa roused himself. It was another day. "Git ready to git off," he said.

The train was already slowing. When it came to a stop, we straggled up the aisle. Benumbed by the long ride, we stumbled off and stepped onto land as flat as a pancake.

Uncle Jules was waiting for us, and helped Papa gather sacks, bundles and children into his new Buick. We found it had three seats, the third being two stools pulled out from the sides. He must be rich to own such a big automobile.

To confirm the impression, he stopped in front of a house much larger than Grandpa's. Green bushes were next to the deep-set front porch, though a cold wind said it was winter. He didn't give us time to look, but ushered us into a parlor without a bed, where a fire was burning in a small fireplace. The fire wasn't made of wood but big chunks of black rock.

We girls gazed open-mouthed at this miracle and pointed.

"It's coal."

I shook my head. "It can't be cold. It's on fire."

Papa and Uncle Jules laughed, and my face burned.

Papa said, "You spell it c-o-a-l, not c-o-l-d."

Aunt Adah came bustling in from the kitchen where she was cooking breakfast, and gave us all a warm welcome.

Soon we were sitting down to a hot breakfast of eggs, sausage and some white stuff called grits, which was eaten with butter melted in it along with the eggs and sausage. Their good food further confirmed the rich impression. Also, instead of oilcloth their dining table was covered with a white cloth such as Mama used for company.

Aunt Adah said, "I know you all must be worn out, so just stay here and rest today, and move tomorrow."

Uncle Jules told Papa, "Caleb, take a nap after breakfast, and when I come home for lunch you can go back with me to the store and pick out your furniture."

Papa looked as if someone had struck him. "Furniture?"

Brusquely, his brother said, "Yes, furniture. You'll need beds, stove, table and chairs, won't you?"

"Yes-s," Papa said slowly, thinking of the spool beds, feather ticks, ladder-back chairs, a marble-topped washstand and high-boy, the pretty dining table we left in the smokehouse. Seeing his brother's look, he said quickly, "Yes, of course. I'm tuckered out. After I sleep a while, I'll feel better."

At Aunt Adah's insistence, we all lay down; she put us girls in a sideroom adjoining the kitchen. Lillian and Gloria got the double bed, but I was on a half-sized one, and could hardly turn over without falling off. In addition, the bed kept moving around every time I closed my eyes, my brain kept making the same sound as the train and any moment I expected the conductor to come, hollering "Tickets!" So sleep came in fitful dozes.

Papa's voice jerked me upright. Rubbing sleep out of my eyes, I slid to my feet. No, it wasn't Papa's voice, but Uncle Jules's.

"Caleb ain't up yet? Musta been tired plum out. No wonder with all them young'uns. How in the Sam Hill will he git them all raised?"

"They'd been better off if you'd left them right where they were. Caleb will never make a south Georgia farmer," came Aunt Adah's voice.

They were in the kitchen, talking about us. My big ears stretched like a donkey's.

Uncle Jules said, "*They* might have been better off, but *we* wouldn't. The store ain't gonna last long unless I get some cash, and the best chance for that is Pa selling the farm. As long as Caleb was on it, he wouldn't, and he'd probably let him have it.

"The rest is entitled to our share, and we need it right now. Sally says their crops didn't turn out good this year, and they need money bad, too. The truth to that is Willy ain't gonna work — leaves it all to sharecroppers while he goes off to town every day."

"That's none of our business, Jules. It may well be that Caleb could have got the farm. They'd certainly been better off. I think you'll regret bringing them down here. He has no boys old enough to help. How do you think he'll farm two hundred acres?"

All at once the room seemed very cold, and I shivered. Uncle Jules meant none of them liked Papa, except Grandpa. They had tricked Grandpa into leaving his home, and when he sold it, they planned to take his money. What would become of him then?

They had tricked Papa too, and got him away from the farm so it would be sold, got him down in this flat land where Aunt Adah didn't see how he could farm. What would become of us?

I had to find Papa and tell him. We had to tell Grandpa, too; he would see he couldn't sell the farm, and we all could live there together. I entered the kitchen, almost bumping into Aunt Adah. I couldn't let her know.

"Goodness, child, you startled me. The rest still asleep?"

I nodded. "Where's Papa?"

"Your uncle has gone to wake him and your mama. Do you need to go to the bathroom?"

I stared at her.

"The toilet."

I nodded. She led me down a hall and opened a door. There was a toilet like the one on the train, a washpan hooked onto the wall and a long, white thing like a watering trough. I pointed.

"That's a bathtub. You fill it full of water, get in and wash yourself. This" — she laid a hand on the washpan — "is a lavatory. You wash your hands here when you finish using the toilet. See, turn it back to stop the water. There's soap and towel. I must go finish dinner."

I considered the comfort of that bathroom. Neither house we had lived in had one. No matter the weather we always had to go to the outhouse, and we washed from pans or laundry tubs. The soap with which I washed my hands was white and sweet smelling, not homemade lye. The towel was pink and fluffy. We used worn-out cloths. If we stayed in this alien land, maybe we could have things like these. But my conscience wouldn't be hushed. I had to tell Papa.

Opening the door, I almost bumped into him. I blurted, "Papa, Papa, we must go back home!"

"What are you talking about, Lowell? Have you gone crazy?" he asked crossly. "Go on into the dining room. They're about to eat."

"Please, Papa! We got to git Grandpa and go home!"

"Your grandpa is fifty miles from here. Now do what I said!" He gave me a little push, went inside the bathroom and closed the door.

I did, but no one was there. Mama was in the kitchen helping Aunt Adah. Neither saw me as I slipped inside the room where we slept. I'd tell Lillian. She would know what to do.

I had to shake them awake. Being on the front side, Lillian reached out and pinched me for waking her, and I cried, "I woke you 'cause dinner's nearly ready, and I wanted to tell you something." I fled back to the kitchen.

Mama said, "Go on into the dining room, and find you a place. We're about to put dinner on the table."

But, again finding the room empty, I went to find Papa. Maybe he would listen to me now. But he was with Uncle Jules in the parlor by the funny fire. Beseechingly, I looked at Papa. I wanted to tell him, to scream out what I heard. But he paid me no attention. This and the pain from the pinch made tears spill onto my cheeks.

"Hey, what're you crying for?" my uncle asked. "We don't allow crying around here."

Papa pulled me onto his lap. "She's homesick. She wants to go back home and take her grandpa."

"That's a pretty come-off! You just got here. You'll have a new home tomorrow. We'll soon have you eating gopher, chitlings and possum! Ha, ha, ha, ha!"

Knowing what he'd done, I wouldn't look at him. Pulling Papa's head down, I whispered, "I got to tell you something. Before it's too late."

Aunt Adah appeared in the doorway. "Come to dinner."

Putting me down, Papa got up and bent to whisper, "Wait till after dinner," while he dried my tears with his handkerchief.

During the meal Uncle Jules teased me about being homesick until I thought my face would catch fire. Seated between Lillian and Glory, I saw Lillian casting baleful looks at our uncle. So she didn't like him either, and she hadn't even heard what I had. I wouldn't tell her because she pinched me.

Under the pretext of reaching for bread, she whispered, "I

didn't mean to pinch so hard. I was only playing." Though her words lifted my spirits, I wouldn't tell her what I heard. The pinch hurt.

Papa was the one to tell, and I would tell him as soon as he'd let me; so when Uncle Jules and Papa got their hats to go to the store, I got mine, too, though Uncle Jules frowned.

On the way I rode between the two, and the first words my uncle said were "Now, Caleb, they ain't no use for you to git any more furniture than you can make out with. No use atall."

"I ain't aiming to."

I said, "We got plenty furniture in the smokehouse back home," hinting to Papa, who didn't take the hint.

My uncle said, "You could have it shipped later on."

He didn't mean for us to go back. I swallowed a lump in my throat. If I could get Papa off by himself I could tell him.

At the parlors, bedrooms and kitchens placed in little groups in the store front, my eyes went wide. There were sofas longer than the train ones, and much softer, but when I ran my hands over them, Uncle Jules frowned. "Don't be handling things," he said.

We merely passed by, and didn't stop at the back either, but climbed some steps to another floor. Here were iron bedsteads, thin mattresses but no feather ticks, dressers, cane-bottomed chairs, stoves and sundry other articles needed in a home. A poor one.

My uncle said, "You'll need a stove," and led us to the very smallest. "This one will do. And a eating table," and showed us a long, pine table with straight legs, very ugly. "Now how many beds, double ones?"

"Well," Papa said, hesitating, "We'll need four. Jenny'll be coming home when her school is out." His eyes brightened.

His brother led him to stacks of iron bedsteads, and Papa chose three black ones with spots of gold paint, and a white one a mite more fancy to go in the parlor, he thought.

The spots of gold paint would be the nearest to gold we would see in south Georgia; we didn't know that, though Papa might have had a foreboding. He had to have a reason for choosing black beds.

Next came the mattresses, the thinnest and cheapest, and springs. Then Papa walked over to a dresser with four drawers and a mirror.

Uncle Jules said, "You don't need that."

"Yes, I do. For the women to primp by," and Papa said it firmly. Finally, his brother nodded.

Walking to the cane-bottomed chairs, he asked, "Let's see, how many?" He counted us and said, "Seven."

Papa said quickly, "You didn't count Justin. He'll soon be big enough to sit in a chair. And how 'bout company?"

"You won't be bothered with company much."

"I don't see why not. All my family's here," and his tone became belligerent. "That's one reason for my moving here. And Pa. He'll want to stay with us some."

"That's right, that's right," his brother conceded, and allowed an extra chair.

Emboldened by this concession, Papa pointed to a rocker.

But Uncle Jules said with finality, "You don't need that."

Papa stared at the cane-bottomed rocker, then sighed. "I don't reckon so. But we'll need a safe for the dishes."

My uncle pointed to a tin-doored, ugly, small group of kitchen safes. Papa nodded, his lips tight.

Uncle Jules heard someone come in the front door and hurried down to the front. Papa started to follow, but I pulled him back.

"I gotta tell you, Papa, what I heard Uncle Jules tell Aunt Adah before we got up today."

"Well, hurry," he said.

I told him. As he listened his face became white. When I ended, he said, "Pa and me was suckers. We gotta git him and go back just as quick as we can." His steps were determined as he started down the steps. We hadn't reached the bottom when we heard a bell ringing.

As the customer went out the door, Uncle Jules came to the back to a box on the wall with a little round black cup in front. He picked up something like a buggy whip hanging to the box, held it to his ear and spoke into the handle.

"Hello! Hello, Sal! We're fine as hair on a frog's back. What's that? He has? (Pause). That's more'n I thought. No, not tomorrow. Caleb's here. Yeah, come in this morning. I have to help him move tomorrow. We just finished picking out his furniture — "

We picked it out, all right. I felt as if I had eaten green persimmons.

When my uncle put down the buggy whip, he turned to us with a big smile. "That was Sally. Pa's sold the farm. Got more'n I thought."

Papa trembled. "Sorta quick, wann't it?" He looked around for a chair, found it and sank down heavily.

I went up close and caught hold his arm. "Papa, Papa!" I whispered, my heart choking.

His dulled eyes found mine. "We can never go back."

Uncle Jules said, "You wann't planning on going back noway, was you? Pa got twenty thousand dollars cash for the farm."

Tears in his eyes, Papa looked at him. "He won't have it long. By the time you and Sally get through with him. Pa was a sucker. I was a sucker. I was more. I was a fool, and I want you all to know I know I was a fool. I just realized it a few minutes ago. I was going after Pa and take him home as soon as we got back to your house. Now it's too late." Papa was on the brink of sobbing.

"How was you gonna do that? You ain't got no car. You ain't got nothing! I'm trying to help you git something."

"You help! We still got legs. If we ain't got nothing else, we got legs! We can use 'em, too!"

"Now, Caleb, talk sense! Sally's house is nearly fifty miles from here. You couldn't possibly walk it. Besides, Pa wouldn't go back with you. He's happy right where he is, and he'd have thought you crazy if you told him your scheme."

"Scheme! You and Sally are the schemers! I hope you two will take Pa's money and burn in hell with it!"

Uncle Jules looked around wildly. No customers were in. He was plainly shocked that Caleb would use language like that, and more shocked to learn Caleb wasn't as big a fool as they thought. Yet, "The move could mean a better life for you and your family, if you'd only git some git-up-and-go about you," he told Papa bluntly.

Papa winced. I had to make him feel better. I said, "Oh, Papa, we'll show them! We'll git rich raisin' cotton, see if we don't!"

Uncle Jules said, "With cotton nearly a dollar a pound, you're bound to. Cotton is pure gold now, Caleb. The sensible thing for you to do is go ahead and move like we planned. Why, from the first crop you ought to have plenty money!"

Woodenly, Papa replied, "It's the only thing I can do." He was at the bottom, he realized, and all he could do was start climbing.

"Caleb, you'll owe me three hundred dollars outta your first bale of cotton," Uncle Jules said, suddenly serious.

That brought Papa to his feet. "Three hundred dollars! For that little tad of furniture? You're outta your mind!"

"Add it for yourself and see!"

Papa did, seeing the prices of each item, and turned away, drooping. Three hundred dollars, and Mama didn't even have a rocker in which to rock the baby. For these few pieces of his cheapest furniture his own brother charged him three hundred dollars! Besides being a schemer, his brother was a cheater. His own brother! A nightmare was beginning. No, it had begun when he agreed to move to this land of robbers.

The farm to which we moved was some twenty miles from Ralston, but it might as well have been a hundred as far as Uncle Jules and his family were concerned. From the day we moved, none of them visited us during the year we lived there, despite the new Buick.

The day we moved he took us, with a driver in a truck following with the furniture. It was almost a silent ride, joyless and dreary. The somber gray sky didn't lend itself to cheerful spirits. Then, too, we were aliens in this wide land stretching away in endless expanse to meet a distant horizon.

Seated on one of the bucket seats, I watched the landscape flow past. The white sandy road ran between groves of pines, fields now deserted, and over little, rattling wooden bridges spanning brooks of water brown as coffee. In some places the brown water was along the roadside, not going anywhere; sometimes the water stretched away into gloom created by tall, leafless trees from which long, gray masses like beards swung in the wind. They were bald cypresses and the gray stuff was swamp moss, Uncle Jules said.

Out of a stretch of road hemmed in by fields we pulled into a wide, barren yard. And there stood our house. There it sat, as gray as the day, showing its nakedness in brazen defiance of any charm. No tree or shrub softened its sharp outlines; it stood alone, a gray etching against the background of gray fields and sky, with a keen wind accentuating its loneliness.

"Well, here we are!" Uncle Jules said with great cheerfulness.

Crawling from the security of the car, we went warily up the worn, warped boards comprising the front steps. As if the house was doing its utmost to bid us welcome, the front door was wide open, also the back; and connecting the two was a wide hall off which six doors opened, three on each side. The rooms were enormous, much larger than those of Grandpa's house.

Uncle Jules said, "A nigger family lived here."

We children had never seen a Negro, except on the train. There were none on the streets in Dahlonega and none where we lived in the country. Since there was no occasion for it, the name had never been mentioned in our house; so Uncle Jules's information meant nothing to us.

When Mama directed the driver to put the furniture on the front porch, Uncle Jules thought it was time for him to leave.

When both truck and automobile were gone, Mama directed that the washpot, which Uncle Jules had grudgingly allowed Papa, should be set up and filled with potash water.

In the backyard we found a pile of odd-looking wood and a well that Papa said was nothing but a hole in the ground with a cistern pipe for a curb and only a chain and bucket to draw water. The top was open to the elements (and mosquitoes, we later discovered).

When the water was boiling, ceilings, walls and floors were scrubbed, the washpot being filled again and again. When the chore was finished the house had a clean, antiseptic smell, and we children had a thorough knowledge of how to draw water with chain and bucket.

After the kitchen was dry, Papa put up the diminutive stove and put the tin-doored safe in a corner. The dining table and chairs were placed in the dining room; our parents put their bed and the dresser in the adjoining room, and set beds in the three rooms across the hall for us.

But we had no sheets, pillows or quilts. Papa told us, "We'll have to sleep on bare mattresses tonight. I'll borrow a wagon and go to town tomorrow to see if they've come. I had 'em shipped. Nell, too." At our glad surprise, he added, "I couldn't bear to part with her."

While Mama and Lillian began preparing a meal, Papa went to see Mr. Weane, the owner of the farm, who lived a little way from us.

From the sacks and bundles we brought emerged dishes, cooking utensils, our bone-handled cutlery and clothes. When everything was put in its place, the rooms were still so empty our voices had a tendency to echo.

A fire was built in our parents' bedroom with the odd-looking wood. We later learned they were pine knots, commonly called lantern knots. Picked up from fields and woods, they were remnants of the longleaf pine from ages past. Rich in resin, they made a fire so bright a lamp wasn't necessary. As they burned, a black pitch oozed from them, which burned so fiercely and gave off such a piney scent we had to move our chairs many feet away.

Surrounded by strangeness, we sat oddly upright in the cane-bottomed chairs, and, homesick too, we gazed morosely into the hot, bright fire.

Our mood was also influenced by Papa's. Since his talk with Mr. Weane, he had been white-faced, stern and almost silent. The new landlord had enlightened him as to his status. He was a sharecropper.

Mr. Weane had also walked him over the almost endless fields he was to tend, giving him instructions and expectations. For such extensive farming Papa knew he was wholly unqualified, but kept silent. Destitute, with a large family to feed, he was trapped. He resolved to do the very best he could with a one-horse-farm qualification on a two-horse farm. But he was scared and well-nigh hopeless.

Suddenly breaking the silence, he revealed what Mr. Weane said and what we were up against in tending all that land. But our status of sharecropper hit him hardest.

To Mama, according to her raising, we had fallen to the lowest rung of the social scale. Sharecroppers were no more than poor white trash.

We older children were aware of a sharecropper status. Since we came from generations of landowners, we had always been counted in the landowner class. The fall was great and our gloom joined that of our parents.

Lillian's voice suddenly broke our dejected mood by singing:

> Twilight is stealing over the sea,
> Shadows are falling dark on the lea;
> Borne on the night winds, voices of yore
> Come from the far-off shore.
>
> Far away, beyond the star-lit skies
> Where the love-light never, never dies
> Gleameth a mansion filled with delight,
> Sweet happy home so bright.

By the time she reached the chorus we all were singing, pouring our longing into song, making life more bearable.

CHAPTER 22

The Land

M R. WEANE was to furnish us groceries until harvest, the cost to be deducted from our share of the crop, which was a third. His idea of groceries was flour, meal, lard, sugarcane syrup and sowbelly meat filled with skippers. Mama had to boil the meat before frying in order to kill the worms. Once dead they floated to the top of the water, which Mama would pour off. We ate it. We had to.

For breakfast we had the inevitable milk gravy but without milk, syrup and bread. No butter. Assuming we would be supplied with a cow, Papa sold our dear Lily. In his talk with Mr. Weane he learned his assumption was wrong, though the Weanes had a drove of cows.

In north Georgia we usually had bread and milk for supper. Now our supper consisted of dried apples boiled with sugar, bread, gravy and the crisped sowbelly.

The Monday following our move, Papa began turning land with plow and mules furnished by Mr. Weane, and as soon as the ground allowed he planted a vegetable garden. In the interval between planting and producing, our table was lean indeed.

Instead of plowing with Nell, Papa had to use a two-mule plow, so she was used only for Papa to ride to town when necessary.

As soon as he began plowing the big fields for cotton, he realized the enormity of the task before him. It was impossible for one man, so he had to use us girls in helping to spread guano and for planting. When the seeds were up, we girls became diggers of grass in earnest.

Such expanse of land none of us had ever seen. The fields seemed endless. From one end of a row we couldn't see the other. We came to know the meaning of the word *toil*. It wrapped its coils about us, strangling us, until we were too weary to struggle against it. The work we thought we did in north Georgia was, in retrospect, play.

No more did we dawdle at the end of each round, nor did we rest with hoe handles under our chins to watch birds flying over. There were no birds flying over except buzzards circling lazily, and who cared for them? We hardly lifted our eyes from the sandy dirt, which the burning sun made so hot that we had to dig holes for cooler dirt every time we moved forward.

[117]

We planted more cotton than anything else, but corn ran close. The rows of corn were set wider apart than in north Georgia so that a row of field peas could be planted between them. The peas were the staple summer vegetable and were eaten twice a day, every day, by every family. The problem was worms liked them, too. No matter how many times the cook washed them, when they were placed on the table little white worms would float in the soup. The peas were the ones Jenny wrote about, but we learned to skim off the worms and go right on with our eating.

Planted amongst the corn, also, were velvet beans which were used for stock feed. In the fall enough had to be picked for seed. A picker soon learned the adjective was sorely misleading; what looked like velvet was minute prickles, causing severe stinging of naked fingers.

Fodder was unknown. Instead, after the corn was pulled and peanuts dug, cows, mules and hogs were turned into the fields, which were temporarily fenced with strands of barbed wire. Rounding up the animals when they were needed was a tremendous job, usually done by younger children on mules.

Different, too, were the peanuts, commonly called penders or goobers, as they were larger than the ones in north Georgia, and next to cotton in value, though the market wasn't nearly as great as now.

In spring and summer hogs and cattle were turned into fenced pastures comprising miles of wooded, swampy land abounding in the tough wire grass, pines, clumps of palmetto, live oaks, haws, hog plums, and thickly overgrown with other vegetation, tangled and wild. On the fringes grew sassafras and gallberry bushes, the latter making excellent yard brooms.

Also in the pastures were, without reason it seemed since they had no tributaries, pools of brown water, wherein dwelled catfish and redeyes, water moccasins and leeches. In the pools were clumps of wire grass, forming little islands; cypresses, with the long moss swaying from them, thrived, forming "knees" around which debris and soil clung, also forming small islands.

The pastures didn't invite exploration; they were real forests primeval. Some sections had never been penetrated by man, and were so repellent they weren't likely to be. Even domestic animals would avoid them, for they were the home of bobcats, coyotes, bears and alligators. Also deer and other less dangerous fauna.

Botanical life, too, was vastly different. Scattered over the terrain were great beds of prickly-pear cactus with long, cruel thorns; sandspurs were the bane of cotton pickers and bare feet; broom sedge, dog fennel, sweet fennel, jimsonweed, Jerusalem oak, coffeeweed and teeweed were common.

Among the numerous wild flowers buttercups, not daffodils, were the first to bloom in meadows; the small cuplike flower was set on a two-inch stem like the violet (we didn't see any violets); if you held one under your chin and it didn't reflect yellow, then you didn't like butter.

In damp places grew weird-looking flowers called pitcher plants, which devoured insects; the foliage was pitcher-like, but the flower, rising on a straight stem, formed a cushion around which were tiny beige flowerets, commonly called hen and biddies.

The oddest plant was the hatpin, which grew everywhere — a tiny white button set on a stem from two to four feet high. These were like tiny stars embellishing the dull country-side.

We came to know lantanas, hydrangeas, periwinkles, Cape jasmines, oleanders, bridal wreaths and magnolias. We children had never paid attention to flowers, but the profusion of these southern blossoms thrust itself upon our eyes, and we began to ask their names.

For shade, the chinaberry or "umbrella" tree, alien to us, was the most common. Often pecan trees were in yards. Many years later farmers developed pecan orchards, which grew into a prosperous industry. In my time pecan trees were counted wild along with black walnuts. In another county we were to see our first palms.

In this flat, sandy land apple trees didn't flourish, but pears, plums and peaches did. It was our introduction to them, and also to figs for which I had an immediate fondness; and occasionally, pomegranates, that odd delicacy, were found.

It seemed in a land of such abundance that there should be no reason for empty bellies. But worms infested vegetables; bugs ate snap beans as soon as they cracked the ground. Mama raised some pumpkins, but worms ate them while the slices were drying. No pesticide was known except Paris green, a poison Papa dared use only on Irish potato vines. After the crop was harvested, he coated the potatoes in slaked lime for a preservative.

And the land swarmed with mosquitoes, gnats and rattlesnakes. Mosquitoes made sleep nigh impossible unless one slept under mosquito netting. Malaria, as a result of the mosquitoes, was prevalent. In daytime gnats swarmed around the eyes and up women's coattails, making life miserable; as a result, pink eyes were common. Rattlesnakes were continually biting dogs, cows, horses and hogs. Keeping yards free of weeds and debris was a necessity since they were not off limits to the rattlers.

Sandspurs were the bane of outdoor activity; their spurred heads tangled opened cotton bolls; they scattered on the ground. When someone suddenly leaped two or three feet in the air, everyone knew he had stepped on a sandspur with bare feet.

CHAPTER 23

Toehold and School

THE SUNDAY following our move, visitors lit on our front porch like a flock of birds. Papa opened the door. "Come in," he welcomed.

"We're the Weane chillun," said a pale, frail girl. "I'm Letty, the oldest at home, and these're my sisters and brothers."

Mutely, we gazed at them. How could any family have so many children? Among them were Luby, a girl Glory's age, and Minnie, mine.

Of course there weren't enough chairs; so Papa offered them to the older ones; we younger ones sat on the floor.

"I've wondered all day," Papa said, "about churches. Where is the nearest Baptist church?"

"Church?" Letty said. "The nearest any church is in Brack."

"Brack?"

"Town, three miles off. The road going past here goes to Brack."

"You mean they ain't no churches in the country?"

Shaking her head, she said, "I been living here all my life, and I never heered of one."

"Huh. You all go to Brack to church?"

"Nobody goes to church round heer."

Heatherns. Plumb heatherns. In north Georgia everybody went. It was hard to think of life without church.

He became anxious. "How 'bout school?"

"Oh, they's a school," she said, as if she had just as soon dispense with school as well as with church, "a mile from here, called Loblolly."

"Loblolly? Sorta odd name, ain't it? You all go?"

"Me and Hartie's too old, but Luby, Peedee, Minnie and Winkie," pointin to a scrawny little boy, "all go. Winkie just started this year."

Mama said "He looks too little to be going."

Giggling, Letty turned to the tiny boy. "Is you? Is you?"

In quick scorn we stared at her. We knew *is* connected to *you* was the language of an ignoramus.

"If ignorance was bliss, she'd be a blister — the whole tribe of 'em," Mama said later. Though sharecroppers, we were superior to them at least in education.

Wanting to become friends, Minnie and I exchanged the usual questions and answers, as had Luby and Gloria, and found we were in the same grades.

Embarrassed at Letty's maltreatment of grammar, Papa talked over us. "Is school in session now?"

"Oh, yes. School begins in October and ends the last of March. Six whole months. I'm glad I'm too old to go."

He smiled. "Six months of schooling at one time would be

hard to take, I guess." But he was pleased. At least the schools were better than the mountain ones. He now asked, "How many bales of cotton did your pa make last year?"

"Oh, he didn't do so good, 'bout ten, I think."

A thousand dollars! His heart jumped with hope. Maybe Jules wasn't lying about cotton being gold.

On leaving, Luby told Gloria, "We'll be by to show you all the way to school in the morning."

Hardly more than two wagon wheel tracks, with a line of dog fennel between, the road ran past the big, white Weane house, and on between wide fields and piney woods, the Weanes called them.

Indicating all the land and woods by a nod, Luby said, "All this is our'n."

We were duly impressed. Their farm was much larger than Grandpa's. Our inferiority received another downward push.

At a mailbox with J. W. Wilkins written on it we were joined by the prettiest girl I ever saw. She was a little taller than Gloria; her hair was a profusion of golden curls crowding around her shoulders; her eyes were bluer than any sky; though her lips were a pretty pink like her cheeks, they drooped petulantly. Her name was Lucie.

By the way the Weanes welcomed her, we knew they were close friends, and we felt left out.

Pointing to a rambling, two-storied white house set amongst pecan trees, Luby said to us, "That's her'n."

She was a landowner's child.

Indicating us by a nod, Luby told her, "They moved into the house the Wash niggers moved out of."

"They living where *niggers* lived?" Lucie was astonished. In frank curiosity she turned her wonderful blue eyes upon us, measuring us in terms of dollars. By her look we couldn't have been worth over ten cents.

Luby said, "They're our tenants now," as if we were their property.

"And the Wash niggers is our'n." Lucie smiled with secret

knowledge, then said, "That Wash, now. He sure's a strong man."

Luby said, "A *man!* He ain't no man. He ain't nothing but a nigger."

Lucie giggled. "Man or nigger, he shore is strong. You oughtta see him handle that stallion of our'n."

Luby gave admiration grudgingly. "I didn't think nobody could."

"Wash can. You oughtta see his brown muscles as he makes that horse do as he says. He shore is strong!"

Just then we came to a short wooden bridge over a narrow brook. On one side near the road was an unpainted building which looked as if it would fall apart any time. Instead of windows, it had solid wooden shutters, but wisps of smoke curled from a small chimney.

Lillian stopped to gaze. "What's that?"

Lucie said, "That's where Wash lives."

Lillian swallowed. "People live in that?"

"No," Lucie said, "just niggers."

"MyGawdAlmighty! How could anybody live there?"

"Oh, niggers live anywhere."

And they laughed at our ignorance.

It wasn't long before we turned off the main road onto a path leading to what seemed another nigger house, only the one room was made of logs. Since these were decaying, the school must have been very old.

As in Wash's house, there were no glass windows, and the shutters had to be left open for light. There were single desks; a big potbellied stove near the front provided heat. The teacher's desk was to the right.

The teacher was a sweet-faced young woman with red hair and blue eyes. She rang a tinkling little bell to open school. There was no lining up and marching, but the students were orderly and took their seats quietly.

We three went to stand before her desk. She gave us a warm smile. "My name is Miss Richards. What are yours and what school are you from?"

Lillian answered for us.

"School is so near closing this term you needn't buy books. Bring the ones you used in the mountain school, and we'll see what we can do," she told us.

When she saw how familiar I was with my first reader, she found me a second one, and introduced me to adding and subtraction.

Not only pretty and kind, Miss Richards was also something of a miracle worker. She stimulated an interest in learning, which made students do their best. She did this through love, not fear, for she had no switches. Though usually kind, she could be tough when occasion demanded, thus gaining students' respect also.

Her best miracle was the program of songs and poems by students she presented at the end of school. She called it a pantomime, but it wasn't really, and no one knew the difference. But it was magical and for better effect it was given at night, which was unusual at that time.

Every pupil had a part, if not a solo one, then we sang in groups, thus not only giving pleasure to the students but also to the parents.

CHAPTER 24

Toil, War, Laws

AFTER SCHOOL ended, we came to know toil intimately; before the sun was up we were in the fields; when we stood on our shadows we went to dinner, and we returned when they were a foot long; when we shouldered our hoes, chuck-will's-widows were calling in the dusk.

What we ate didn't matter; opening our mouths, we poked food in, swallowed, repeating the process until our stomachs told us they were filled. Exhausted, we fell into bed, only to be awakened at dawn to resume the relentless task of hoeing.

But we did no field work Saturdays and Sundays. By April the weather was very warm, and on Saturday afternoons we girls would take soap and rags to bathe in a washing-hole Lillian had found in a creek near our house.

Like all water there, the creek was brown and filled with leeches. Every time we came out we had to smack leeches off us. Having flouted wildcats and catamounts, Lillian wasn't about to let little things like leeches keep us from the only pleasure we knew. For since moving Lillian hadn't preached one sermon. Nor had we played at all. Coming to this strange land must have shocked all play from us.

By the rivers of Babylon, there we sat down,
yes, we wept, when we remembered Zion.
We hanged our harps upon the willows in the midst thereof.
For there they that carried us away captive required of us a song; and they that
wasted us required of us mirth, saying,
Sing us one of the songs of Zion.
How shall we sing the Lord's song in a strange land?

—Psalm 137

Moreover, we didn't attend church. We felt that our old clothes were not fine enough.

It was in April, too, that the United States declared war on Germany. Since moving to Grandpa's place, we had heard nothing of the war in a land called Europe, and by the spring of 1917 we had forgotten it.

Now busloads of soldiers began passing our house, going from one camp to another or to a train in Ralston. At the sight we shivered with excitement. They were going off to kill Germans.

"But some won't come back," Papa said sadly. And one day he had to leave the fields to go to Brack and register for the draft himself. For the first time the war stabbed our own hearts.

After our garden began coming in we had more and better food. Also, Mrs. Weane came to see Mama, the two liked each other, and as a result, Mr. Weane let us help milk his many cows, giving us half of what we milked, and this was enough to supply us with milk and butter.

During this time, too, we had our first taste of turkey. Because

[125]

a passing car killed one of the Weanes' turkeys and we saw this and reported it to Mrs. Weane immediately, she sent us half of the cooked bird. This was a great treat to our meat-starved bellies.

She also started Mama with a flock of chickens, and Mama soon began selling eggs and fryers, which allowed us to buy little things.

In their elegant white house the Weanes knew no privation. They had a real parlor with a soft sofa and chairs, a gramophone and a self-player piano which never ceased on Sundays. Their table was always laden with good things to eat, and the daughters had many fine dresses of silk, georgette and crêpe de Chine. The boys had suits with white shirts and ties.

To give credit due, Mr. Weane made all his large family, except his wife, work in the fields. The girls did field work the same as we did. Anyone pretending illness to get out of work was given a dose of red pepper tea. Very little illness occurred in that family.

The fine house drew me as flowers do bees, and I took advantage of Minnie's friendship. Where good food was, Lowell was. However, the federal government, because of the war, limited the amount of flour, sugar and coffee each family could have on hand. This didn't bother us since we couldn't buy the quantity allowed. But, patrolling the country in automobiles (more people owned them here), law officers often raided homes of suspected hoarders, among which was the Weanes' big, fine house with its well-laden table. Stacked in the attic were flour, sugar and coffee, and the Weanes too were soon eating corn bread to a great extent.

Law officers became familiar. In 1907 Georgia had passed a Prohibition law. This hadn't bothered the mountain people very much, but here the State Prohibition officers often passed our house, hunting whiskey stills and bootleggers. Once we saw them taking a man and his wife to jail for selling whiskey. Since this couple was generally known to be wealthy, seeing them carted off to jail frightened us children. If officers took wealthy people to jail, what would they do to poor people like us? We had to be sure not to break a law.

"What are laws?" we asked our font of wisdom.

"Laws," Papa said, taking on his teacher's expression, "are rules to live by made by federal, state, county and town governments. If you break one, you have to go to jail."

"How can we tell if we do?"

"The Ten Commandments are laws made by God. All laws of all the governments of this country are based on the Ten Commandments. If you live according to them, you'll be safe."

From Sunday school we knew what the Ten Commandments were. So if we broke one, we would not only break God's law but also the government's. It seemed we were hemmed in on all sides, and all we could safely do was work in the fields, eat and sleep.

Mama told us another rule. It wasn't exactly a law or one of the Ten Commandments, she said, though it was in the Bible. She repeated it often and saw to it that our family abided by it: Cleanliness is next to godliness.

We knew what that meant, all right.

CHAPTER 25

A Gift; Lillian's Decision;
Jenny Comes Home

M RS. WEANE wasn't the only visitor Mama had. A month or so after our arrival, a timid knock came on our back door one Saturday afternoon. When Mama opened it she saw a Negro woman with a puppy.

Smiling shyly, the woman said, "I'se Lizzie Stokes, Wash's wife. We'se the folks moved outta here," indicating the house.

"Oh. Won't you come in?"

"Wellum, I see you all don't have a dog, so I brought this here puppy, if you wants him."

Four pair of children's arms were held out to receive the gift, which was solid brown with loving eyes and eager, licking, pink tongue. Lizzie set the puppy on the floor where we children immediately dropped to receive instant puppy love.

Indicating a chair, Mama said, "Please set down. Can I give you something for the puppy?"

Glancing around our almost bare kitchen, Lizzie said, "No'm, you'se welcome to him. I thought you might like a dog. Can't git along in the country hardly 't'out a dog."

"We had to leave ours in north Georgia — where we come from — no way to bring her. Smart dog, too, Fetch was."

"Sho nuf. Wellum, how you like dis war gwine on?"

"I don't. It might take my man."

"Mine, too. I got three little chillun. Don't hardly know what I'll do if he goes."

"I got six. But my oldest girl is teaching school in Wilcox County. She'll be home when her school is out."

Lizzie gave appropriate sounds of admiration. "Ugh-h-h, a schoolteacher! You sho nuf mus be proud o' her!"

"Yes. She was always smart in her books."

Behind Mama's back Lillian stuck out her tongue and crossed her eyes, then suddenly said, "I'm going to be a teacher, too, soon as I git more education."

We stared at her. She didn't look like a schoolteacher.

Disappointed, I ventured, "Ain't you gonna be a preacher?"

She tossed her head. "Reckon not. I want to be a teacher like Miss Richards."

Knowing Lillian's record of studying, Mama said, "You'd better buckle down and start studying."

"I aim to." Lillian was now fourteen, and was experimenting in balling up her hair, but there were no boys around to cast eyes at, so she had stopped giggling. In fact, she hardly ever laughed now.

There wasn't much for any of us to laugh about. Our lives were long rows of monotony, chained together with sun risings, sunsets, the eatings, the sleepings, the long shadows, the short shadows, the cries of doves in the piney woods, the lone pine surrounded by acres of field, with one or two limbs telling it still lived, the lollings of buzzards, circling and circling, the sun burning down, browning us until we looked like Indians. Cotton weather. Cotton, cotton, cotton, the fields and fields of white gold.

One Sunday the quiet was broken by Uncle Willy's Ford chugging to a stop in front of our house. He and Aunt Sally had brought Jenny home. She was sick. With them were Grandpa and Aunt Sally's twelve-year-old stepson, freckled-faced and bashful.

Papa met his father in the yard and both men hugged each other a long time. When they turned to go into the house, tears were sliding down their cheeks.

Mama wouldn't allow any of us to touch Jenny, and she put her to bed immediately. That dampened our joy in seeing our sister and relatives, especially when Mama shooed us outdoors.

There we spied Aunt Sally's stepson, who wouldn't budge from the Ford or tell us his name; so we climbed in with him to get better acquainted. After all, he was almost our cousin. His house was halfway to where Jenny taught school; it was in Ben Hill County. The following year it was to become as enticing to me as Mr. Weane's house.

CHAPTER 26

Malaria, Ice Cream, the Fourth Brother, Roots

WHEN JENNY'S SCHOOL was out she had gone to Aunt Sally's. She was like me about food — she liked to stay where good food was. After a week or so, she had a chill one morning followed by a high fever in the afternoon. Uncle Willy said they ought to take her home. She had chills and fever.

Thus we came to know malaria, transmitted through a bite of the anopheline mosquito. Newcomers were especially subject to it, probably because natives had been bitten so many times they were immune.

In addition to malaria, Jenny had caught a fellow, a soldier, by the name of Zing Hurd. We didn't know which was affecting her more, the fever or the fellow. But she wasn't up to being teased. Between her shaking and burning, she lay silent and weak.

Mama was experienced in doctoring miscellaneous aches and pains. She resorted to a strong purgative in any doubtful illness; so, in Jenny's case, being baffled by this contradictory disease of freezing and burning, she prepared a large dose of Epsom salts for Jenny, and we gathered around to watch her drink it. She was on a quilt on the front porch. She sat up to drink, but began gagging the instant she lifted the glass to her lips.

Lillian said, "Don't think of the salts, Jenny. Think of Zing. He's a soldier, and he's fighting for you. Say Zing, Zing, as you drink!"

Turning up the glass, Jenny drank, lay quickly down and as quickly leaned her head off the porch.

Lillian screamed, "Say, Zing, Zing, Zing!"

Jenny cried, "Zing, Zing — brr-rr-up," and vomited.

Mama sent for Mrs. Weane, who brought medicine more bitter than Epsom salts — quinine, white powdery stuff to be taken a teaspoon at a time after meals, followed by anything to take the bitterness out of the mouth.

Jenny said she couldn't.

Unsmiling, Mrs. Weane, the mother of more than a dozen children, said, "Take it or die."

Jenny took it.

Soon she was out of bed and on her way to recovery, but she had to continue taking the quinine for months. As she improved her appearance did too. She was now over seventeen, and very beautiful. With her slightly oriental eyes and black hair piled high on her head, she looked like a queen.

Papa contrived to get an old, topless buggy for Saturday trips to town, a necessity since he had to sell Mama's eggs, fryers and his added vegetables for a little cash. The buggy looked better after Nell was hitched to it. Being a beautiful roan, Nell added to the looks of even a plow.

After Papa's return one Saturday, Jenny announced her intention of driving to town. Papa never said a word, so she told me to bathe, head and all, in the creek, and I could go with her. We were soon on our way. To my knowledge Jenny had never driven, but we came safely into town, and Jenny found a place to hitch Nell.

Making a beeline to a department store, she looked at the ready-made dresses. "I got to buy some to wear to school," she said, but autumn was far off, and all they had was summer ones. She bought a white organdy with a wide, pink ribbon sash. On second thought, she bought a white organdy with a wide, blue sash for Lillian, and slips for both.

"Don't know where we'll wear 'em. You all don't even go to church — living like pure heatherns."

"They ain't no church 'cept in town, and we ain't got fine clothes to wear to that."

"Fiddlesticks! Papa's got a suit, Mama's got that silk dress and hat, both got Sunday shoes. But I don't know 'bout you young'uns."

Telling the clerk our ages and describing our sizes, she bought white voile dresses and slips for Gloria and me, patent-leather slippers and socks. Instead of stockings, socks for children were just beginning to be made. For Gregory she bought a cotton suit, barefoot sandals and socks. For Justin she bought a white dimity dress, but since he was a baby, he could go barefoot, she said.

For Lillian she also bought a pair of shoes like her own, only bigger — blond kid, high-heeled and laced all the way to the top — and a pair of lisle hose, also a pair of hose for Mama and socks for Papa.

Though we could hardly walk for the bundles, we went into a store the likes of which I had never seen, and sat down at one of several pretty round tables of fancy iron with chairs to match.

She laid our bundles on the floor beside us. When a clerk came, she said, "Bring us a dish of vanilla ice cream."

Soon he set before each of us a cute little dish in which was some white stuff like a blob of dough. In the dish he put a tiny spoon. Jenny dipped hers into the white stuff, got a spoonful and put it into her mouth, looking very pleased as she swallowed. She looked at me. "Eat it! It's good."

I took a spoonful into my mouth. It was awfully cold, but I swallowed it, getting a good taste. "It's the best stuff I ever eat."

Leaning over, she whispered, "It's ice cream. Hadn't you ever tasted it?"

I shook my head, eating.

She looked sad. "You know, you all are becoming as ignorant as these south Georgians, and they are the most ignorant people I ever saw. And the nastiest! Eating goats, gophers — " She broke off to lean over again and whisper, "They even eat hog guts!"

I wouldn't believe it, though Jenny never lied.

After the last trace of ice cream vanished (I'd have licked the dish but Jenny wouldn't let me), she bought a big sack of penny candy to take home.

On the way, she said grimly, "We're all going to church tomorrow."

Everything she bought was a little big but wearable, though Lillian had a time getting her shoes on, not that they were too short but they were so narrow. After they were on, she had to practice walking, and we laughed and laughed at her tottering. She wanted to dispense with the shoes and go barefoot, but Jenny said, "No. Absolutely not. You're a young lady now, and they don't go barefoot. And you ought to have a corset." Lillian was horrified.

The next morning Jenny balled Lillian's hair, and when she got her new clothes on, she looked so different we could hardly believe the young lady was Lillian. She was beautiful.

We went to church in a wagon Papa borrowed from Mr. Weane. We found plenty of automobiles in the churchyard and very few buggies and wagons.

We also found we weren't the only north Georgians in the community. Close enough to visit were two families we had known well in Lumpkin County. We weren't the only ones bitten by the cotton bug.

Until distance put an end to it much visiting was done among the three families. After church one of them would come home with us for Sunday dinner (which curtailed the sale of Mama's fryers) and an afternoon visit or we would go home with one of them. Either way meant plenty of fried chicken, macaroni and cheese and apple float.

To crown our growing satisfaction, when the church held its revival the featured singer was a distant paternal cousin with the same surname as ours, thus bringing a touch of glory to our name. In such ways our roots began to sink into that sandy country of piney woods, buzzards and sandspurs.

One day Papa spent a long time currying Nell, loving her as he worked. Satisfied at last, he rode her off to town and was gone a long time. He returned walking and white-faced.

"I swapped her for a cow, two hogs, and thirty pieces of silver. She was like one of my own. I'm a Judas."

Mama said, "We had to have a cow. As for the hogs, the Lord knows our bellies could stand some meat besides chicken."

But we had to go to church with a mule hitched to the wagon. And not until the arrival of the cow and hogs did our loss begin to lessen.

The cow was so gentle we immediately named her Pet. We tied ribbons around her neck and could hug her all we wanted. Even Gregory could milk her. Half Holstein, she gave so much milk we had more than we could use. We could now stop milking the Weane cows, a triumph since they were taking half of what we milked.

The hogs were ugly, black-spotted on a washed-out red, long-nosed, ribey and mean. "Lost brothers to the ridge runners," Papa said. "They say they can't be fattened, but I aim to try." He penned them up, north Georgia style, in a pen near our barn, and began feeding them.

A few days later Mama heard the hens and rooster squawking in terror. Running into the yard, she saw the hogs; one was chasing the hens while the other had caught one. Looking around for a rock to throw, forgetting there were none, she found nothing; so she ran toward the hogs, waving her apron. To her horror, the hogs turned and made for her. Her screams joined those of the chickens and brought Jenny on the run.

She grabbed a yard broom from under the house, and beat off the hogs, which ran into a field. She helped Mama into the house. Though they hadn't harmed her physically, she was hurt in another way.

Since the rest of us, except Justin, were in the fields, Jenny ran for Mrs. Weane, who hurried to help. Then Jenny went after Papa. Far into the night there was a lot of going in and out of Mama's room. Finally Papa walked Mrs. Weane home. Mama would be all right, but would have to stay in bed a few days.

The next morning Papa took a shoe box, dug a little grave near a lantana and gently laid the box in. Solemnly, he covered it with dirt, making a little mound. Tears in his eyes, he said, "He would have been your fourth brother."

CHAPTER 27

His Brother's Keeper

IN AUGUST cotton began to open and we began picking. But the bright hotness brought other than the white purity of opening cotton, such evil as to strike our hearts with cold horror.

After Lizzie brought us the puppy, she continued to come to our house occasionally. After we got Pet, Mama would take them any surplus buttermilk. Also, in his bewilderment over tending the tremendous farm, Papa sought advice of Lizzie's husband Wash, since Papa was unwilling to reveal his ignorance to his landlord. Thus it was that we came to know, like and respect the Negro family.

Papa, Lillian, Glory, Gregory and I (Jenny was still weak from her illness) were far from home one afternoon when, to our amazement, we saw Mama running toward us, calling, "Caleb! Caleb!"

Mama never came to the fields. Something dreadful had happened.

Easing off his cotton sack, Papa went to meet her. We saw her throw her arms around Papa, talking very fast.

Justin or Jenny must be dead. All of us threw off our sacks and began running toward them, but Papa waved us back.

"My GodAlmighty!" Lillian whispered. "What can it be?"

We could only shake our heads. We saw Papa talking to Mama, then she started back toward the house. When he rejoined us his face was white.

As he looked at our round, wondering eyes he knew he had to tell us something. "Jed Wilkins just come by the house." Pause. "On his way to town." Pause. "Scared your Ma and Jenny half to death. Told 'em to lock all windows and doors. Seems — seems — he said — " Pause. He licked his lips. "I don't believe it!" he burst out. "I don't believe it!"

"*What*?" Lillian shrieked.

"What Jed said, that's what!"

"What did he *say?* " Glory asked, more calm than any of us.

"He said Wash — he said Wash," he cast about for another word and not finding it, blurted, "raped Lucie!"

He could have saved himself the effort. We didn't know the word's meaning. He tried to convey it. "He said Wash hurt Lucie, did something meaner than kill her. That's what her pa said. But I can't believe Wash would hurt anybody, much less a little white girl."

Vigorously, we agreed.

"What will they do to him?" Lillian asked.

"They'll put him in jail, that's what they'll do!"

Being put in jail was the worst punishment anybody could get.

Papa said, "Let's git back picking cotton. It's none of our business. None atall!"

With heavy hearts we began picking. Suddenly straightening, he said, "Wash wouldn't do such a thing! He just wouldn't!" He stared into the distance, then muttered, "Am I my brother's keeper?" Then he eased the cotton sack strap from his shoulders with shaking hands.

His gray eyes found us. "I got something to do. Go on picking like I was here. If anyone comes asking for me, say I've gone to the bushes. I may not be back this evening, so go home when the sun's setting."

We watched until he disappeared in a field of tall corn, then halfheartedly resumed picking.

"Papa was headed toward Wash's house," Lillian said.

Fear seeped into us and we fled home.

There we found Mama and Jenny torn between anxiety and fear. When we appeared running, fear won. Jenny locked the doors. For a long while we waited in almost complete silence for Papa's return.

He had to identify himself before Mama would open the door. He said, "Unlock them doors. We ain't got nothing to be scared of. I just come from Wash's house. He ain't home. I saw Lizzie, and I hope them men don't catch him."

"What men?" Mama almost shrieked.

"The Ku Kluxers, Lizzie said. She said they'd kill him!"

Mama knew about the Ku Klux Klan. "What have they got to do with it?"

He gave her a look. "They're down here. Probably Mr. Wilkins and Mr. Weane are — "

Mama nodded, looking at us, then back at him.

"Lizzie said Wash took a load of peas to town this morning and ain't come back yet. But he could be guilty. He could have come back and waylaid Lucie. But Lizzie said he'd never do such a thing and I don't believe he would. She's taking on awful and scared to death."

Solemnly, he looked at Mama, then stated, "Bela, we're living in a heathern land. Negroes don't stand the chance of a snowball in hell. I'd like to help somehow, but Lizzie told me to go home."

"A Negro told you that?"

"She said if the Ku Kluxers caught me at her house, they'd kill me for being there. She made me come home, said she didn't want us having trouble on their account."

"Bless her heart!"

He fell silent, thinking, then blurted, "But then, why would Lucie tell that? She couldn't have mistook him for another nigger. He'd been on their place too long. He could be guilty."

We girls still didn't know what was done to Lucie except she had been hurt. At the thought of her we were very sad; she was too pretty to be hurt. "She liked Wash so much, too," Lillian said. "She used to brag how strong he was."

Papa shot her a look. "She did?"

"She told us how he could handle her Papa's stallion and nobody else could ever do that."

"How big is Lucie?" he suddenly asked.

Lillian said, "A little bigger than Glory."

"About twelve or over," Papa guessed.

He jumped up and paced the floor.

Mama said, "There's nothing you can do, Caleb. These people are heatherns, and to them we count no more than Wash. You stay out of it!"

"I'm going to the Weanes' to find out what's going on. I'll be back in an hour."

He was, and shaking with fury. "They're gonna lynch him! I went on to the Wilkins's. Women and men there by the hundreds. Lucie's in bed —they ain't even had a doctor to see her! Them people reminded me of a flock of buzzards around a dead cow. The only thing left to do is pray for Wash and his family. They ain't found him yet. As long as there's life there's hope, and I hope he got away."

But we prayed useless prayers. They found him next day and lynched him.

Some weeks later it became generally known that the little girl who looked like an angel had lied, or, could it have been a wish fulfillment? Whatever, they killed an innocent man.

CHAPTER 28

Mount Olive Community and Collards;
Jenny, the Teacher

SINCE THE LYNCHING, Papa was determined to move as soon as the crop was gathered. By that time he had another tenant farm in Aunt Sally's community. It had Mount Olive Baptist Church, was closely settled and within three miles of the town of Fitzgerald.

But Mr. Weane claimed Papa's expenses had been more than his share of the crop, and we couldn't move till the money was paid.

In righteous anger Papa told him, "I'm moving! You've swindled me out of my cotton money, but I can't prove it. If I could, I'd take you to court. You got the cotton, but I'm taking my corn."

"A sharecropper can't leave a farm till he pays what he owes the landlord. That's the law."

"Don't say law to me! You don't keep the law. Man's or God's. You ain't nothing but heatherns here. I want no part of you. Bring on the law. I'll have a word or two to say to the law," Papa said.

Mr. Weane didn't bring the law, and with the help of the north Georgia friends we moved to our new home.

At first sight we liked the two-storied, weathered gray house. From the shrubbery-filled yard to the fancy lightning rods on its top, the house had a sense of home.

The four large downstairs rooms were quite ample for our scanty belongings. The kitchen held stove, safe and dining table with space to spare.

The well was covered with plank curbing and had a windlass like the one on Grandpa's farm, but, like the one at Weane's, it contained wiggletails.

There were ample barn, cribs and smokehouse, and the whole place didn't look like a sharecropper's.

"Mrs. Russell, our landlady, told me her son and his family lived here until he had to go to war, so his wife and little girl moved in with her. She has another son in the war, too, and both are in the navy," Papa told us and explained about sailors and soldiers, then added, "Mrs. Russell lives right up the road, across the main road leading to town."

Widowed for years, she made it plain to Papa she wouldn't furnish groceries. She would furnish tools, mules, wagon, guano and seed. Though cotton was the money crop, we could plant what other stuff we pleased and could have half of all we raised. Her farm was big enough for two crops, one for us, one for her. Papa would plow for her, which he didn't mind, her being a widow. Far from being rich, she had no prospects of becoming so, and no class chasm lay between us. Her house was also unpainted, yet was ample and built for a landowner. Since we weren't living under the yoke of great expectations, we had hope for better times.

But we were facing starvation. Papa had to sell the hogs for a barrel of flour and enough clothes for us to begin school. Since Pet was dry, we had no milk or butter.

In the garden we found rows and rows of a green vegetable like cabbage, only not headed, just big, loose leaves. Mrs. Russell called them collards, and said we were welcome to eat them and anything else we found on the place. We found nothing else, but ate the collards. Since Papa had moved his corn, we had corn bread and collards twice a day for many, many months. Mama sold eggs and fryers to provide things like soap (no soap-making here), lard, coffee and sugar; so we had flour and lard to make gravy for breakfast, but no doubt the collards saved our lives.

When he moved from one county to another, Papa had to report the move to the army authorities in Fitzgerald so they could add his name to the draft list.

Not long after we moved Mrs. Russell came to explain, she said, where we could get our wood. "Git it from the woods next to the big field where you'll plant cotton. On no account, don't go into the woods back of the big corn field."

We soon learned why. Her two brothers living in town had a whiskey still in the forbidden woods. We also found the farm was kept under surveillance by state Prohibition officers.

We learned about the whiskey-making from the brothers themselves; they stopped by our house to get water once, and continued to do so. To our surprise they didn't look like bad men, and Papa said they weren't, just too lazy to work. That set Mama's seal of disapproval upon them.

*

The Sunday following our move and a week before school began, up drove Uncle Willy, Aunt Sally and Grandpa. And Jenny, who had returned to Aunt Sally's soon after the lynching.

Jenny told Mama, "Guess what! I'll teach at Dorminy this year, and I can live at home!"

Mama flew into Jenny's arms. "I'll have my girl back home! Oh, Jenny!" She burst into tears, and Papa encircled both with his arms.

When the joy subsided Jenny added, "I'll teach the third and fourth grades."

Dorminy school was the one we would attend. As Glory would be in the fourth grade and I'd be in the third, Jenny would be our teacher, which would make her our boss. I saw Glory scowl, but I was proud that my teacher was my sister. At first.

Having three rooms, the school was the most modern of the time. Built of brick outside and plaster within, it had indoor plumbing, a marvel indeed.

Jenny was another Miss Keene. One of the first things she did was to get a bunch of switches from gallberry bushes and stand them near her desk. This made me a mouse all year long. Just as Miss Keene had, Jenny made so many rules students would forget them, and she would call the broken rule to mind with a switch in her hand.

Once again we saw blood brought by the teacher's switch. Not only an ordeal to watch, it also brought back all the horror we had known under Miss Keene. Again school days became dreadful for Gloria and me. Gloria told Papa, but in those days parents usually sided with the teachers, and he withheld his opinion.

Most of the way to school, we four had to walk a railroad track. It wasn't easy walking.

Just before school's dismissal one day, Glory, interested in an assignment, blurted a question to Jenny.

Getting a switch, Jenny said, "Gloria, I'm going to whip you. That was the third time you spoke aloud without permission."

Standing up, Glory said, "You're not going to whip me. I'll tell Papa on you!"

Starting toward her, Jenny said, "I don't care if you do. You broke a rule and I'm going to whip you!"

Just then the dismissal bell rang and Glory darted out the door with Jenny going after her with switch in hand. She called, "Gloria, don't run from me! I'll whip you that much harder when I catch you!"

Well on her way, Glory shouted back, "You won't catch me!" Outrage lent wings to her feet, and all the way home she put so much distance between her and us that Jenny soon gave up trying.

"I'll whip you after you get home, see if I don't!" she kept calling after Glory.

Remarkably, so far, Lillian had kept her own counsel, but she had stood it as long as she could and blurted, "You don't have the authority to whip her in her own house, Miss Jenny! And you don't have the right, even if you should catch her before we git home."

"Yes, I do! From the moment we step out of our yard in the mornings until we set foot into it in the afternoon, I have the authority to whip either of you!"

"You may have it, but you can't do it! Not me, you can't, and you'd better not try it!"

Still a mouse, I swallowed my alarm. Lifting a hundred pounds of guano had made Lillian strong. I knew who would win that fight.

Jenny said, "I'll report your talk to your teacher!"

Measuring her sister with hot eyes, Lillian spat out, "Tattletale!"

Jenny's chin lifted. "I *am* a teacher!"

Lillian's temper flew. "Yes, you're a teacher! But who helped make you one? I did. Glory did. Lowell and even Gregory. We did your share of work at home while you was off in school. We had to work so you'd have money to go. You've hardly lifted a finger with any work at our house. You're Miss Jenny, Miss GodAlmighty, the schoolteacher. Well, I'll tell you, Miss Schoolteacher, I aim to be a schoolteacher, too, but I'll never treat my pupils like you treat yours. And I don't aim to get out of doing work at home just to be one!"

"I pay board!"

"But don't work!"

"Teaching is work."

"Ha! You wouldn't know what work was if you met it in the road. Try plowing all day, turning land! That's work!"

"I refuse to stoop to a quarrel. But I'll whip Gloria when we get home."

Lillian's mouth drew into a straight line, and remained shut the rest of the way. As for me, I never opened mine.

When we reached home, we found Papa with Gloria on his lap, big as she was. She had fetched him from the fields. "What you aiming to do with that switch?" he asked Jenny.

"Whip Gloria. She broke a school rule."

"Throw it down!"

"But she broke a school rule!"

"She broke one of yours. You got too many!"

"But *I'm* the teacher!"

"And *I'm* the father!" Papa thundered.

Flinging down the switch, Jenny stormed out to seek Mama's sympathy. Papa followed, and what happened remains unknown. But never again did she threaten to whip any of us. Nor did she tell on Lillian. The next year she accepted a position back in Wilcox County, which was as it should have been; for a person is not without honor except in his own family.

However, while she was home we enjoyed benefits from her board money. Our flour barrel was never empty; we children were bought Sunday clothes so we could attend Mount Olive Baptist Church.

Though our parents had Sunday clothes, they didn't attend, for the first time in our lives. Perhaps the cause was loss of status. Since we all couldn't get into the buggy, we walked. We also had to walk the railroad a good way. Walking crossties in too tight shoes proved so agonizing to Lillian that she wouldn't put her shoes on until we came in sight of the church, to Jenny's chagrin.

To heal the breach caused by their heated words, Jenny had bought Lillian a wide-brimmed, Milan straw hat; where crown and brim joined was a wreath of ripe wheat interspersed with tiny blue flowers. We had never seen so beautiful a hat. When Lillian dressed in her Sunday clothes she wasn't the Lillian we knew. She was a beautiful young lady.

Gone, oh, gone were our days of play! In the meadow of Grandpa's farm we had left Mrs. White, Mrs. Green and Mrs. Brown.

CHAPTER 29

Papa Fills the Flour Barrel; Jenny's Downfall

WHEN SCHOOL TERM ended, our field work began. Since he had to plow for Mrs. Russell, too, Papa was forced to ask Lillian to help with the plowing, as he had on Weane's place. The hoeing fell to Glory, Greg and me.

In order to renew her teacher's certificate, Jenny had to attend the summer sessions at the teacher's college in Ralston, where she stayed with Uncle Jules and Aunt Adah. Her leaving meant we would no longer have her board money.

We soon felt its absence. Though Pet had freshened, giving us milk and butter, our financial situation became so desperate Papa hunted a job in town for the few weeks between planting and hoeing.

He found one as clerk in a grocery. To think we'd actually have money each week made us whoop with joy. But our elation was short-lived.

Since I now had to rely on my brothers for play, I slept with them in the bedroom of our parents; so one night I heard Papa come in with a slow step. Walking the three miles to and from town, he had to leave before sunup and return after we were in bed. On this night he didn't light the lamp.

Mama, too, was awake. "Why don't you light the lamp?"

"I don't have the heart to. I'm fired."

Silence.

Then, "But, Caleb, why?"

"I gave a man too much sugar for a dime."

Another silence.

Then both burst into laughter. They laughed and laughed, and our flour barrel was almost empty.

Pride in my Papa poured through me, and my heart lifted. He was fired because he was a good man, not bad. He gave overweight, not under. My papa was a good papa.

For the rest of our lives together our family quoted "too much sugar for a dime" more than Franklin's "He paid too much for the whistle."

However, his goodness didn't fill the flour barrel so when the whiskey-making brothers came to see him one morning, he was willing to listen.

They had a good run of whiskey in the making, but because the Prohibition men were now their constant shadows they were afraid to finish the run. If Papa, respectable, honest, above reproach, would, he could have half the profits. He would and did.

Against Mama's will. To her, right was right and wrong was wrong, and never the twain should meet. She refused to speak to him. She spoke to the atmosphere. Before *she'd* break a law, civil or moral, we could all die of starvation. She repeated this every day, all day.

Marking the first time, dislike for her entered our hearts, for we agreed with Papa. In silence, he bore her words, the burden of breaking the law and her wifely back in bed.

We children were especially kind to him. We made a point of being very obedient and seeing every wish of his carried out with diligence and a certain amount of self-righteousness, for none of us liked the way she was treating him; and we stayed away from her as much as possible. Since we were busy in the fields, this wasn't hard to do.

Finally, he held the profit of evil-doing in his hands. Borrowing a wagon from Mrs. Russell, he went to town, and returned with a barrel of flour and several tow sacks of food. Surprising us all, he bought us some clothes, even Mama, and enough gewgaws to delight our souls.

Still maintaining silence, Mama hardly glanced at the pretty dress he bought her, and even while eating the food breaking the law bought, she preached her theme: "I'd die of starvation 'fore I'd break a law!" Watching her chew and swallow with relish, we looked at her in contempt.

But Papa answered her with never a word of retaliation. He also ate the food with relish, and never expressed one regret. He ate heartily and with obvious pleasure at the result of his labor. He had done what he had to do like a man.

Among the things he bought for us girls were crocheting needles and thread, so every time we had a chance to sit down we would crochet.

While I was crocheting one day, Lillian came in and began slapping me playfully, as she was wont to do. As usual, I welcomed her attention and reached over to return a slap. I felt a sharp pain in my thigh. Looking down, I saw the needle buried deep. Horrified, I began screaming.

Mama came running. Seeing what was wrong, she ran for Papa. Both came running. When he saw how deep the needle was, his face turned white. Only an inch could be seen. He just stood there, looking.

Mama said, "You'll have to pull it out, Caleb!"

Taking his pocket knife, Papa cut away my clothes. Remembering the needle's hook, he ever so gently pulled the needle out without tearing my flesh much. Because of shock the ordeal wasn't painful. He looked at the wound, saturated it with turpentine and that was that. In a few days the wound healed.

Mama's "mad" with Papa was over. So was my enthusiasm for crocheting.

Before Jenny went to summer school, she had some photographs made and gave Mama one. At the time, Papa wasn't home, which was a good thing, for to us all the picture was shocking.

The prim, the good Miss Jenny didn't have any clothes on, just a net draped around, not over, her beautiful shoulders, and where her breasts began to show was a bunch of pretty flowers. To our ignorant eyes, she may as well have been naked.

When Mama showed the picture to Papa, he shouted, "Burn it! I'll not have such a picture in my house! I never thought to see the day I'd be ashamed of one of my chillun! I want no daughter of mine in my house who'd make such a wanton picture. Tell her I said so!"

How sweet were those words upon us children's ears! At last, the saintly Miss Jenny had fallen from grace, and how we gloried in her downfall!

Mama put the picture in her trunk, and wrote Jenny not to come home for a while because Papa didn't like the picture.

So when summer school ended, she went to the community in which she would teach the coming school year. Though it was in an adjoining county, it was still at a safe distance. None of us minded her absence except our parents, and I suspect Jenny didn't mind being absent.

CHAPTER 30

God's Second Choice; the Circus;
Lillian's Proof

LILLIAN was fifteen that April of 1918. She had transcended childhood and was now a beautiful young woman. Like a butterfly emerging from its cocoon, Gloria, too, was struggling out of childhood, not because of age but because of Lillian. Since Lillian wouldn't play, Glory wouldn't.

So, perforce, I turned to my brothers for play, and soon learned the difference between a boy and a girl. The difference was a great convenience to boys since they didn't have to squat to pee, and I knew what I wanted to be: a boy. I tried hollowing out a joint of cornstalk, but that didn't work, then I tried bamboo, unsuccessfully. I wanted to be like my brothers, but couldn't find anything to make me, so I turned to our font of wisdom, Papa.

When I told him what I wanted, his mouth opened and he stared at me a long time. I thought he wasn't going to answer.

He scratched his chin reflectively before he said, "Now, Lowell, they ain't a thing, not a God-blessed thing you can use. God made boys first, and He didn't have enough clay left to fix girls like boys, so you'll have to stay a girl. They ain't a thing you nor me nor nobody can do about it."

Then girls were God's second choice.

I had been cheated and was angry. "Why didn't God make girls first? Then boys would have to squat and not girls."

In his best parental tone, he asked, "Are you too lazy to squat?"

I shook my head and tried to explain, "Squatting takes too long. A girl has to pull up her dress, pull down her drawers, then squat. Girls are just God's second choice."

Drawing himself up in the old lawyer stance, he said, "You mustn't think such thoughts. Them kind of thoughts ain't to be thought."

Astonished, I said, "They come in my mind. I don't tell 'em to."

He put on his wise look. "Would you let a chicken roost in your hair?"

I knew what a chicken roost looked like. "No, I wouldn't."

"Well, don't let them kind of thoughts roost in your mind."

"How can I make them fly away?"

"Think of something else right quick — like Christmas. Then they'll fade quick." As he turned to go, he added sternly, "Stop watching Gregory and Justin pee!"

Of course I didn't stop until their urinating became so commonplace it was no longer of interest. But the feeling of being God's second choice lingered until a much more exciting thing happened.

On the Fourth of July a circus would be in Fitzgerald and

would hold a parade down Main Street in the morning. After its afternoon performance, the town was going to block off Main Street and have a big Fourth of July celebration.

In addition, a pilot had landed an airplane right beside the road on the way to town, and anybody could see it that wanted to.

By the time Papa finished describing the wonders, we were wild with excitement. Who would go? Papa for one, he said, not wanting to miss the day for the world. Lillian, Glory, Gregory and I would be bound to go, but Justin couldn't walk the three miles; so the less said in front of him about the trip the better. Mama wouldn't go, of course. She never went anywhere.

The Fourth of July was a real zippity-do-dah day, bright with sunshine, birds singing, flowers blooming. As we set out for town, Papa's steps were as eager and sprightly as our own. We didn't mind walking the dusty road for three miles.

Papa and Gregory wore their overalls, but we girls felt it was almost a Sunday occasion. Since it was impossible for Lillian to walk very far in her high-heeled, too tight shoes, she went barefoot. Since she did, Glory and I did. But we wore our Sunday voile dresses and Lillian her orange-and-gray checked organdy. We felt dressed up despite our bare feet.

Though we had never seen an airplane, we knew what it was the minute we saw the strange object in a meadow beside the road. We walked all around it, and climbed on its wings, which were made out of the same kind of cloth as tennis shoes. There were a top and a bottom wing held together with a lot of wires and sticks.

The pilot's seat had no top, and how could the pilot stand the rain?

"He has to," Papa said, "because he has to fight German planes while flying. He has a gun right this side of that stick where he can fire the gun and fly all the same time."

"They guide the plane by that little stick?" Glory asked.

"Yes."

"What if they was in the air and the stick broke?"

"I guess the plane would fall to the ground."

We children decided we wouldn't be pilots, and went on to

town for the big wonder; for Papa said elephants, lions, tigers, clowns and a band would be in the parade, and we didn't want to miss that.

There were so many people lining the main street it seemed like Judgment Day. By pushing a little Papa made room for us so we could have a good look at the parade.

First, we heard the band playing the rousing tune of "Dixie," and everyone began singing:

> I wish I was in the land ob cotton,
> Old times dar am not forgotten,
> Look away! Look away!
> Look away! Dixie land!

Then they came in sight, red and blue uniforms, brass flashing, the big drum giving a big, loud boom after each line of the song. The cheering people almost drowned out the music, and we hollered along with the rest.

Then came the elephants, their big ears flopping, dressed in their bright red and green saddles; after them, came the cages on wagons pulled by milk-white or coal-black horses with red tassels bouncing. In the cages we saw lions, tigers, leopards and monkeys.

Following on white horses were beautiful ladies dressed in glittering clothes which hurt the eyes to see. All up and down the line of march funny men tumbled, turning somersaults and cartwheels. They had real white faces, big mouths and noses, and were in ragged clothes. Papa said they were clowns to make people laugh. Some did, but we didn't. We felt sorry for them.

As the parade wound to the ball park where the performance would be held, the crowd followed. But Papa told us sorrowfully, "We can't go in the tent to see the performance. It cost money and I ain't got any. But we can go sit on the benches and listen."

So we did, and could hear the music coming from a tent almost as big as the ball park, and once we were sure we heard a lion roar. But our hearts were heavy.

No more than Papa's. His face wore his saddest look as he said, "Next year, if crops are anyways good, we'll have money to go inside."

Our spirits lifted somewhat. Tired of just listening, we went back to the main street. It was a good thing we did. Someone was giving away balloons, candy and cold drinks; men were busy roping off the street, greasing some pigs and setting up a red, white and blue greased pole with a flag floating at the top. Anyone climbing to the top would win a prize and anyone catching a greased pig could have it, a man said.

Papa said, "I shore would love to have me one of them pigs. We don't have one to kill this fall. But I'm so slow and old I'd never catch one." He looked at Gregory and shook his head; hopefully, he eyed Lillian who could move like a scalded dog when she had a mind to. She was strong enough to hold a good-sized shoat, which those greased pigs were.

She caught his eyes. "Now, Papa, I got my Sunday dress on. Besides, I'm a girl, a grown girl, a young lady!"

In plain disgust he looked at us girls. "I can't see why in tarnation one of you couldn't have been a boy. Or if Walter had only lived —"

"Who's Walter?" Greg asked.

"Your brother, born 'tween Lillian and Glory. He'd a been just the right age to catch me one of them shoats." He sighed deeply.

A roaring overhead made us look up to the sky where that airplane was soaring like a buzzard. Out of it someone was throwing hundreds of blown-up balloons of all colors. People went wild, trying to catch them.

A man climbed onto a wagon. "Ladees and gentlemen!" he hollered. "I'm gonna turn loose six shoats at that white line you see. Anybody catching one can have it. 'Course you think they's a trick in it, and you think right! Them hogs have been coated with axle grease, and you have to catch 'em with bare hands. Come on, men and boys, try to catch you one of these fine hogs!"

Men and boys jostled their way through the crowd to the line. Suddenly, Lillian joined the jostling and made her way to the line. We saw the man come down from the wagon and talk to her. We saw her talking back. The man shook his head, but she kept talking.

At this unheard-of behavior, a gasp went up from the people, but being in a holiday mood, they shouted, "Let 'er run! Bet she can beat 'em all! Let 'er run!"

The man climbed back on the wagon.

When Lillian toed the line with the male contestants, a loud round of applause rose deafeningly. People began to call out, "Run, girl, run!" "Show 'em, gal!" and various other words of encouragement.

As for us, we stood petrified. Papa's face turned fiery red when she started through the crowd, but now all color drained from it. He stood as a stone, his eyes fixed on Lillian. He didn't know whether to be ashamed or proud, but he knew the reason.

As the squealing shoats were turned loose they were given a sharp slap on their rears to incite speed, and they had a good start before the man said, "Go!" to the contestants.

The pigs showed surprising speed; people lining each side of the street made the hogs go forward, though the width of the street gave them leeway for much zigzagging. Since they were glistening with axle grease, it was easy to keep them spotted if eyes moved fast.

Not so with the chasers. The males wore blue shirts and overalls, and were either tripping over each other or sprawling on the ground in snatching at the pigs.

Only Lillian stood out. Her orange checked dress billowed out behind her; her hair, loosed from its pins, streamed out like a banner. Like the others, time after time she went sprawling with hands clawing empty air; but she was doing as well as the males.

Then a pig was caught, then another, proving the pigs could be.

With hearts in our mouths we watched Lillian. When we saw her sprawl forward again and make no effort to get up, our hearts fell clean to our toes. She was all hunched up, and Papa began running to her. Petrified, we stood, and saw a man go to her and bend down. Fear loosed our feet and we ran after Papa, arriving as soon as he.

The man was helping her to her feet and holding onto something with his other arm. Our hearts almost stopped, but shot as high as the sky when we saw the man put a shoat in Lillian's arms.

The people began shouting and cheering until we couldn't hear a word. She handed the pig to Papa, and we made our way to the sidewalk, people making way as if Lillian was real important.

On the sidewalk she faced Papa, crying a little and wiping her nose and face with her hands, which smeared axle grease on her face. "I may not be a boy," she panted, "but I can do anything a boy can. I caught that hog for you!"

He laid a hand on her shoulder. "You're far better than any son *any* man could have! And you're a far better daughter than I deserve!"

He looked at his second daughter with her black-streaked face, her Sunday dress ruined by gaping holes and axle grease, her honey-colored hair blowing about her face, the blood trickling down a leg from a skinned knee, and love for her flooded him.

Handing the prize to Gloria, he took his bandanna and gently wiped her face, then tied the handkerchief around her skinned knee. Someone handed him a rope with which he securely tied the prize before placing it on the sidewalk.

Somewhat awed by Lillian's feat, people made room for us to watch the boys shinny up the greased pole. Only one reached the top, and his prize was a free ride in the airplane. Personally, we didn't envy him.

The glory of the day was fast fading and faded faster when some men had a water fight with fire hose hooked onto fire wagons. Tiring of spraying one another, they suddenly turned the water on the people. All of us were drenched, and Papa said we'd better go home and get on some dry clothes and pen the pig.

People passing in buggies and wagons gazed, some even slowed, at the man in overalls and straw hat, leading a hog by a rope; a small boy with golden ringlets; a tall girl in a torn and dirty dress with a bandanna tied around one knee; and two young girls in dirty white dresses. All looked as if they had fallen into a creek. Had our somewhat ludicrous appearance been known to us, it wouldn't have mattered, for we had seen and heard wondrous things.

"Papa," I asked, "what is the Fourth of July?"

"A holiday to celebrate the time us Americans told England she owned us no more — July fourth, seventeen seventy-six is when it was. The reason was, we decided we didn't like tea, and dumped three shiploads into the ocean at Boston. Boston is a town like Fitzgerald, only it's in Yankee country up north," he frowned, disliking the idea that Yankees could do any good thing.

"Boston," Lillian said, "is in the State of Massachusetts like Fitzgerald is in the State of Georgia. It wasn't tea they didn't like but the tax the English put on it — taxes without representation, they called it."

Surprised, Papa said, "I didn't know you had all that in your head!"

"Schoolteachers have to know all these things, and a lot more."

"You ain't no schoolteacher."

"I aim to be after another year's schooling. The principal at school said I'd make a good teacher."

She didn't look like one. Her shoulders were already stooped from following a plow, her splay-toed feet were unconfined by shoes. "What made you decide that?" he asked.

"I decided a Baptist church wouldn't let a woman preach. Besides, I'm a leader in B.Y.P.U. at Mount Olive, and that's sorta like preaching."

"What's that?"

"Baptist Young People's Union. Meets every Sunday night before preaching. We each have a part and have to tell it in front of everybody else, but you can add other things to your part, if you want."

"That church is a fast church," he said, frowning.

"No, it's not the church, Papa. It's the times. Times are changing — getting faster."

That didn't make him like Mount Olive. He had gone once and once was enough. If times were getting faster, then that church was going at a gallop. Though both were Missionary

Baptist, Mount Olive was as different from Concord as a citron was from a watermelon.

Mount Olive had no shouting, not even an "Amen" corner. The songs were so fast a person could hardly keep up; played on a piano instead of an organ, they sounded ragtime. Preaching service was shorter, hardly lasted an hour instead of two.

He disliked it all, particularly the meeting of young people, boys and girls together without a chaperone. No good would come of it. He didn't like it. Come to think of it, he didn't like the whole land, no part of it. If he had had any sense, he'd have stayed on his pa's farm. "I was hornswoggled out of that. Pure hornswoggled! By my own family!"

In with the times, Lillian only smiled at his ranting. Wann't no use crying over spilt milk.

CHAPTER 31

Lillian Becomes a Teacher; Jenny's Beau

THAT WEEK Papa received his draft call. He would be among the men called to go next. We girls couldn't farm alone, so he sought a place to rent and found a farm available in the fall for three hundred dollars a year, which was cheaper than a house in town. Besides, if he came back, he would need a farm.

Jenny and Lillian prepared to support the family in his absence. When teacher examinations were held in Fitzgerald, Lillian stood and passed them with a grade high enough to be assigned a school in Jenny's county, though the schools were many miles apart. Lillian's was near enough for her to come home on weekends, but Jenny's wasn't, though she said she'd give a big part of her salary if Papa became a soldier.

That year we made some money, and, reluctantly, we moved to our new home. Surrounded by a white sandy yard edged with chinaberry trees, the house had only four rooms, two large and two small, and was connected to an old kitchen by an open breezeway which we used as a washing-up place; the decrepit old kitchen was a junk room.

We had no room to spare. The two big rooms became our bedrooms; the one with the fireplace became our parents' room, in which they had to put another double bed for the boys. Painted blue, the other had two double beds for us girls. Mama put the dresser in there to give it an air of a parlor, she said.

Our parents' room opened into one of the small rooms, which became our dining room; the other small adjoining room was the kitchen.

The Stover house had once been a beloved home. Once painted white, the house was shaded by two huge chinaberry trees, one on each side of the front porch, which ran the width of two bedrooms and was made pretty by scrollwork.

Next to Grandpa's farm, this place became dear to our hearts, no doubt because of our better living conditions. As we became renters instead of sharecroppers, we stepped to a higher rung of the social ladder. Also, living there placed us within a mile of Dorminy school, Aunt Sally and Mount Olive, and still three miles from Fitzgerald. No more railroad walking.

On November 11, 1918, the war ended. The world rejoiced and so did we. Papa wouldn't have to go away to fight the Germans. This special joy made our hearts light and free as air. All we had to do now was raise cotton.

Lillian began to buy things for the family anyway. The first thing was a Victrola with a lot of records, which endowed us and the whole community; for people would come from miles around to listen to our "talking machine" nearly every night.

The records opened the door to a world of music other than hymns. Some were of famous singers; the ones we preferred were "Listen to the Mocking Bird," "Snow Deer," "Alexander's Ragtime Band," "Ogala," "Liza Jane," "Are You From Dixie" and "Alabama Jubilee."

Having constant company made more chairs necessary, so Lillian bought two rockers, fancy with scrollwork and shiny like the train walls. Since the Victrola was a table model, she bought a table for it, with a shelf beneath on which to keep the records.

Being a teacher compelled her to buy nice clothes; among the dresses was a navy blue tricolette with floral designs in multi-colored beads all over the front. I asked to touch the beads, which she graciously allowed. There was a black silk with long Georgette sleeves.

Papa didn't like this one. He said Lillian's arms might as well be naked as encased in that mosquito netting. But she said everyone was wearing Georgette these days, and we even had a record by that name, so he puffed out his cheeks and looked wise to hide his ignorance.

That Christmas she bought our gifts from Santa Claus, and gifts for our parents. It was the Christmas the first talking dolls were on the market. Such a wonder was out of my reach. I would be happy with any doll.

On Christmas morning I was astonished to find a big doll dressed in pink bonnet and dress and real shoes, and when I turned it face downward it cried "Mama!" I also had a box of chocolate cream drops.

The boys had a big, red wagon and other sundry things like a jack-in-the-box and a ball each.

Gloria got no toys, for when Lillian quit playing, she did. Since she went with Lillian to church, Lillian wisely bought her a Sunday dress, shoes and stockings.

We also began to have more expensive Sunday dinners. Jenny saw to that. The reason was that she had a new beau who ate with us. Never had she invited any to do that. This one must be special. She began coming home every weekend, and began acting like a daughter and sister again, gathering us all in with her talk of Cassius Fraser, the new beau.

What part of the county his father's family didn't own, his mother's did. The two families had hewn the county from wilderness, and Jenny would be lucky to become a member of such historical families. His family history and property didn't impress us because of our ignorance. But his hearty laugh and jolly manner did. We instantly liked Cass. Because he paid us children attention, he made us captives. We loved his cheerfulness, I think for the reason that we were such strangers to it.

That first Sunday dinner consisted of baked hen with dressing, snap beans (a rarity in winter), creamed potatoes, deviled eggs (I thought they'd be sinful to eat), macaroni and cheese, and apple float. And Mama cooked a pot of rice.

Rice was something new to us children. I had never heard of it. But Papa planted some in a swampy field; after threshing, the amount was about a bushel. This Mama hoarded for special occasions. It proved to be one of the most delectable things I ever tasted. If I had had to choose between rice and peanut butter, it would have been a very hard choice.

For many Sundays Cass was a dinner guest, and the menu varied only slightly. Years later he said he never ate so much macaroni and cheese and apple float in all his life, nor had he since.

CHAPTER 32

Influenza; National Affairs

THOUGH THE RAGE of war had ended, the rage of influenza had not. In January a neighbor hurried to our house; he had had a telephone call from the people with whom Lillian boarded; she was very sick with influenza and Papa was to meet them in town with a wagon and mattress for Lillian to lie on. Hurriedly he left, running the mules all the way.

But he was long in returning. Mama walked the floor in anxious waiting, after she prepared a bed, and saw there was a good supply of turpentine and kerosene on hand.

All that doctors and other people knew about influenza was that it was similar to pneumonia, and it killed just as surely. All over the nation people were dying like flies from it, and undertakers were hard pressed to supply enough caskets. Mama had battled pneumonia and won, and she was determined to win this battle with influenza, though the name made people quake with fear.

When we saw Papa driving slowly down the lane to our house, our hearts flew into our mouths. Mama began crying. It was as if death had already struck.

Lillian didn't know anything for many days. All she did was lie with closed eyes; her nose constantly dripped blood, and she made odd little coughs. Hovering over her constantly, Mama kept hot cloths saturated with lard, turpentine and kerosene on Lillian's chest; she kept putting spoonsful of sugar and turpentine into her mouth, manipulating her throat until she swallowed. She kept her feet warmed with heated woolen cloths, and called on every bit of her medical knowledge for help. Still, death lurked in every corner of the room, and ours was a very silent and fearful house.

One day a car drove into our yard, and a man and woman got out, holding Jenny between them. When Papa and Mama hurried to them, Jenny lifted heavy eyes and whispered, "I'm sick, Mama."

"Flu," the man said tersely, and introduced himself and his wife, Mr. and Mrs. Blaney, with whom Jenny boarded.

"I already have her sister in bed with it — she's mighty low," Mama said as they helped Jenny into the house.

"We heard. Mrs. Stone, the woman with whom she boarded, died. We left two in bed with it. My mother is tending them while we bring Jenny home," Mrs. Blaney said.

Together they got Jenny in bed beside Lillian, then looked at each other.

"We must go," Mrs. Blaney said. "Our two boys are bad off. Is there anyone I can call to help you?"

"No. I got my husband and two other girls. God bless you both for bringing Jenny."

"You're welcome. We only hope God will be merciful and let all our sick get well. And we can pray."

"Yes," Mama said, "we can pray."

For many nights a lamp burned all night in our house. Mama slept in dozes; she, Gloria and I hovered over the bed, constantly tending and watching while Papa and the boys did the outside work. We were hardly aware of eating.

Then one day Lillian's eyes opened to consciousness and the

flush of fever was gone. Jenny had never lost consciousness and she improved daily, though both had to stay in bed.

As soon as Mama knew Lillian and Jenny would be all right, she collapsed with the flu; then the two boys. That left Papa, Gloria and me to nurse the sick, cook, tend the stock and milk, but not for long. Gloria took sick.

Since so many were sick, Mama said, rice was to be cooked for the sick ones. My heart sank. I wasn't sick.

A few mornings later, Papa couldn't get up, and I alone was healthy, active and riceless. I felt cheated. I didn't mind tending the sick (they were always wanting something), toting chamberpots, feeding and watering the mules, milking the cow, straining the milk into pitchers carefully washed separately from the dishes, feeding the hog, washing dishes and trying to cook. What I did mind was being riceless.

Cooking was no simple matter. Having just passed my eighth birthday in December, I was totally ignorant of it. Fortunately, Jenny was well enough to call instructions from her sick bed. Nevertheless, my biscuits were hoecakes, my gravy like starch and filled with lumps. Only my rice turned out well, and while I was dishing it up for the sick, I wished I could get the flu, too, so I could have some.

Jenny was the first to get out of bed, and was soon able to take over the cooking, which I was very happy to have her do, while I did all the outside work.

Hopefully every morning on opening my eyes, I felt of my forehead to see if I had a temperature. When I found I hadn't, disappointment dragged me to a dark abyss. There I was, envying and smelling the rice going down the gullets of the sick while I remained as healthy as our cow. I couldn't bear it.

Before anyone awoke one morning I kept turning my face, first one side, then the other, to my pillow, hoping to get it hot enough to fool my sister into thinking I was sick.

When getting-up time came, I didn't, though I knew I should make the fires. Since Jenny was just getting over the flu, she had no business getting out of a warm bed in a cold house. But my desire for rice overcame my guilty conscience.

Jenny arose, made the fires, then came to seek me. "I'm sick,"

I told her, but couldn't look her in the eyes. "I want some rice for my breakfast," I tried to say weakly.

Placing a hand on my forehead, she said, "M-m, a little warm." As she turned kitchenward her back was disapproving, but not minding too much since I was assured of eating rice, I lay in blissful anticipation.

This became reality, and I filled my long-denied belly with boiled rice, covered with melted butter. When I appeared in the kitchen with my emptied plate, Jenny wasn't surprised. When I announced my cure, and was going to milk, feed the mules and hog, she nodded her head.

"No more than I expected," she said.

"The rice cured me," I said.

"I'm not surprised," she replied and smiled at me in understanding. I grinned, grabbed the milk bucket and fled barnward.

I never did get the flu.

The year of 1919 was momentous in our lives and the nation. Indeed in the nation unheard-of changes were brewing.

The year began badly for us, but with the battle against influenza met and won, we felt we could do most anything. In February Jenny and Lillian returned to their schools, Papa began spring plowing and our household settled into its old routine, except that people stopped coming so often to hear our talking machine.

Being a renter instead of a sharecropper, Papa was free to plant what he pleased. For his money crop he decided on watermelons and, as a sort of security, a few acres of cotton. For our personal use he planted a large vegetable garden and plenty of Irish and sweet potatoes, and sugar cane so we could make our own syrup. One thing he didn't plant. Collards.

The family became aware of community social life, and Lillian an enthusiastic participant. Social activity centered around church and school affairs. Minor and relatively private recreations were watermelon slicings, candy pulls, peanut shellings and cane grindings. There were no such things as serenading newcomers, cornshuckings or logrollings.

Being free of the struggle to get enough food on the table, our parents began to pay attention to national affairs. From their discussions we children learned.

In addition to being embroiled in the peace settlement, the nation was embroiled in the fight to pass two Constitutional Amendments, the Eighteenth and Nineteenth, both of which would change this nation's way of life. The battle for ratification was proving successful, much to the consternation of the male majority. It was almost certain that very soon women could vote and there would be no alcoholic beverages, legally, that is.

Not being a drinking man, Papa wasn't affected by the Eighteenth Amendment, but the Nineteenth brought forth his ire. "The world is on its way to hell on a greased road. Just like a woman, give her an inch and she'll take a mile. Yeah, let 'em vote! They're already cutting their hair short, skirts, too, so men can see their legs. A bunch of hussies!"

Lillian said, "Men ought to be glad women *are* shortening their skirts. They can see whether a girl is bow-legged or not."

Papa laughed. "I usually found out anyway," darted a quick look at Mama and began to sing:

> Come all you rounders if you want to flirt,
> Yonder comes a lady in her hobble-skirt.
> You can hug her and kiss her as much as you please,
> But you can't get her hobble up above her knees.

Mama cut in, "That'll be enough of that!"

Not only Papa but also most of the men disapproved of the woman emerging from the war years. Object of male derision and persecution, she was an angry woman, defying conventions, battling furiously for the rights to vote and to own property separately from her husband. Basically, the postwar woman was battling for the status of a human being.

The male majority devoted themselves to ridiculing, scorning, vilifying and persecuting those women suffragists. But the women fought with greater ferocity, and a new day for women was on its way. In 1920 their right to vote became law.

In January of that year also, the Eighteenth Amendment became law.

[161]

CHAPTER 33

I Get Sick at Last; Lillian and Jock

In EARLY 1919 I wasn't aware of national or local affairs. I wasn't aware of anything. I was sick at last. But not with influenza. I had malaria.

In late winter I was aroused from sleep before the household awoke by an uncontrollable shaking. I was freezing to death; my teeth rattled, and it seemed my bones, too. I couldn't even call Mama.

With Lillian and Jenny off teaching, Gloria and I had the room to ourselves, she in one bed and I in the other; so it was that no one was aware of my condition until Mama came to see why I hadn't come to breakfast, an unheard-of circumstance.

She piled more quilts over me, which had no effect whatsoever; the shaking continued all morning; at noon, fever took possession, and I lay in a stupor. Occasionally, I would rouse, but everything seemed a dream and no thought of rice or other food entered my brain. But one thought did: My family's indifference to my illness.

For me the world had stopped, yet the household went about its usual business, not paying me much mind as this thing shook me nearly to death, then cast me into a firy furnace every day. Sometimes I was aware Mama made me swallow something very bitter, and others she made me swallow something that made me feel cooler (peppermint drops for fever). In the intervals it seemed I was left alone.

Mornings I bore the shaking alone; afternoons I sank into the stupor of fever. Once I roused to see Jenny and Lillian primping at the dresser. They didn't even notice my eyes open, but I never had time to call out, for the stupor dragged me back into blackness.

One morning I awoke without the shaking chill. My head seemed clear, the sick feeling was gone and I was hungry. I sat up and slid my feet to the floor, but darkness swept over me.

When it receded I was on the floor with my back against the bed. Holding on to the mattress, then the bedstead, I gained my feet. Nothing happened. I took a tentative step, then another. By holding onto objects I groped my way to the kitchen, where I surprised Mama cooking dinner.

"Lowell, what are you doing out of bed?" She felt my forehead. "No fever!"

"I didn't shake today," I croaked.

Turning back to her tasks, she commented, "You're getting well."

When I told her I was hungry she opened a pint of canned tomatoes, put them in a bowl and I devoured them.

Strengthened, I wandered out to the backyard in the shade of a big chinaberry. Amazed, I stood and gazed at the green fields. When I fell ill Papa was just turning land. Now the crops were ready for laying-by. Forlornly, I gazed across a green field of waving corn. How beautiful it was!

Arriving for dinner, Papa saw and hurried to me, gladness in his face. "Are you well?"

I nodded, gesturing toward the fields.

He laughed. "You been sick a long time. Didn't think you'd ever git well. You missed all the planting and hoeing. Bet you're glad of that, eh?"

"No, I ain't," I croaked.

He gave me a wink. "Planted watermelons this year. Gonna make some money — a lot of money so we can go to the circus, but you'll have to git your voice back first so you can holler."

Aware he was confiding a dream to me, I felt my heart swelling with pride. I nodded and smiled. Gregory and Justin came running up, happy to see me out of bed, and I was surprised at how tall they were. It was as if I had been away a long time.

"Let's go to dinner!" Papa said.

While I was in bed, Gloria had to do most of the hoeing. She hardly glanced at me at the dinner table — mad because of all the hoeing. Both Jenny and Lillian were in summer school at the teachers' college in Ralston, and I missed them, especially Lillian.

[163]

All afternoon I stayed in the shade of the chinaberry, playing farming. With an old spoon I laid off field after field, and gazed with deep satisfaction at the newly turned dirt. I had missed seeing newly turned fields, the upward shooting of new green and being part of the bustle and hope at planting time. So I played farming.

To my dismay, the next morning the familiar chill awoke me, and all that day I was as sick as I had ever been. But the next morning I had no chill and felt well again. Thus the illness continued, and I had to adjust my life to "well day" and "sick day."

I wanted to get well. Summer school would soon be over and my older sisters would come home. I hadn't seen them except through the daze of fever since they returned to teaching, and I was eager to see them.

When they did come home, they paid me scant attention. They would clean the house, then sit sewing pretty things for their hope chests. When I asked what those were, they laughed and said a hope chest contained things hoped to be used if a girl married.

Jenny knew her things would be, for she and Cass were engaged. As to Lillian, we were all surprised at her sudden interest in sewing. They spent many hours, the dark head and the fair one, bent over their sewing in our bedroom.

Assuming I was deaf or asleep on my "sick days," they didn't lower their voices, thus I discovered one day why Lillian was making a hope chest. She was in love with Jock Teasdale.

"But, Lillian," Jenny said when Lillian told her, "you're a schoolteacher, and he's nothing but a sharecropper's son. How *could* you fall in love with *him?*"

"Love has no reason," Lillian said, and sighed.

"Papa will never allow you to marry him."

"He won't even let me date him. I've been dating him on the sly, and we see each other at B.Y.P.U. and church. He's the president of B.Y.P.U., and a leader of the church. Why, he's made our B.Y.P.U.! We've won the banner four times in a row because of his work."

But Jenny heard only the first two sentences. "How can you sneak so?"

"I love him!"

Anxiously, Jenny said, "Lillian, listen to me! The feeling you have for him may not be true love. You could be mistaken — please wait for a better prospect!"

"It is so true love! Why, I'd die for Jock Teasdale!"

Exasperated, Jenny burst out, "I don't see how you can love him! He doesn't have a dime!"

Throwing aside her sewing, Lillian stormed, "So, you disapprove of him, too! Just because Cass comes of a property-owning family makes your feeling for him true love, eh? And because Jock's family doesn't own a dime, my love for him isn't the real thing, eh? Well, Papa isn't exactly rolling in wealth, either, nor does he own an inch of land. Why do the Abbotts think they're so high and mighty? You can all go to hell!"

Jenny's face flushed. Haughtily, she said, "The Abbotts have always been counted high and mighty. Papa is the only one of his family who never amounted to anything! And do you know why?"

"Yes, Grandpa sold Papa's cordwood so he couldn't go to college and be a lawyer. Then his holier-than-thou sisters and brother tricked him away from Grandpa's farm so they could get the money. That's why!"

Jenny shook her head. "He married Mama. That's why!"

Horrified at such disloyalty, Lillian gasped, "Jenny!"

Knowingly, Jenny nodded. "Mama's people were poor white trash, though Grandpa Walters was a Baptist preacher. Mama has been detrimental to Papa ever since they married. Listen, to breed a thoroughbred horse, you don't mate a dray horse with a thoroughbred. You have to mate thoroughbred with thoroughbred. The blood must be equal."

Lillian's voice began to rise. "You're comparing our mama to a dray horse!"

"Yes, I am. Why do you think Papa has failed in everything he has tried to do? A woman must be more to a man than a brood mare in order to be a good wife. She must know how to maintain and raise their status in society. Mama doesn't have that knowledge. She's too primitive. Papa could have married another girl with a good family and money, but wouldn't. I'm trying to prevent your making the same mistake. I don't want you to throw yourself away on a man without good family or a dime. I want you to have a man worthy of you!"

Mama loved Jenny more than any of her children.

Furious at Jenny's words, Lillian shouted, "How dare you talk against my mama? You're just like the rest of the Abbotts! You rate people by the dollars they own! If a man has no money, then he isn't worth a damn! For your information — and you can tell the rest of the family, I'll marry Jock Teasdale the minute he asks me!" She flounced out.

"Wait, Lillian! I didn't mean to make you angry!" If Lillian heard, she never answered. Jenny didn't pick up her sewing, but stared into space. Then I saw her cheeks wet with tears.

"Oh, Jenny!" I cried, "Don't cry! He might not ask her."

Startled, she whirled to face me. "We didn't know you were awake."

"You woke me."

"Feel better?"

"I don't know. Lillian — what if she does really and truly love Jock? Wouldn't it be better for her if she married him?"

"You're too young to understand such things!"

"I only know what Papa told me. He did cut that cordwood for college money, and Grandpa sold it. He wanted to be a lawyer something fierce. And he said Mama was the prettiest thing he ever laid eyes on."

"Even so, he did a foolish thing when he married her. Oh, I hope Lillian won't do anything so foolish! Well, he hasn't asked her yet. He may not even love her."

At the thought my heart went out to Lillian. "If she loves him, I hope he loves her. She loved a man once who didn't love her," I said, remembering Lillian's sorrow over Erastus Redder.

Her face brightened. "There's a way to tell. If I could only see them together — m — mm — m" Her eyes narrowing, she said, "I think Papa has a lot of watermelons wasting in the fields — " and she hurried to the kitchen to find Mama.

What could wasting watermelons have to do with Lillian's being in love with Jock Teasdale?

Jenny didn't think much of Mama. She said she was poor white trash. That was how all the Abbotts thought of her. Papa had married a dray horse. But I couldn't believe that was the reason he never had money or much of anything. Mama was good. Why, she was next to God in goodness. How could the Abbotts say she was poor white trash?

Jenny believed it, too. Was that the reason she stayed with Aunt Sally so much? She had also stayed with Aunt Tish and Aunt Sally while going to town school, and they dinned it into her head about Mama being poor white trash. That's why she took up for the Abbotts.

Lillian hadn't stayed with our aunts. It was generally known they didn't care too much for her because she favored Mama's people. That bothered her not one whit. She didn't care much for them, either. She thought them peculiar and different from other people. If they "looked down on" her, they weren't the only ones looking down. She also resented openly their attitude toward Mama. She owed them no favor and didn't expect any from them.

Angry as she was, she didn't tell Mama what Jenny said. She didn't even consider telling. Each person had a right to his own opinions, and Lillian knew Jenny had bared her most private ones in trying to prevent her making a mistake like the one Papa had made, according to the Abbotts. Mama might be poor white trash, but Mama was our mama, an unalterable fact. To her we children owed our lives.

Lillian reasoned she was as much Mama as she was Papa, and none but a traitor would betray his own blood. She also knew Grandma Walters' parents were owners of slaves and a big plantation before the Civil War; and had not Grandpa Walters' father been killed in the war, he might have become a land-owner, too, and his posterity couldn't have been called poor white trash.

No Abbott had been killed in any war. She had never heard of one being a soldier. Ruefully, she admitted to herself and later to me, she was more proud of her maternal blood than the paternal; for despite Papa's reason for a thwarted life, she believed he could have found a way to attend college. If one searched diligently enough, a way could be found. Had not she become a schoolteacher? She was just as sure a way would be found for her to marry Jock.

Sunday afternoon we had a watermelon slicing. In addition to Lillian's friends, relatives and neighbors were invited and of course, Cass. By the crowd gathered in our front yard, it seemed that all accepted. Among those present was Jock Teasdale.

Ensconced in a rocker on the front porch, I was practically ignored, but my eyes kept busy, roving from person to person and resting on Jock longer than on anyone else.

Slender and of medium height, he seemed to be the most popular of the young men, for others were constantly stopping to converse with him. Though his face had an open, pleasant expression, he wasn't sufficiently outstanding to warrant the capture of Lillian's heart. I had expected more, someone like a Prince in the fairy tales I read so much, or even a blond version of Jack Dempsey. Disappointment swept me.

Jenny was right. Lillian certainly deserved more than this. I couldn't picture the flamboyant Lillian married to just an ordinary man like Jock. But she loved him and, as she said, love has no reason.

Apparently, she would have no chance; as I watched him my heart grew heavy for Lillian; in all the games the young people played he never once sought Lillian as a partner, but bestowed his favor on a girl by the name of Minnie Bass.

Lillian seemed to take no notice of Mr. Teasdale's slighting her. She laughed and talked a lot with other young men, and in games she didn't lack for partners. She ate watermelon with a dark, handsome young man named John Whitmore, who was also a teacher. Though he was no more princely-looking than Jock, I preferred him.

Not only my eyes but also the eyes of Jenny, Papa and Mama often strayed to Jock, and they were pleased by what they saw; for he was ever by Minnie's side, his head bent attentively to her.

No doubt Lillian was flirting with all those other boys to cover her heartache. My own heart felt like a rock. If Lillian loved him, I wanted him to love her.

When people began leaving Minnie left with her parents; among the few staying to help clean up was Jock, who made more trips to the hog pen with rinds than anybody else. After all traces of the watermelon slicing vanished, the only person remaining was Jock. From my vantage point I saw him go up to Papa and say something, then the two went to the backyard under the cedar trees.

Cass had left, too, so Jenny, Mama and Gloria joined me on the porch; the boys were playing in the yard. Lillian was pretending to be petting the dogs. When the two men went to the back, she joined us.

She didn't seem a bit nervous or upset by Jock's talking to Papa, but the rest of us were and kept darting looks at her. With a little smile on her lips and her eyes on the distant piny woods, she just sat rocking, paying us no mind whatsoever. Could Jock be asking for Lillian as Cass had for Jenny?

Finally, the two came from around the house. In saying goodbye they shook hands, smiling. As Jock rode out of the yard he waved, and all waved back. As Papa took a chair on the porch we looked at him, our hearts in our eyes.

He was not to be hurried. Carefully, he cut a chew of his Brown Mule tobacco, put it into his mouth, and began chewing.

"Well?" Mama asked.

Lillian stopped rocking, her eyes still on the piny woods.

"I just rented the Teasdales that big field back of our house for next year. Make more by renting than planting."

Lillian turned, her eyes found us, and she laughed heartily.

CHAPTER 34

Jenny Marries; a New Brother;
the Jingle of Silver

IN THE SPRING of 1920 two family events occurred. In April Cass and Jenny were married in a simple home ceremony. In May Mama gave birth to a baby boy.

Cass and Jenny began housekeeping in a little three-room house on his father's farm. Concentrating on her new life as she had on studies and teaching, Jenny decided to teach no more. A married woman's place was in the home. We all agreed with her.

A few weeks after the marriage Papa was needing cash. He told me when we were alone one day, "I sure miss Jenny's money."

"What you mean, Jenny's money?"

"She always give me money outta her every paycheck."

I was astounded. We never knew.

At my expression he further said, "That's how I could always buy flour since moving here, and clothes." He went on to name other necessities Jenny's money bought. But I was thinking: Jenny gave Papa money for flour and shoes while Lillian bought Santa Claus, a talking machine with records, rocking chairs and other things enriching our lives. Her money brought great pleasure, but bread was also necessary.

For Mama's confinement, instead of a doctor Papa got a white-bedecked Negro midwife, and the birthing was carried through without ill effects, and much cheaper.

While Mama was in bed the midwife did the cooking, and her main complaint was the hardened dough in the bread tray. "I knowed a man onct who wanted to marry a girl," she told me, "and went to the girl's home, demanding to see the bread tray. When he saw a tray jist like dis'n, he wouldn't ax her ca'se he knowed she'd be a dirty housekeeper."

Mama had her own clue to a nasty housekeeper. She said, "If a kettle is not shining, then you'll know the housekeeper is nasty."

All my life these two odd bits of information have lived with me. Since I became a housekeeper, though all my house might be neck-deep in dirt, I've always washed my bread tray after using it and kept my kettle shining clean.

But the midwife's opinion didn't detract from our delight in the new baby. Like me, he had inherited the Brane family dark hair and eyes, so Mama named him Jeems after her father and Brane after Papa's mother, and we called him Brane.

After the midwife left, he cried constantly and we children became wary of him. Mama said he had the three-month colic, and fed him the hardened dough, softened with milk, from the bread tray, and it cured him. He began to fatten and coo and we began to bow before his sweetness.

Though "sick days" had now left me, I still had to take quinine, liquid instead of powder; but since I didn't act sick, I had to take my place in the fields.

Papa allowed Gloria, Gregory, Justin and me each a vegetable garden from which we could sell the produce to have money of our own. Mama allowed Gloria and me a setting of eggs from which we could sell the roosters and unlikely pullets. Both parents made it plain we were to tend our own gardens, but we could spend the money as we chose.

After our gardens began producing, on Friday afternoons we would prepare the vegetables and load the two-mule wagon. In addition to our vegetables, Papa took his, and Mama always sent eggs, fryers and fresh butter. Before sunup the next morning we went to Fitzgerald to sell.

We children soon learned to love the feel of quarters, dimes and nickels and the sound of jingling silver in our pockets. We also discovered selling was fun. Coming into town from our direction, we entered the Negro section first. Beginning at the first house, Papa would holler, "Chickens, eggs and butter! Green beans and onions to go with your corn bread! Sweet potatoes, Irish potatoes! Come and get 'em! Fresh from the garden with dew still on 'em!"

Negro women would pour out of their houses, their faces shiny, bright kerchiefs on their heads and silver tied up in bits of cloth. No men ever answered Papa's calls, only women with silver, no bills.

Once a girl said, "Mist', gimme a nickel's worth of sweet taters."

Papa replied, "Well, just lift the sack and smell!"

After a big laugh from everyone including the girl, Papa allowed her one medium.

We never got to cover all the streets because our wagon would be empty before we could. We wished many times we had enough to cover the whole town.

Because of having known Wash, Papa was able to have empathy with the friendly, gay, brown people, whose poverty never hindered their instant laughter and merry calls to us and each other.

"Hey, Miz —, how's you dis mornin'? How you gitting along?"

The usual answer to this was, "On my feet."

They greeted each new arrival personally. No one went unnoticed. Thus Papa learned their names, and would join in their calls with "Here comes that sleep-head, Miz —. Bet she wants a chicken for her Sunday dinner!"

"Naw, I don't! Ain't got dat much money today. Naw, suh. All I'se got's a quarter. What can I git de most of for dat?"

Papa would look over what we had, then let her have a mess of beans and a small onion. "You can't eat beans without onions," he would say. He had no scales to weigh by ounces and pounds, and sold by "messes."

Holding up a fifty-cent piece, a woman asked, "What can I git for dat?"

"How many mouths you got to feed?"

"Six wit my own. Five chilluns. I ain't got no man."

Papa put on his stern look. "What become of the man who helped git the chillun?"

"He daid. Got kilt by lightning. I wash and iron for people. Dat don' pay so good."

Many called out, "She tells the truf!"

[172]

Papa said, "For fifty cents you can have a big mess of Irish potatoes with some onions for good measure."

No wonder our wagon emptied so quickly, but we had enough silver to satisfy us, Mama had a fair price for her stuff, Papa had enough for coffee, flour, sugar and tobacco; and many bellies had food.

When Lillian returned from the first session of summer school, she opened another world to us, the motion pictures. On Saturdays, first she went peddling with us and seemed to enjoy it as much as we did. Watching us zealously counting our silver, she said, "It'd pay me to stop teaching and start peddling."

When the wagon was empty, we'd head downtown. Since Papa refused to accompany us, we left him at a grocery store while we enjoyed ourselves. First we would stop at a drug store for an ice cream cone, then go to our paradise unlimited.

Since the price of an ice cream cone was five cents and movies for children, six cents, we had money left to buy cloth from which Mama made our dresses, and underwear, and the boys' shirts.

Wonderful indeed was the world of motion pictures, and we came to live for Saturday afternoons. The program consisted of a comedy (Mutt and Jeff, Felix the Cat, Keystone Kops, or Larry Semon), a serial and a Western.

Horrified by watching a girl tied on a railroad track with a train nigh upon her, we could hardly wait until the next Saturday to find out if the train really did run over her.

From the Westerns came our first knowledge of a land called the West, a strange, almost treeless country filled with gigantic rocks and bad men.

The game of Cowboys and Indians or Cowboys and Outlaws became very popular with my brothers and me, and our lives lost some dullness because of the wondrous world of motion pictures.

CHAPTER 35

I Share Lillian's World; I Find a Rock

M ORE AND MORE people were buying Fords, but all we had was that topless buggy, so Sunday mornings, if weather permitted, we children from Lillian on down to Justin, walked the mile to Sunday school and church. Sunday nights Lillian and Gloria had been going to B.Y.P.U. and church for quite a while, and one day Lillian asked me if I would like to go with them. Of course I would. From that time on, I went every Sunday night.

There were two groups in B.Y.P.U. Lillian was the leader of one, and Jock of the other. They took turns in giving the program. When's Lillian's group led, she began giving me poems to say. But Gloria wouldn't take any part, and sat with her head hanging down most of the time. Lillian and I couldn't understand her shyness, and were a little ashamed of her.

I couldn't help but notice Lillian and Jock had much to say to each other after B.Y.P.U. and church; while Glory and I sat in the buggy, Lillian and Jock would talk apart from others. Since the watermelon slicing we hadn't heard her mention his name, though the Teasdales were renting the big field back of our house with Jock doing all the plowing.

Soon after returning from summer school, Lillian was notified by the trustees that she had been appointed principal of Ridgeway School, where she was teaching. Though she was Miss Abbott, principal of Ridgefield School in that community, the moment she entered our door she was Lillian. We still took turns sleeping with her, including Brane, when he was old enough. She took her place in our home, helping in field and house as if she wasn't a school principal. Nor did we regard her as one. She was Lillian.

From our washplace under the cedars breaking yard and field, she watched Jock plowing. Catching me watching her, she said, "I've a right to." After a pause, she asked, "Lowell, can you keep a secret?"

"Nobody but you knows I know about Santa Claus."

"This secret is much more important, but I'm so happy I need to share it."

"You *know* I keep a secret!"

"Promise you won't tell, anyway."

I crossed my heart and hoped to die.

Though we were alone, she lowered her voice. "Jock and I are going to be married."

My mouth and eyes flew wide open. "But I saw him with Minnie Bass at the watermelon slicing last summer!"

"He used her as a cover. He knows our family disapproves of him. He also knew you all were watching him. Why do you think he rented that field so close to our house?"

I shook my head.

"He wanted Papa to see how good he works." Sadly, she shook her head. "Makes no difference how good he works. It's his blood."

Recalling what Jenny said, I nodded. "You have to match good blood with good blood to make thoroughbreds."

Her eyes narrowed. "Are you on their side or mine?"

"Yours! That's what they think," I said and realized her secret was indeed important. For a good while I had been free of the burden of "sick day." Now I saw Lillian's secret would place another burden upon me, though I was glad she would marry the man she loved. But, oh, why couldn't she have chosen another?

For generations the Abbott family's tradition was to marry good blood. In their young days Aunt Sally and Aunt Tish had rejected men they loved because of the quality of their blood.

Since Papa broke the tradition by marrying Mama, why should he now forbid his daughter the same right? But he did.

"If you marry Jock, what will Papa do?"

She sighed. "He said he'd disown me," then she brightened. "But here's the best part. I won't be here! After Jock gathers his crop, he's going to Griffin to find a job. When he does he's coming for me!"

She would be farther away than Jenny. We'd never get to see her. It was as if a cloud came over the sun.

[175]

Seeing my downcast face, she added, "Later on, you can come see us for long visits."

As always, she knew a silver lining.

Since I now relied on my brothers for play and companionship, Papa naturally included me in plowing lessons. Soon he was letting us turn land, side cotton and bar off corn. We used the crippled mule Rhoda because she was slower than Kate, and we had no trouble keeping up with her. We liked plowing, but since we were novices, Papa always plowed nearby so that all four were not far from each other.

In siding cotton one day I plowed up a pebble as large as Papa's fist, and instantly stopped the mule to marvel at such a find, for Aunt Sally was right about there being no rocks in south Georgia; there were only small pebbles, an odd tan as smooth as glass. This one was also. "A rock! A rock!" I shouted.

The boys wondered why I was so excited over a big pebble.

Stopping Kate, Papa came to see, almost running. Holding out his hand, he said, "Let me see it!" Turning it over and over in his hand, he said, "That's the biggest rock I've seen down here. Greg, do you remember rocks?"

Greg looked bewildered, and Papa continued, "And I know Justin don't. In north Georgia, where we come from, there's a lot of rocks, white 'uns, white as milk with gold in 'em and great big gray 'uns, some bigger than our house. And mountains."

Fondling the big pebble, he sat down against some cotton stalks and motioned us to sit. "Lowell, you 'member how blue them mountains was from the front porch on your Grandpa's place?"

I nodded. Just by closing my eyes I could see them.

Taking his Brown Mule tobacco and knife from his pocket, he cut each a chew. "Here, have a chaw."

Instantly, Justin spit his out, but Greg and I were big enough to plow, so we were big enough to chew tobacco, and we chewed while Papa continued.

"And snow?" he questioned me.

I nodded, remembering.

"Christamighty! What I'd give to see some snow! In winter we could sit by a good ole hickory log fire, and look out the windows and see the whole earth covered. *Snow.* Talking about pure beauty! Nothing can hold to that soft, white stuff called snow. Covers the whole earth, the holes, the grass, the ugliness, and all you can see is rabbit tracks. That's when a man can hunt!" He chewed thoughtfully.

Eying the boys, he continued, "On cold, winter nights with wind whistling around the house, I'd git out the popcorn popper, fill it full of popcorn and hold it over them hickory logs till that popper would nigh jump outta my hand. Then Ma would take that popped corn and roll it in 'lasses — not this heart-burning stuff of this heathern land — but honest-to-goodness sorghum 'lasses. Talk about something good!"

His eyes turned sorrowful. "Heck, you boys don't know what popcorn is. Don't even have the seed in this Godforsaken land. When I asked for 'em at the seed store, the man thought I was tetched in the head. No rocks, no mountains, no snow, no nothing here."

Spitting, he wiped his mouth on the back of his hand, and a light kindled in his eyes. "In a land full of rocks, mountains and snow a man can live — has something to look at and look to — real winters of snow, icicles and rabbits." The light died and it seemed as if all the sorrows of the world came to burden his shoulders.

"Hornswoggled, that's what I was. Hornswoggled by my own family. And Pa, too. Brought down to this land of piney woods, hot sun and gnats!" He brushed at the swarm around his eyes.

"And sandspurs, Papa! Don't forgit them!" I added, plucking one from a bare foot.

He got up, brushed off the seat of his pants, and said, "Well, this ain't gittin' the grass outta the cotton," and headed for his plow, his shoulders drooping, his steps slow.

Gregory and I got to our feet, but Greg just sorta went over backward and lay there. The ground seemed to be rising up right in front of my face, and I quickly sat down before it hit me. Before we knew what was happening, nausea hit us, and we vomited and vomited while Papa stood helplessly by.

After our stomachs and heads cleared, Papa sent us to the

[177]

house with his admonition: "Don't tell your Ma I give you a chew. I'd never hear the last of it. Didn't know it'd make you sick. I won't give you no more."

That was all right with us. We didn't want any more.

CHAPTER 36

Papa's Tomfoolery

ONE DAY while we were resting and watching larks sail in the sky, Greg said, "I wish we could fly like birds."

"Why," Papa said, "you can."

Our eyes opened wide. "You mean really fly?"

"Why, shore. All you have to do is flap your arms like birds do their wings. Stand on that bank yonder, flap your arms up and down half a dozen times, then jump. See if you don't fly!"

Flapping our arms up and down, we stood on the bank until we felt we had enough "juice" to fly on, then jumped. To our disappointment we only landed in the sandy dirt six feet below, and climbed back to Papa accusingly.

Seeing our faces, he stopped laughing to say, "Aw, you didn't give yourselves enough time. It takes a lot of practice to fly. Wait till we have more time."

What more time did we have than after dinner while Papa was lying on the front porch resting?

Greg said, "Then we'll have more food to fly on, too. You know what I'm gonna do when I git up in the sky? I'm going to sit right down on one of them big, fat white clouds and sail right across the sky."

"I ain't," Justin said. "I'm gonna git on one of them buzzards, so I can have me a good ride."

I imagined flying would be better than swimming. "I don't wanna git on nothing. I just aim to fly, fly and fly." I could feel the cool breezes as I swept through them. I bet I wouldn't sweat a drop! I'd just sail and sail through the cool, cool blue.

Exhilaration filled me as I plowed the long rows of cotton in the burning sun.

Hardly had the last mouthful of dinner been downed before we were out in the yard running. Around and around the house we went, running as fast as our will could make our legs go, our arms pumping up and down, up and down, faster than windmills. Any moment now, we would rise off the ground and skim through the air, as soon as we could make our legs and arms go faster. Our feet were barely touching the ground as it was.

Suddenly, Papa sat up, blinking as he saw us racing around the house, our arms flapping up and down as we ran. After watching several rounds, he called out, "What in tarnation are you *doing?*"

"We're gonna fly like birds!" Greg shouted as he disappeared to the rear, I right behind him, and little, chubby Justin behind me.

As we ran around, Papa's head followed us like an owl's, and in the glimpse I caught of him as we passed I saw his face all screwed up with laughter. Finally, he called out, "Stop, you're gonna kill your fool selves!"

In utter frustration we flung ourselves down in the yard, panting like dogs after chasing a rabbit. Our blood pounded in our ears, our faces were as red as a hickory log fire and sweat streamed from us, making the sand cling to our skin.

Greg was bawling like a baby, but I didn't have the breath. Justin could do nothing but lie there.

Somewhat ashamed, Papa said, "I told you it took a lot of practice. You just can't fly when you want."

Between sobs, Greg said, "We can't never fly! I'll never sit on a white cloud and sail across the sky!"

"Now I wouldn't say that!" Papa admonished. "Best thing to do is catch one of them mocking birds, put it in a cage and study its wings, then make you some like his'n."

Hope made Gregory stop bawling, and we all sat up and looked at the mocking bird hopping along the ground.

Immediately, Justin rose and waddled toward it. When he was within three yards, the bird cocked a knowing eye and flew, though Justin called lovingly, "Birdie! Birdie! Birdie!"

"Now that ain't no way to catch a bird," Papa said.

"How, then?"

"Git a handful of salt and sprinkle it on the bird's tail."

For the rest of the summer Mama couldn't keep salt. But we could never catch a bird; so we never learned to fly.

CHAPTER 37

Papa Fails; Gloria; A Baby Sister

PAPA LOST money on his watermelon crop along with other farmers. They heard of the good northern market and planted many acres. When time came to ship, they found the northern market almost nonexistent. That summmmer watermelon slicings had never been so popular.

But the other farmers didn't have three hundred dollars' rent to pay. If it hadn't been for his cotton, Pa couldn't have paid it. As it was, he barely had enough.

The fall of 1921 Papa lost money again on his main crop, sweet potatoes. It was a heavy blow, for he thought sweet potatoes were a sure thing. By the time ours were ready to sell prices hit bottom, and Papa couldn't pay all the rent.

The owner suggested Papa go back to cotton the next year. "Why, I bet you'll make enough to pay every cent you owe off cotton. Can't beat cotton."

But Papa was scared. He had never seen prices so low, yet when he bought clothes, flour, sugar, coffee, the prices he paid were out of all reason.

"I might have knowed it! It's that new Republican President. He's just a slick politician! The little farmers won't stand a chance now," he ranted.

In 1922 Papa planted acres of cotton and acres of penders, but when selling time came he made only enough to pay for guano and seed.

"Cotton prices are lowest I've ever seen," he said.

Four cents cotton
Ten cents meat
How in the world
Can a poor man eat?

We ate all right. We had milk, butter, bread, vegetables and chickens. But we couldn't go around naked.

After Lillian began teaching, Gloria had to shoulder more man-sized work, plowing, strewing guano and helping Papa cut wood with a crosscut saw. If she resented this, she never said so.

Indeed, she talked very little to anyone. She went about her work in a silent, aloof manner. She was almost a young lady, but she never went through the giggling stage, as had Lillian. Nor did she pay attention to boys. In fact, she paid little attention to anything.

When crops were laid by that year, Uncle Jules and Aunt Adah came one Sunday. They now had two girls and three boys. They also had the same big car. Aunt Adah saw that Gloria needed to get away from our poverty for a little while; so she asked Mama if Gloria could go home with them for a three-week visit, and Mama consented.

During the visit Aunt Adah made Gloria a pretty Sunday dress with a yoke of eyelet embroidery. Then she gave her a prom party, the remembrance of which gave Gloria pleasure the rest of her life. However, upon her return home, she again sank into her silent, aloof manner.

While Gloria was on her visit, Mama let me stay with Aunt Sally a while, always a pleasure. But my vacation abruptly ended one morning when Gregory and Justin came in the wagon.

Standing, Greg urged the poor, lame Rhoda to a gallop by hitting her with a fishing pole. Clinging to the wagonside for dear life was Justin; otherwise, he'd have bounced out in no time. Bringing the wagon to a sudden halt, Greg shouted, "You gotta come home! The stork brought Mama a baby girl last night! You gotta come home and see her. Git your things!"

His excitement caught me. I had to see my baby sister. When I saw the tiny, wizened baby, I knew I'd swapped my birthright for a mess of pottage, for, once home, I had to stay, a great disappointment.

The baby was sickly and was no pleasure. The puny Florine, like me, was not one to attract immediate affection, and remained the most unnoticed baby Mama ever had, unless it was me.

As soon as Mama was able to resume her work, the midwife left, and the household settled into its old dull routine until Lillian returned from summer school. She paid little attention to the new baby, but talked to me while she sat sewing for her hope chest.

She was still waiting for Jock to come for her. He had found a job, but could save very little money. They wrote each other, making plans for the future. It would take more time than they thought, if Lillian would wait. She would. She filled her hope chest before she returned to be principal.

When Papa told the owner he couldn't pay any rent, Mr. Stover, knowing the low prices, was sorry. "I can't have you stay on my farm free," he told Papa regretfully. His leniency was at an end.

So was Papa's hope.

We had tried. We had worked like dray horses, all that labor for nothing. It seemed we were just born losers. Circumstances were against us, but we didn't know that.

Several factors were effecting changes. Impoverished nations could no longer import; the replacement of horse by automobile narrowed the market for stock feed; production exceeded demand, resulting in decreased farm income to such an extent that millions of small-scale farmers were forced to seek urban employment.

Unaware of the world's economic situation, Papa took the blame for his failures on himself. Believing them to be the result of his own incapability, he was so stricken he never said a word to any of us while he went about searching for a place to move to. Since he knew what Stover's place meant to us all, he just couldn't bring himself to tell us that we had to give it up.

CHAPTER 38

Sharecroppers Again

T HE PLACE he found was the misery of all miseries. He was ashamed to tell Mama. He was afraid to tell Lillian. With her strange aloofness, Gloria wasn't one to invite confidences. Both Greg and Justin were too young and Brane was just going on three. I was the only one left, so in despair he told me.

He and I had gone to town alone that day. On the way home, he said, "We have to move, Lowell."

"You mean leave Stover's place?"

He nodded.

"Oh, Papa!" I was crestfallen.

He said, "But I found another place," and was silent.

"Is it prettier?"

"Lowell, it's the worst place in the whole world, the very worst. But it's the only one I could find, and the owners don't care if we make just a dime, they git a third."

He paused a long time before adding, "Lowell, the owners are white trash. I wouldn't be caught in public with them for nothing. Fact is, I don't even want people to know I'm their sharecropper."

He stopped, swallowed hard, then, "Christamighty! *Their* sharecropper! A pretty pass to come to! A pretty, sorry pass!" His eyes stared into blankness, then he turned to me. "Promise you won't tell Ma! I don't want her to know."

"She'll have to! She'll move there, too!"

"I'll tell her, but not now. I gotta think of a way. You're the only one I've told. Promise not to tell her or any of the rest!"

I crossed my heart and hoped to die.

He seemed to feel better. "You 'member the shanty Wash lived in?"

I did. No glass windows, the shack had looked as if a wind had blown some planks together.

"This house is as bad or worse." He sighed. "Sharecroppers

agin. Ma ain't gonna like it. Low-down as white trash, just poor white trash — that's what we've become. It's hard to believe how low we've fell."

I could see the despair in his face; for a moment he gave way to the onslaught, slumping in complete dejection and letting the mules plod on without guidance. Then, straightening, he said, "You young'uns will have to change schools. But Ashton is a genuine high school with busses to ride chillun to school."

We would ride to school! That, indeed, was an unheard of luxury. Hope stirred. "Let's go see the place," I suggested.

Instead of turning into the lane leading to the Stover place, we rode three miles further, then turned to the left into a more used road which went past a white frame church.

"Methodist!" Papa explained. "Oaktowers. 'Fraid we'll be in a Methodist community over here. You all will have to go to it — no Baptist churches. But we can still go to Fitzgerald on Saturdays. It's still the closest town."

On the road were some big, fine houses, most of which were painted white — old, old houses reminding me of the Weane house, only much finer. It seemed we were moving into a community of rich people. The Methodists must have more money than the Baptists.

At a crossroads cut in two by a railroad, we turned into a road on the right. To the left, on the other side of the railroad was a big, white, two-storied house.

"Our nearest neighbors. The Robersons. Fine people. They ain't snobs," meaning they would recognize us as living.

Almost parallel to the railroad, only a good-sized field between, our road ran like a white, sandy ribbon under pine trees. On the right was a swamp, dark and dismal.

Papa said, "You young'uns have to stay outta the swamp."

That wouldn't be hard to do.

Pushing back the swamp and letting the sun shine full strength on the road, the woods gave way to an open pasture on the swamp side; on the other was the big field ending at the railroad. Pointing, Papa said, "Part of the land we'll tend. Ain't but a one-horse farm — hardly that."

Across a small wooden bridge and only a few yards further

stood a log cabin, silvered gray by weather and time, and almost as dilapidated as Wash's shanty. The road ended at the house. It was ours.

Papa stopped the wagon in the yard, and tied the mules to a peach tree. With trembling knees I climbed from the wagon and saw at once the house was divided by an open hall six feet wide.

To the left, steps led to a stoop four feet square. At the front was a huge cistern pipe placed vertically. On a cross plank was tied a pulley with chain holding a galvanized bucket swaying in the wind. The uncovered well meant the water would be infested with wiggletails.

The door from the stoop led to the kitchen. At least water wouldn't have to be toted far. The kitchen itself was just large enough to cook and eat in, cooking in one end, and eating in the other, but the tiny room was walled and ceiled, a luxury, and a small glassed window gave light to cook by and another gave light for eating.

From the kitchen a door led to a large room with a big fireplace; it too was walled and ceiled. "This," Papa said, "will be my and your ma's room." A glassed window faced the pasture. "Let's see what's across the hall."

There was another large room, but the logs were the walls. The outside ones had been chinked, but the owner hadn't bothered to chink the inside one separating the room from another one, and the logs rose only two thirds of the way to the roof, which had no ceiling.

"This will be you young'uns', I guess."

The sorriest of the house, it had only an open space for a window; a wooden shutter attached from the outside swung idly in the wind. I viewed sleeping here with consternation.

In order to reach the adjoining room, we had to go out the door we had entered and through another opening into the hall. This room was as tiny as the kitchen, walled on three sides and ceiled, and had two glass windows.

Gazing about this room Papa said, "Lillian will want to fix this up for a parlor."

I nodded, without hope, for I was looking at the log wall with wide spaces between the logs through which anyone could peep without hindrance. There wouldn't be much courting done in that parlor. But then Jock would never come to the house, and Lillian never courted anyone else. But this would be her room.

Outside, we saw a big barn in better condition than the house and a barn lot. To the left was the big field adjoining the railroad. "That ain't no hayseed railroad, but the main line of the A, B and C. Trains go by here day and night at a fast clip, so you young'uns will have to stay off the railroad tracks."

To the right of the barn was another wide field of some twenty acres; adjoining it was a little strip of land, broken into patches, ending at the fenced pasture. That was all the land. I couldn't believe it.

Seeing my look, Papa said, "Guess I'll have to sell Rhoda. Shore hate to do it. She's a fine mule, even if she is crippled. I can't feed two when there's no use."

This was bad news, for Rhoda had been a faithful worker; gentle, affectionate and obedient to us children, she was dear to our hearts. But Kate, a big, black mule, fast-gaited and spirited, yet gentle, had been bought first, and she wasn't crippled.

The decision to sell Rhoda was the first decisive step toward the actual moving. Papa could find no easy way to tell Mama, so at last, in desperation he told her. She didn't rant and rave, as he expected, nor did she blame him; she had inherited some of the Presbyterian philosophy from her mother: What is to be will be. But the fall from the status of renter to sharecropper hit her hard, and she joined Papa in quiet despair.

We were soon busy with moving preparations. Rhoda was sold; Papa traded his two-horse wagon for a one-horse; we packed our belongings; and we spent nearly a day cleaning the new residence, washing down walls, scouring floors with boiling lye water and cornshuck mop. The house at least smelled clean.

Then, load by load, we moved. Only too soon we were making the last trip. Papa and Mama in kitchen chairs in front, the rest on an old quilt in the back. Thus we rode to the low status of sharecropper. We not only looked but were the sharecroppers of the deep South, poverty-ridden and hopeless. And we knew it.

I was more hopeless than the rest. We had so little land none could be used for gardens by us children. There would be no

Saturday peddling for silver; there would be no motion pictures or ice cream cones; for by the time school closed next year Lillian would be married to Jock and living in Griffin. She wouldn't be present to furnish us money.

When Jock left to work in Griffin, Papa and Mama breathed a sigh of relief, believing that was the end of him. They not only wanted Lillian unmarried to Jock, they also wanted her unmarried to anybody, for she was the only hope of money they had. Since Jenny had married, Lillian always gave Papa money from her pay check. Only I knew that would end when Jock came for her — as soon as school ended, he wrote.

The weekend following our move was the first time Lillian saw our new home. She was ashamed and dismayed. "Why, I wouldn't have any of my friends see this hole for all the gold in the ground," she said.

Wryly, Papa answered, "They ain't no gold in this ground. They ain't nothing but crawdad holes."

When Cass saw the farm, he too was dismayed. "You'll never raise cotton on this ground, Mr. Abbott. Too low. Why didn't you come to me? I could have got you a farm close to us — a good farm where you could make some money."

Papa shook his head. Hating to admit his inadequacy, he chewed his Brown Mule thoughtfully, but the basic honesty of Cass was contagious. Slowly, he said, "The truth is, Cass, I just wann't cut out to farm like they do down here. On Pa's farm I made a good living, growing our own food and enough cabbage and apples for clothes and things. Why, I made enough off that old rocky farm to send Jenny to college. But down here, I just can't git the hang of it somehow, and the situation has gone from bad to worst."

Cass said, "The way your family done you made you lose heart, that's what. But if you was close to me, I could give you a hand."

Stubbornly, Papa replied, "You have a family of your own."

Cass and Jenny were the proud parents of a son.

Even he was having a tough time making ends meet; the boll weevil had invaded the cotton, taking a heavy toll. For what little cotton was left, farmers got such a low price they could barely pay their guano and seed bills. Too much of everything was being raised, for no matter what crops they were selling, farmers found the market glutted. How could they cut production when money crops were their only hope to live?

The poor were surely growing not only poorer but desperate. The problem existed for farmers all over the nation, with wheat as well as with cotton. The distress grew until it became a political question of the first magnitude. Something had to be done for the farmers.

Jenny considered returning to teaching, but she had no natural milk for the baby, and had to put him on cow's milk from a glass bottle with a rubber nipple. In the gnat- and fly-infested country where there were no screens, she had to be very particular in keeping all bottles and nipples germ-free or risk giving the baby dysentery, a disease that killed babies as quickly as lightning. She couldn't risk leaving him with anyone while teaching, so she remained at home.

Slowly, Cass now suggested, "Fitzgerald has a cotton mill."

We had heard of lintdodgers; they weren't as low as niggers, but even sharecroppers were counted higher. Papa's mouth grew thin and straight. "I ain't sunk that low, yet. If I just had the money, I'd go back where I come from, to them good, old red hills of north Georgia." He sighed. "But I ain't got the money — ain't got nothing but a passel o' young'uns."

Cass laughed. "They can't help that."

"No," Papa agreed, "but I can't either."

No longer able to attend Mount Olive Church, Lillian, being Lillian, made friends quickly with the young people of the new neighborhood by attending, but not joining, the Methodist church. When they discovered she was the principal of Ridgeway School, could sing and was interested in their social doings, they quickly accepted her in the choir and social activities.

Sure enough, she tried to fix that side room into some semblance of a parlor, though she never invited her new friends to her house, always managing to go to theirs. On the floor she put a green straw rug which was too big, and went up three feet on the wall on both sides; she put her bed in there with a nice counterpane, her two rockers, the center table on which she set the Victrola. But when she was hanging scrim curtains, a piece of flooring gave way; the chair leg went through, tipping the chair and spilling Lillian hard on the floor.

Fit to be tied, she crawled to her feet. "God damn such a place! What did Papa mean by moving to this Godforsaken hole?"

"It was all he could find," I said, defensively.

"Then, thank God, I'll soon be away from it all!"

"Oh, Lillian, you don't love us anymore!"

"I love Jock," she said shortly, which cut my heart in two.

Then I saw she was looking at me oddly; she sat down suddenly, covered her face with her hands and burst into loud wails. "All of you," she gulped, "all of you — are too much for me. I can't bear it! I can't bear seeing you live in such misery!"

I could only stand, speechless, looking at her.

Her wailing ended; wiping her eyes, she looked at me. "Papa is so helpless!"

I could not speak, for I knew not how to answer.

In the field by the railroad Papa planted cotton, since that was the higher ground; in the field near the barn he planted corn; in the little patches he planted sweet potatoes and a garden; we had no space for sugarcane or rice.

Looking over the small crop, Papa said, "The less land, the less work we'll have to do." But he didn't smile.

We children found the new school fascinating. Attending was a pleasure and we rode to it in a school bus. Justin was now in the second grade; Gregory in the fourth; Glory and I were in the sixth, which she had failed the past year.

Ashton was indeed superior to Dorminy in grades and curriculum. Constructed of field stone, it was a genuine high school with grades through eleven (there was no twelfth). It had a girls' basketball team, a boys' baseball team — both usually winning — a tennis and basketball court, and playground equipment, such as swings and slides, for younger children.

Though Glory and I weren't in high school, our room was on the second floor of that building. We felt proud to be so close to high school.

Our teacher, Miss Spivey, was easy-going but also very able. Through her guidance we learned to parse sentences, and became entangled with fractions, decimals and long division.

At the end of school a field day was held, in which Dorminy participated. Even the elementary grades were included in sport contests such as potato races.

When Lillian's school ended in April, she came home with anticipation lighting her eyes. Immediately she set to sewing, for summer school, she told Mama, but I knew better.

On a Saturday in May she and I went to the mailbox which was at the intersection of our road and the one to town, a good way from our house. Opening the box, she saw the letter with familiar writing; she tore it open, her eyes jumping to the words.

I watched her, saw the eagerness fade, the fresh bloom of girlhood die and sorrow stamp its seal in their stead.

She never wept, no sound of anguish escaped, nor did she even tremble. She sat down in the grass beside the road, with the open letter in her hands. With unseeing eyes she stared off into the swamp.

Had she wept and wailed, I could have wept and wailed. But since she sat as still and silent as the Indian graves in north Georgia, I sat still and silent, feeling the loneliness of the wind in the treetops, the dismal dirge of the swamp frogs and the mourning cries of doves in nearby woods.

Reaching out, I took the letter and read:

Dear Lillian,

I hate to write you this letter, and thought a long while before writing, hoping things would work out. But they haven't, so I must write to tell you we cannot be married; for since coming here I fell in love with another, and owe my heart to her.

Please forgive me, if you can. Had your family felt differently, I wouldn't have left Fitzgerald, and we would have married long ago. I am not blaming anyone, please understand, but myself. Had I been a better man, your family would have, no doubt, approved.

Try not to hate me as much as I hate myself for having to do this to you; for I still think you are the best girl I ever knew, and know in my heart you deserve a much better man than I can ever be.

Life can do cruel things, for I never dreamed I'd ever love another but you; but we cannot control our hearts. As you often said, "Love has no reason."

You have my heart's best wishes for the very best of everything all through your life. Please try to forgive me, I beg, yours in eternal friendship,

Jock.

As I read, I wept and wailed silently; for both Lillian and me, our grief was too great for noise or motion. Only death stills hearts and tongues; and hope, dreams and faith had died there at the mailbox.

After a long while, long enough for ants to investigate our feet and legs, she said in a whisper, "It was no more than I expected. I was born to grief and sorrow. I wanted to be a preacher," she said in a flat, lifeless voice, then shouted out, "God, you *know* I couldn't be a preacher! But I became the next best thing, a teacher. I'm a good teacher! You *know* I'm a good teacher!" Her hands clenched and sweat began streaking her upturned face, and I shivered in the hot spring sun.

Looking into the sky as if she saw Him there, she said, "I couldn't have the first man I loved. I bore that, and didn't complain. You know I didn't. Now You didn't let me have the second, and I am complaining, God. I loved Jock. You know that! He was the best, the sweetest love I'll ever have! I know what You want me to do! But I won't do it! I won't!"

She stood up and raised clenched fists. "You hear me, God? I aim to be loved!" Fury and frustration shook her. "I'll show You! You hear me, God? I'll fight You!"

She sank to the earth, beating it while her body jerked and twisted in silent grief.

Dumfounded, I sat motionless and silent.

After a while she lay still, then sat up and wiped her face on the tail of her dress; her hair had fallen loose; so she took out the remaining pins and retwisted the bun, and all the while we looked at each other, tacitly knowing her heart and mine were one and the same.

Upon our return to the house she announced she would attend both sessions of summer school. She set a furious pace at the sewing machine; she made a pastel pink crêpe de Chine evening gown and, instead of hemming it, she took it to town and had it picoted around the hem, low neckline and side panels; she bought a strand of pearls to wear with it; she made a burnt-orange organdy, full-skirted and tight-waisted; a lovely brown-and-white checked voile trimmed with brown organdy ruffles; and other summer dresses, fluffy and full. Before she left she locked her hope chest without a glance inside.

We didn't see Lillian from the first week in June until the first week in September, but Uncle Jules and Aunt Adah made a special trip to our house to tell Papa she hadn't visited them once from her dormitory, and she was having a gay, gay summer going to dances, movies and parties with the fastest young set in town. She was acting as if she were no kin to the Abbotts.

CHAPTER 39

An Island unto Ourselves;
My Secret World

It began to rain so often boll weevils swarmed to our cotton, and grass grew by leaps and bounds. When it wasn't raining we'd pick up the squares boll weevils caused to fall, and burn them — futile work, for squares continued to fall as bountifully as the rain.

On the rare sunny days we tried to hoe out the huge clumps of grass; so our hoeing continued though it was far past laying-off time.

Then it began to rain every day. Day by day Papa would stand gazing at the downpour, white-faced, grim-mouthed, the bleakness of despair in his eyes.

During that time we were an island unto ourselves. We saw no other human being, and we were surrounded by a great expanse of rain. Our house was filled with gloom; everyone seemed to walk on tiptoe, and voices were heard only when necessity demanded, and there was never any laughter.

I alone had one pleasure. Lillian had brought home a discarded library book, *The Riders of the Purple Sage* by Zane Grey. Since I had also seen motion pictures of the West, I was enchanted. Not content with mere reading, I had to create of that land a world of my own. I began writing two stories, though I didn't know a gulch from a canyon. Writing was a wondrous world in which anything could happen and did. I had found a magical world and could share it with no one. All those rainy summer days found me sprawled on the straw rug, writing in left-over school tablets and lost in a world of enchantment.

CHAPTER 40

Lillian Comes Home

THE FIRST WEEK of September Lillian came home, and I forgot my wonderful world for many years.

She was almost a stranger. We hardly knew her because of her new hair style, dignity and diction.

Her hair was parted in the middle from front to back, then each side pulled into a knot beneath her ears, very becoming to the new Lillian.

Nothing about her reminded us of the old hoydenish Lillian. She respected herself and expected respect from others; as a person she knew she was important and honorable, and carried herself in a stately manner; gone was the stoop from plowing; her body was as straight as physical education could make it. Gone, too, was her girlishness. She was full-grown, and more beautiful than any movie star.

Her arrival lightened the gloom, bringing the brightness of another world; for she recounted her summer to us, her dates, her parties and dances, and a smattering of all she learned.

When she recounted the dances, Papa surprised us by saying, "When I was young and gay, I never missed a dance for miles around."

Mama said, "I didn't know that."

He laughed. "There's a lot of things about me you don't know."

She said, "I wouldn't be atall surprised."

We all relished the telling, for when Lillian finished it seemed as if we had been to the parties and dances ourselves.

CHAPTER 41

The Land Flowing with Milk and Honey

Lillian seemed to have brought the sun with her also; for it ceased raining. When the mud dried somewhat, Papa went to look over his crop.

The corn liked rainy weather he found, for we would have plenty. But only a few bolls of cotton were opening under the hot sun. Sixteen acres, and there would scarcely be a light bale.

When he returned to the house he was white-faced and silent. It seemed doomsday was upon us.

Lillian said, "I can give you more money out of my pay."

Surprisingly, Papa said suddenly, "No, that ain't the answer. I've took enough money off you and Jenny. I shoulda been the one giving instead of taking. I'm at the end of my rope, the very end."

Gloom thick as soup settled upon us. What would become of us?

The booming voice of Cass shouting, "Whoa, whoa, there mules!" lifted the gloom as high as a bird soaring. Hurrying to the yard, we found Cass climbing from the wagon. We were never so glad to see anyone.

After a glad welcome, Cass said, "I've come after you all to go home with me. Pa's brother Tom is here from North Carolina, and Pa's killing a lot of hogs tomorrow for a big barbecue. Jenny's home making a lot of pies and cakes. We want you all there!"

There were no "ifs" or "Will you come?" The "We want you all there" was a command, brooking no excuses. I guess the "We want you all" got us. Someone wanted us.

Our hearts lifted sky-high, as high as the blue cloudless sky overhead the next day. I had never seen so many people, even at protracted meetings. All relatives of both Cass's parents were there in addition to us.

Above all the noisy crowd came the booming voice of Cass's Uncle Tom. Bragging about North Carolina. According to him, the State of North Carolina was a land flowing with milk and honey. By the looks of him his words were not idle. Driving a big Reo, he wore a fine suit with green folding money in his wallet and pockets that jingled with silver.

During the barbecue eating, I noticed him and Papa in a long conversation. I was happy to see Uncle Tom's talk was bringing smiles to Papa's face. When they finally quit talking, I saw them shake hands.

As soon as the eating was over, I saw Papa talking to Cass, then he gathered us together, and said, "We're going home." There was a lilt in his voice we had never heard before.

"The day's only half over," Lillian protested. The rest were reluctant to go, too.

"I've important things to do in the morning, and have to go. If we leave now, we'll be there by dark."

"What things?" Lillian asked.

"I'll tell you on the way home," and he laughed exuberantly.

Was this the man who had been at the end of his rope only yesterday? Had he suddenly lost his mind?

But we had hardly got out of earshot of the barbecuing people when he said abruptly, "We're moving to North Carolina."

He had lost his mind.

Only Lillian had a voice, which asked, "But the money?"

"I'll git the money."

All the thirteen miles home we listened as Papa told us what he learned from Uncle Tom. They were begging for workers in North Carolina; wages were high; a man could have anything he wanted by just working. Durham was the place to go, Uncle Tom said, the Piedmont section. Plenty of jobs there and plenty of money, and we were going just as soon as we could get ready.

As he talked elation filled him. "Just think! No more burning sun, no plague-taked gnats and no more damn cotton!"

I gasped at the bad word, delighted.

"We're going! We won't stay in this hole no longer than we can git away. And let me tell you, it snows up there! Think, just think! It *snows!* We'll git to see snow agin! Another thing, apple trees grow up there! And there's mountains higher than in north Georgia, and rocks! Huh, just about all the rocks in the world are in North Carolina!"

Snow! Apple trees! Mountains! Rocks! "Just like on Grandpa's farm!" I said, excited now.

"We won't live on no farm. We'll live in town where there's honest work for an honest man and good schools for chillun. Just think, Lowell, you won't have to pick no more cotton!" He laughed, alive again.

"I'll have to go first, git a job, then send for you all," he told us at supper. "It'll take weeks to do that."

With her usual practicality, Mama said, "You have no money. How you gonna git there?"

"I'll git the money."

"You can't go looking for a job in overalls. You'll need a suit, white shirt, a good tie and Sunday shoes and socks."

"Ma, I know all that. I'll git them all. Now, Lillian, are you going to stay down here and teach school or go with us?"

Without a moment's hesitation, she said, "I'm going."

"All right. After I leave, you'll be in charge of the family. You'll have to see that the cotton is picked and the corn gathered. You'll have to make all the moving arrangements. You'll have to act like a man."

She laughed. "I been acting like one since we moved to this damn country. Guess I can keep on for a few more weeks."

Bright and early, Papa went to the source of money: his Pa, sister Sally and her husband Willy. He told them they had hornswoggled him into moving to this Godforsaken land, and it was their responsibility to help him get out and get somewhere he could make a living for his family. Sally admitted to the hornswoggling. Tish, now married to Jode, Aunt Sally and Uncle Jules were the ones, with Uncle Willy adding his influence, and they all borrowed most of Grandpa's money.

But Papa didn't have to borrow any. Aunt Sally and Uncle Willy bought, for cash-on-the-spot, Kate, Pet, Mama's chickens and everything else we couldn't move, including the dogs. They were glad to buy our share of corn. Possession would be given when Papa sent for us, and they were to help us and see we got on the train.

In his new suit, white shirt and blue tie, Papa looked as pretty as he had while Clerk of Court. All went to town to see him off. As the train pulled off none cried but Mama. At the thought of leaving this hated land we were just too filled with joy to shed a tear over what we knew would be a short separation.

Lillian shed her schoolteacher personality as a snake sheds its skin. We had a lot of work before us. We picked cotton, gathered corn and began packing. This time we wouldn't be loaded with sacks and bundles, but would ship everything not needed on the train.

Since Papa's decision to move, Gloria joined in the talk and laughter as much as we. She had been weighed down by poverty, and this new hope of a better life lifted the burden.

"Gloria is acting better," I told Mama.

"The new land will be good for her. For Florine, too. According to your Papa's letters, the climate will cure her."

And it was and did.

Papa had been gone hardly a week when he wrote that he had a job at twenty-five dollars a week. The job was with the

University of North Carolina in a little town, and he had rented a house. We were to come as soon as the cotton was picked and corn gathered. It was cold up there and Lillian had better buy us all some coats.

It was October before we were ready, and the last few days were spent with Aunt Sally and Uncle Willy, for the furniture had been shipped with our personal belongings. Cass and Jenny stayed, too.

That was the sad part of our moving — leaving them. It would be a long time, if ever, before we'd see them again; the distance was too great to make in one day even on a train. It couldn't be made in a wagon at all.

Our last letter from Papa told us he would meet us at the train station in Durham, and sent us the train schedule we were to follow. It would take us two days and nights to get there.

At seven o'clock one evening we once again entered the wondrous land of a train car. As the train began to move, we felt like the Hebrews being led out of Egypt. Like them, we were going to a land flowing with milk and honey, only ours would also have rocks, mountains and snow in winter.

R

DATE DUE

OCT 1 1 1977	JUN 1 9 1980	
NOV 8 1977	AUG 7 1980	
JAN 1 7 1978	SEP 4 1980	
FEB 1 6 1978	Jan. 12, 84	
MAR 1 7 1978	MAR 6 1984	
MAY 1 2 1978	APR 1 2 1984	
OCT 19 '78	JUL 3 0 1984	
OCT 6 1978	NO 06 85	
8 1979	JA 27 '86	
FE 20 '79	JE 12 '86	
APR 3 1979	SE 25 '86	
MAY 9 1979		
JUN 1 4 1979		
JY 11 '79		
FEB 7 1980		
APR 1 1980		
MAY 1 5 1980		
JUN 9 1980		
GAYLORD		PRINTED IN U.S.A.